THE POWER OF TEN

VIS A. LIEPKALNS

authorHOUSE®

AuthorHouse™
1663 Liberty Drive, Suite 200
Bloomington, IN 47403
www.authorhouse.com
Phone: 1-800-839-8640

This book is a work of fiction based on non-fictional characters and events.
Unless otherwise noted, the author and the publisher make no explicit guarantees
as to the accuracy of the information contained in this book and in some cases,
names of people and places have been altered to protect their privacy.

First published by AuthorHouse 12/9/2008

ISBN: 978-1-4343-8080-7 (sc)

Library of Congress Control Number: 2008906849

Printed in the United States of America
Bloomington, Indiana

This book is printed on acid-free paper.

Table of Contents

Preface

Any similarities between the events in the chapters of this book and real events are not coincidental. With some literary, romantic, and dialogue enrichment, and given the imperfections of the human memory, I have tried to make sense of my experiences and the people within them. With their names changed to protect their privacy and mine, I put ten of them in the same room. These people share a common desire to understand each other; they make that effort mainly through stories about events in their childhood that shaped their character one way or another. A common theme in their stories is child abuse and stress—and redemption through survival, adaptation, and sacrifice. They contribute powerful and fulfilling learning experiences to each other that give them the synergy to move on.

In the process I have also tried to find common ground: between lovers and the object of their passion, between kin who feel funny just hugging each other, between rock music and "classical music," between faith-based assumptions and scientific reasoning, between historical icons and real people, and between our perceptions of existence and non-existence. I'll stop there.

You can read it like a novel, or you can read it like an anthology. The narrative chapters (most of the book) are designed to generate images and recall experiences in readers' lives. The rest of the book is designed to make us think. Take it to the beach. Just don't leave it there; this book is environmentally friendly.

The lyrics to "Nessun Dorma" from Puccini's *Turandot* have been quoted from the *Biblio Lirica Ricordi* edition (1986). The discussion about the song "Desperado" is based on the lyrics published in *Eagles, Their Greatest Hits* (The Swallow Turn Publishing). The sources for discussions of other songs are "The Original Pine Top Boogie

Woogie," by Clarence "Pine Top" Smith (The Edwin H. Morris Co./NY); "Send in the Clowns" by Stephen Sondheim (Rilting and Revelation/NY); "One Hand One Heart" by Sondheim and Bernstein (Amberson/NY?); and "Camelot" by Alan Jay Lerner and Frederick Loewe (Chapell & Co.). "Minuit" by Paul Winter is quoted phonetically from the *Wolf Eyes* album (Living Music), words by Keita Fodeba, translation by Susan Osborn and John Guth. "Astral Weeks," "Sweet Thing," and "Ballerina" were written by Van Morrison (Van-Jan Music, the CD I have was produced by Lewis Merenstein for Inherit Productions).

The authors of other songs and titles are given credit in the text, except for "Johnny's Song"—I wrote that.

I apologize in advance for any errors, omissions, or errors of omission. I'm sure we can talk things over.

In almost all references for facts and historical accounts I have used books rather than the Internet. I have found *The World Almanac* (World Almanac Books), the *New College Encyclopedia of Music* (Westrup, Harrison and Wison, eds., Norton/NY), Cohen and Major's *History in Quotations* (Cassell Publishing/London) and Bill Bryson's *A Writer's Guide to Getting It Right* (Broadway Books/NY) particularly valuable and useful.

I also referred to the *Civil War Handbook* by William H. Price (L.B. Prince/Fairfax VA), and to what I learned from my visit to the Andersonville Prison Museum in Andersonville, GA. Special thanks to the Umma Gumma of Fulaniland; he's a great man.

Thanks to the "Big Six"; a great scholar, athlete, friend, and gentleman.

I am eternally grateful to my family for their love and my meaning and purpose.

Finally, I would like to thank the Harwich Library and its Writing Club for being wonderful.

Vis A. Liepkalns, PhD
So. Harwich MA, 2008

This book is dedicated to
Alma Katrina Pukulis-Cernaks
and George Cernaks.

CHAPTER 1

Prologue

She looked back, and the convoy of overloaded carts, wagons, and dilapidated vehicles of all description led back as far as she could see. It was muddy, and those walking alongside kept slipping and falling. She kept one hand on her baby wrapped in blankets at the corner of the wagon so that he could know her presence. The horses were bobbing their heads left and right as if to power their way with their will. Uncle Vilhelm was holding Aries by his bridle, and as long as Vilhelm and Katrina were there beside them, the horses would not panic. As they approached the river there seemed to be thousands gathering in groups at the bank to get across. She saw that the barges, overloaded with fleeing refugees and their possessions, were blocking each other. She thought, "This is not going to work; the baby is hungry and crying." She grabbed the child with its blankets, wrapped them around anew, and ran toward a clump of trees in a direction in which, she had been told, there was a bridge for the soldiers. That was the last Villy and Katrina saw of Emily and little Wellington, until Ellis Island and America.

A Way with Words

Ozzie cruised hesitatingly on the country road looking right and left; a woman behind him in a Hummer had been tailgating him for a while, and was probably furious. He had gotten the address of a psychologist in the yellow pages and was checking the numbers for 1789 Flounder Road. "Let's see, 1776, 1780… it can't be on this side… odd numbers on the other side.

"I'm a really odd number," he said. Another five minutes or so of cruising to the blaring of the anger unmanaged, honking behind him, and he saw it, the shingle:

"Gunther Von Ehrenstein PhD, Clinical Psychologist"

Wellington Ozelts, Ph.D., was nearing the end of a career downward spiral wherein he had lived and worked in five different cities as an Ivy League academic, community college professor, high school teacher, concert hall usher, and taxicab driver. There was a pattern here. Many of his "former colleagues" had moved up in their careers. They were upwardly mobile, but he was "dying." And even if he couldn't fix it, he had to find out why it had come to this. After the children had gone off to colleges, and later, steady employment, his wife had begun a relationship with a pesticide salesman. There was no longer a reason to believe in her husband, a disfranchised academic, albeit a good father.

She had grown more economically independent and weary of his relentless resignation to fate, and the dark humor with which he appeared to accept it. She wanted more. If she wasn't continuously adored and entertained, she "punished" him by nagging or silent treatment. He eventually devised a "fool-proof" plan of escape whereby he would park his car in front of the house; then, with a remote control device installed along the drape hangers, she would trigger a device that would dismember the vehicle. That would keep the local police busy for a while and give him time to start, once again, a new life in Florida. Yesterday, he'd heard that after six months she was still under suspicion for his disappearance but living happily in Des Moines, Iowa, with her pesticide salesman under her new married name, Basezinger.

The office was a small cottage set back from the road. He backed the car into the dirt driveway so if he chickened out of this uncharacteristic initiative he could make a convenient getaway. He locked the car, one of the last Chrysler sedans before Mercedes bought out the company, and walked inquisitively toward the door. It was a metallic screen door that opened easier than he had planned, and he almost slipped on the doormat.

"It would be funny if I fell on my ass here," he said out loud to no amusement of a soccer mom patient who looked up quickly, but then down again into her magazine. He faked a yawn just to display recovered composure and sat down on a deep, soft leather chair.

Ozzie was more tired than he realized and almost dozed off, when a distractingly short man, with thinning, unkempt white hair, but a well-trimmed goatee and thick glasses, opened the door across from his sofa and called out his name authoritatively, in an academic German accent.

"Dr. Ozelts, please, you wanted to see me, yes?"

They walked past an empty desk that apparently was his secretary's because he explained that she was on indefinite leave due to carpel tunnel syndrome obtained typing the manuscript to his seventeenth book.

"A pity; she was such a good worker," Von Ehrenstein remarked in passing.

God, Ozzie thought, *Seventeen books! How many explanations to craziness can there be?*

The office was well ordered but surprisingly unpretentious except for a number of what appeared to be citations and diplomas covering most of the wall behind his desk. There was a large Granny Smith apple sitting precariously on a paper napkin on the right corner of his teakwood desk. Von Ehrenstein grabbed a notepad from a drawer and a Bic pen, flipped over a page with a flick of the wrist and wrote something quickly left-handed. Then he looked up and asked Ozzie with a confident and comforting smile, "Did you have a problem finding my office? Most of my first time patients are late. I congratulate you."

"Thank you," Ozzie said. "That large sign with your name gives you away."

Dr. Von Ehrenstein wrote something down and smiled again.

"Are you comfortable with your life, Dr. Ozelts? How can I help you?"

"That's why I'm here, I guess, Doc. I'm a highly educated man, with a doctorate in string theory physics. I thought I was going places, and now as I reflect on the trends in my life, it's actually been a slow descent down the social and economic scale. It's not that I didn't work hard; at times I almost broke down from the pressure to succeed. My wife has left me; my children are economically independent. It's time for an assessment and maybe even an adjustment before..." And then Ozzie paused and said, looking straight at the Doctor for effect, "...before I shoot myself."

"That kind of comment we take seriously in this office, Dr. Ozelts."

"Sorry, I have a warped sense of humor, Doc. But I might try it... just to get the last laugh."

Von Ehrenstein calculatingly reached over and slowly grabbed the Granny Smith apple and almost bit into it while looking at his notepad, as if the apple allowed him time to suppress his sense of humor. But he returned the unbitten apple to its precarious perch at the corner of the desk. Then he wrote something down, restored eye contact with Ozzie, smiled ever so slightly, and smoothed his goatee.

Ozzie retreated into seriousness and recounted his career in gory detail, including miscalculations, confrontations, misunderstandings, demotions, and even affairs and friendships along the way. Dr. Von Ehrenstein listened intently and took notes occasionally.

After Ozzie had finished, there was a silence that Ozzie calculated to be at least twenty dollars on the meter, and then Von Ehrenstein spoke:

"It is perhaps somewhat premature in this case, but I can tell you that I have seen your particular syndrome before and have published case histories about patients with experiences similar to yours—some of whom, unfortunately, chose a non-viable solution. Your problems stem from poor communication skills; the left side of your brain is highly educated and intelligent but the right side of your brain is helpless in a society where words are as important as deeds. Yes, the words, Dr. Ozelts: communication is at the basis of your problems.

"I think I can help you. But first… you must cooperate and embark on thought processes to help yourself. Suicide must be eliminated as an alternative, and a new life must present itself as a more attractive option. There is still time to learn…time to change."

Ozzie thought that the doctor's conclusion was too routine, maybe even simplistic.

"If I continue to play this game, I'll lose, Doc. This isn't even my language anymore. It's somebody else's idiolect."

Ozzie took a deep breath. He felt the need to explain further.

"There was a car tailgating me on the way here; it was a Hummer. A 'hummer' is street talk for an oral sex act. Now how am I supposed to step lightly around that? 'Good morning, guys, how's your Hummer doing, Ms. Bentley, and that Dick, your husband?'

"'Mrs.' and 'Misses' are 'Mss.' Everybody, from the president on down is 'guys,' except a woman who is not a guy. And the incessant pounding of rap and the insouciance of elevator music are metaphors for the reduction of meaning and purpose to redundancy and glitz, for power and profit.

"'To be' is no longer to be: it depends on what you mean by 'is.'

"What… happened… to the rules?

"Anyway, I feel like I'm gradually being nudged toward a cultural strangeland. I had no part in this, Doc. My learning was wasted."

"Your learning was not wasted," Von Ehrenstein interjected. "Your awareness proves that, Dr. Ozelts."

But Ozzie shifted in his chair and continued ranting.

"Do you know how I lost my last teaching job? I was standing by the photocopier, you know, making copies of handouts and exams. A petite female student dressed in 'formal religious attire' comes up to me and asks me, 'Do you know where there's a place to pray? I must pray now.'

"Well, at first I was kind of stunned. It's not a common question I get. I have a doctorate in physics. I'm not an expert on the logistics of praying. But I took matters into my own hands and told her she could pray anywhere, anytime, and to go pray in a small book storage room across the hall. To make an absurdly long story short, she goes to the dean of the school wailing and whining about how I didn't respect her right to pray in dignity. Subsequently, I was dressed down by the student in the presence of the dean, humiliated, and eventually resigned in disgust. This is not academics, Doc. This is social intercourse, and I'm getting screwed."

"Dr. Ozelts, your voice has changed during this session. You are regressing into a stage of anti-social resentment and aggression!'

Ozzie spread his hands in a gesture of agreement.

"You're right, Doc, I'm spiraling out. I can't handle this."

Dr. Von Ehrenstein sat back and allowed Ozzie to wind down. As Von Ehrenstein leaned back, his seat made that crunching sound that freshly polished leather makes as it is pressured, and he stroked his goatee and paused, testing Ozzie with a penetrating look. Then he lifted his eyebrows. Something "big" was coming up.

"I have an idea…Would you accept my suggestion that you spend 'a working vacation,' so to speak, at the University Neuropsychological Research Center at Cedar Point? There, perhaps a hiatus from the mainstream of society and some innovative group therapy with my colleague would help to overcome some of these neuroses. My colleague is Dr. Myles Leonard, a world-renowned authority on ambivalent behavior. He is looking for qualified participants. Cedar Point is a beautiful setting along the coast, and you can think of this as some time off from this increasingly self-destructive pattern. I will look into the possibility of assigning you to his research program as a paid participant. And since you do have an academic background, your fees and a temporary salary would be generated from a grant to the institute. Does that interest you, Dr. Ozelts?"

Ozzie eyes were drooping. He was tired, and he felt like he had revealed too much of himself too quickly, but he knew when he came in here that he was taking that chance.

"You have your will of me, Doc. I can't figure anymore."

Von Ehrenstein placed both hands flat on his desk, pushed himself upright, and addressed Ozzie conclusively.

"I assume that is a 'yes'… yes? You will find Dr. Leonard's methods a bit unorthodox perhaps, but he is a brilliant group strategist. If there is a way for you, he will find it."

They shook hands, and Dr. Von Ehrenstein showed Ozzie out of the office.

"My new secretary will be contacting you on the details of your registration in the UDISI program at the Institute."

"UDISI?"

"That is an acronym, Dr. Ozelts, that you will find appropriate, I'm sure."

Von Ehrenstein turned his attention to a short, attractive young woman with her blond hair in a long ponytail, who stood up as she saw them coming.

"Ah, you must be the secretary from the agency…" Von Ehrenstein exclaimed.

Ozzie left as Von Ehrenstein continued to introduce himself to his young recruit.

Outside in the dirt lot he saw a beige Hummer parked under a tree.

"That has to be the one tailgating me on the way here," he said to himself.

Fumbling in his pocket for his keys, he noticed that his fly was half-open under his corduroy sports jacket.

"A Freudian zipper," he quipped as he zipped up.

He unlocked the car door, plopped down on the seat, and turned the ignition, but the car wouldn't start. The fuel gauge needle was down to the "E."

He turned the key twice again until the engine started and sped out of the lot leaving a cloud of dust behind.

CHAPTER 2

The Word Merchant

Myles Leonard recovered his informal self, picked up his notepad, and paid his respects to the staff leaving the conference. He was preoccupied about choosing the participants of the next group in his counseling sessions as he sauntered his way downstairs and out to his pick-up truck. A group for him wasn't a Mozart work; it was more like an "Oscar Peterson" or a "Bill Evans": starting with a basic theme, then improvisations flirting on the edge of success and failure, and then somewhere toward the end, a crossroads where it all comes together or… falls apart.

He had to congratulate himself on his selection of participants this time; their potential was greater than anything he had seen before in almost thirty years of doing this. The case histories and CVs of these talented underachievers suggested that they were just what the UDISI research program should be targeting. He had read their files with Dr. Benedict. Benedict was the institute's director and a trained psychiatrist; he had final approval of participants. But reading about personnel was one thing—to experience them interpersonally was another. They'd had only one real "disagreement," and that was about Ms. Debbie Storm. Benedict thought she might be disruptive to Leonard's leadership, but he finally relented after Leonard insisted that he would be equal to the challenge.

That's what excited Leonard about his job: the construction of a group dynamic and flow, to the point where what he called "mutual therapy" kicked in between participants. If you bring the right people together and provide proper facilitation, with enough group-internal empathy—including his own—to "grease" acceptance, there was a good chance for positive learning and change. Empathy, like water, will seek its own level. It's really about approaching a family model dynamic (even though he would be loath to apply his own family as a model). His concept was to provide the ten participants with a synergistic empowerment for understanding and learning by their belief in each other. He could work with ten. Jesus was over his head with twelve; look what happened with Judas and Thomas. But he was right to structure his sessions around the golden rule, a statement of empathy.

Thus preoccupied in thought he was nonetheless able to wave to faces he recognized in the parking lot on the way to his truck. *There's Director Benedict getting into his Audi.* "Pompous bastard," Leonard muttered. Leonard's pick-up truck was a converted Dodge. It had all the amenities of a mini-mobile home, with a bunk bed, a little fridge and a propane stove. It was a survival vehicle, and he called it "Betsy." He was between two women now, so either of them could throw him out. But Betsy would always let him in. He took out his keys and opened the creaky truck door, leaned into the seat, threw his notes onto the passenger side, and stuck the key into the ignition. But then a quick, sharp pain came out of his chest and ran toward his neck.

He stopped pressing on the gas pedal and took a deep breath. Outside the weather was sunny but windy, and the cypresses and cedars were swaying.

"Jesus, if this is '*the Big One*,' those trees will be the last thing I see. God, not now, I'm not ready yet; let me finish this."

9

The pain subsided, and he used his own counseling techniques to switch his mind to the stable mode. He talked to Betsy:

"It's time for a *Rolling Rock*. Betsy, get me to the 'First Aid Station.'"

The "First Aid Station" was the King's Pub up the coast road; it was his daily stop, where a few beers, a thick steak, and spontaneous conversation helped him unwind from the intensity of his work. He felt better after some slow deep breaths, although there was still some discomfort ("probably just a touch of angina"), and he started the truck up. "Betsy" descended down to the gate, turned right, and drove north up the coastal road. About five miles on the right there was a small sign, "King's Pub," with a logo—a crown on top of a beer mug. Leonard turned right past some souvenir and clothing shops and parked his truck near the back door as was his custom. He disembarked from his truck, slammed the driver side door shut, and ambled in through the back screen door. To most, it smelled like stale beer and greasy food, but to Leonard, like friendship and acceptance. He headed for his customary table, all the way down and to the right of the front door, where present and former associates, present and former students, and present and former friends, could stop by to imbibe, argue and debate with "The Word Merchant of The King's Pub."

"A large 'Rolly' please, Larry!" Leonard yelled out on the way to his table.

Larry was the main barman, short-order cook, and bouncer at King's and a long-time solicitor of Leonard's table.

"What's new, ol' buddy?"

"Haven't heard much, Leonard; here's your Rolly—first one's on the King."

"On the King" meant "on the house." Rumor had it that Spanish royalty originally owned the piece of land King's was sitting on, but no one was sure. That's how the name got stuck to the establishment. But as one of Leonard's associates at his table put it, "The crown has now been passed to Leonard."

The first attendant at the table tonight was Alexander. Alexander was of Greek origin, broad-shouldered and tall, with dark hair and eyebrows and thick, green-tinged glasses: the Onassis look, but larger, maybe two hundred forty pounds, with a New World *modus operandi* accompanying his Mediterranean masculinity. He was a salesman of pharmacological products, a pill pusher: "pink ones, yellow ones, purple ones ...and my vacation in Acapulco." He had once been a serious student of research but quit his post-doctoral studies for the more lucrative sales sector. The institute and this area of the state were on his beat, and he stopped in frequently because he was a womanizer, and toward the deep end of the evening Leonard's table tended to draw a fair contingent of feminine conversationalists, bored with their single-minded escorts.

"Alex.... have a seat. What's the pill pushing benefit-risk ratio today? Larry, another Rolly down here!"

"Odds on for a benefit, Leonard...how about the risk to benefit ratio of talking people into living another day?"

"Touché, ol' buddy." At which, Leonard and Alex enjoyed a laughter of bonding.

Then the front door opened, and Suzanne, Leonard's mistress, walked in with her friend Ellen. Suzanne was wearing a white blouse and a quilt-like pullover; she had her usual woven cotton cord handbag over her shoulder. She wore rimless John Lennon–type glasses. She was a woman of confidence and definite opinions. Leonard liked her because her assertiveness and feminist theories about men and their little conspiracies brought out the childhood rascal in him.

Ellen was a large woman from Houston, Texas, with pudgy cheeks, dark hair, and signature glasses with thick, black rims. Ellen was working with Suzanne at the Institute's Women Studies Program. She was one of Suzanne's constant chaperones, a fact which made Leonard slightly uncomfortable.

"Larry, two more Rollys!"

"No, I'll take a gin and tonic please, Leonard."

"Larry, scratch one Rolly... and bring a gin and tonic for Ellen. Sorry, buddy!"

Suzanne sat next to Leonard to his left, and Alex was to his right. Suzanne loved Leonard and knew Leonard loved his work. She was hoping someday to wrest him away from his current wife, June. Although June and he were now hardly even on speaking terms, Leonard couldn't quite convince himself to leave his college-age boys.

Suzanne leaned over and asked Leonard something about how the group selection was going and how he personally was holding up. Leonard answered her question honestly.

"This is the best group I've ever assembled in one room. I couldn't have done better if I'd have picked the seven first astronauts, or the eleven disciples. I want to do everything in my human capacity to help them."

"You mean twelve disciples, dear," Suzanne said.

"We're not counting Judas for the time being, although even he needed help," Leonard said, smiling mischievously.

As they were about to debate the complexities of "the Judas Identity" Leonard waved toward the back door where Bernie was charging in. Bernie wore his usual three-piece suit and silk tie. He was just over six feet tall but looked taller because he was a businessman from New York and wore high-heeled shoes; he worked for IBM and sold computers to large firms. He had dark hair and very thick eyebrows so it seemed that he talked to you from under them, and he had a rather generous mid-section from years of prosperity. Bernie wasn't the most erudite conversationalist, but he brought to the table the modern version of "a jolly good fellow." Leonard liked him because he sensed that Bernie was trapped in his profession, and anyone trying to change was interesting to Leonard. Bernie stopped by the bar to shake Larry's hand and pick up a draft of Rolly. With his ticket to this evening's unwinding, he sat himself down opposite Leonard.

"How goes it, my friends?" he asked the table.

"Hi, Bernie. We're trying to negotiate with the large empty spaces of the universe. 'Please stop expanding in the presence of our happiness,'" Leonard pleaded, raising his glass.

"Well, good luck with that one, ol' buddy." And Bernie raised his glass with a loud laugh in return.

"Let's take one issue at a time. Setting aside the inconvenience of the expanding universe for a second, Bernie, do you think Judas got a bad rap? He was just doing his job."

"Well I guess so, Leonard. Somebody had to 'rat' on Jesus, or the whole thing falls apart. I mean, if Jesus gets out of town, the climax of the New Testament doesn't happen."

"You're forgetting one thing, Leonard," Alex interjected. "Judas took the money."

"Ahhh, the money," Leonard continued. "OK, but what was wrong with being straight with Judas, including him in the New Deal? Look here Judas, I know this is dirty work, but somebody has to do it; just get this job done and we promise you something that's priceless..." Leonard characteristically folded arms, leaned over, and made eye contact with Bernie and Alex. "...we promise you something better than money."

Now all ears at the table were perked up.

"Forgiveness! You can be famous forever, and..." Leonard paused and made a sweeping motion with his right hand. "...we will rid you of the guilt."

Suzanne made a knowing glance at Ellen, who nodded: Leonard was rolling.

"If he and his colleagues had been in my group I'd have them toasting and hugging each other in a couple of weeks: 'all right, fellas, let's forget all this stuff about Judas' guilt and bring some empathy into the picture.'"

"Why would they even need you, sweetheart? Jesus eventually forgives everybody anyway," Suzanne, said smiling and nestling up to Leonard.

Leonard looked at her, threw his head back, laughed, and hugged her with his left arm. He had drawn a cherishable conclusion out of his protégée.

He then theatrically addressed the whole establishment, "Moving on, then, ladies and gentlemen, next topic... You, with the baseball cap backwards, out! ...You, with the tattoos, please refrain from further drawing attention...and, ... oh yes, how about another round to celebrate our sense of being alive, Larry!"

CHAPTER 3

A Blessing in Disguise

It was a bright, beautiful September morning when Ozzie arrived at the Cedar Point Institute—not a cloud in the sky. He drove up to the main administration building and parked in one of the places provided for visitors opposite the wide front steps and four tall, white, Ionic columns.

He stepped out of his car and, bringing some papers and toiletries, a basic white-collar wardrobe, and a Swiss knife, walked into a large lobby with a high, domed ceiling. A security guard asked him what he needed and he answered that he probably needed to register as a paid volunteer for a research program, then he feigned a spastic twitch of his shoulder as a gesture of physical humor. The guard kept a straight face and directed him down a corridor marked RESEARCH PROGRAMS. He saw a door jammed open, marked

REGISTRATION, to his right and entered. A librarian-type receptionist or administrative assistant walked up to the counter.

"Can I help you?"

"Yes, I'm Wellington Ozelts, and I have been sent here by Dr. Von Ehrenstein to participate in the UDISI program."

"Oh, yes, Dr. Ozelts, we have been expecting you. Dr. Benedict, our vice-president in charge of research programs, would like to interview you before your assignment. If you don't mind, I'll notify him that you've arrived."

Ozzie waited and, curious as always, looked around. Everywhere he looked there was light. And everywhere he listened there was a quietness. *A friendly enough place, but I don't think I'll find a barrel of laughs; I'm not doing 'church' here.* Ozzie's stepfather was a minister, and just thinking of his presence made Ozzie feel the cold dampness of church cellars. Then from behind him came a booming voice in a comfortable southern drawl, a voice of hospitality, warmth and gentleness.

"How are you, Dr. Ozelts? I'm Dr. Benedict. I have been looking forward to meeting you since Dr. Von Ehrenstein sent me your file."

Ozzie was taken aback first by Dr. Benedict's height—he was taller, and very slim—and then by the formal academic courtesy. Since he had left academia, most people Ozzie met were indifferent to education in general, and doctorates in particular. Dr. Benedict made small talk as they both walked to the elevator, mostly about the nuts and bolts of the institute and its construction, mission, and funding. They took the elevator to the third floor, and not far after walking kitty-corner and then turning right, they entered a beautiful office. Ozzie had never really had an office of his own but he had seen many offices in his time, and this was a beauty with flowers and artwork from various cultures and periods. Everywhere he looked there was something.

"What is it about administrators and their offices?" he murmured. "If office size and style are measures of status, you must be the boss."

"Excuse me, Dr. Ozelts?"

"Nothing, Doc... Nice office."

A dark-haired, chubby secretary with reading glasses was busily typing when they walked in, but without missing a beat announced several calls Benedict had received while out. Dr. Benedict waved slightly and said, "Thank you, Connie. Hold my calls for a while again, would you please, dear? Dr. Ozelts and I will be in conference."

The office was constructed from old walnut wood and the ceiling, embedded with soft indirect lighting, made Dr. Benedict look even taller. Ozzie was at once amused and comforted when Dr. Benedict sat back and put his feet up on the desk and crossed his legs. Ozzie sat down on a sofa that felt more like a large bean bag. Benedict let a relaxing breath go and asked, "OK, Dr. Ozelts, or would you prefer 'Wellington'?"

"No one except my grade school teachers has ever called me 'Wellington' And I eliminated 'Well' as a nickname because it's a parenthetical, so I came up with 'Ozzie.' My mother named me 'Wellington' because she wanted to name me after a winner. The way things are working out maybe a parenthetical would have been more appropriate. Oh, Well."

Benedict smiled at the self-effacement. "We'll go with Dr. Ozelts initially, and then the alternatives, depending on company and context. How's that?"

Then Benedict checked that Ozzie was comfortable, and continued, this time with a more authoritative and academic attitude.

"This research program is geared toward the understanding of the interactions of individual personalities with their society. It does not deal with clinical psychoses and neuroses as such. When I wrote this grant as a principal investigator for the institute I wanted to incorporate the concept that at a certain level, and in some critical cases, society and social pressures are equal participants with the individual, in the etiology of cases referred to mental health institutions. However, it is not the research program's goal to change society; on the other hand if we can produce a conclusion from this program which would get the attention of those who can change it or refine it for the benefit of the disengaged and displaced—that would be in itself gratifying. We're dreamers, no… more like visionaries.

"Having said that, we have a duty to the research program participants, and I prefer to call them 'participants,' to help them understand and adapt to where they can recover at least some of their identity, meaning, self-respect, and purpose. Have I lost you yet, Dr. Ozelts? A full copy of the UDISI grant proposal will be provided for you by Connie on your way out; 'UDISI' is short for Under-achievement and Displacement of Individuals with Superior Intelligence."

Ozzie couldn't help asking, "Why me, Doc?"

"Well…I mean Dr. Ozelts, your Ph.D. was in physics, that shows a high degree of intelligence and ability to observe. That's why I took interest in your file. I'll level with you, Ozzie. We need you to interact with the other participants under the guidance of the staff here. From your experiences, and your unique perspectives and abilities, your potential to interact and contribute to the group is something we couldn't pass up. Furthermore and as far as I'm concerned, your best qualification is not that you broke down from your, shall we say, disengagements from society, but that you *didn't* break. As far as I can tell from your file, you're taking this whole business rather well."

Ozzie needed to ask another question. "Why would a Ph.D. in physics be useful in a counseling research program? My thesis work was in String Theory, back when it wasn't popular or even publishable. I couldn't get a job to save my life. Had to settle for a chemistry lab as 'lab rat.' My last real job was a bagger in a super market, and I couldn't keep that one either. It's getting to the point where dying is more than just a metaphor."

Benedict wasn't fazed by Ozzie's remark and moved on.

"Ozzie, just as String Theory tries to make sense of chaos and underlying forces, we here try to make sense of the social forces and personal interactions that brought the participants to this program. All of you have been selected for this program because you are people with high levels of intelligence and abilities, some with sub-clinical neuroses but, for the most part, no outstanding psychoses. Yet you have not adapted, produced, and impacted to capacities that would be expected. These are some of the problems we want to address for the benefit of society and the individual. The details of techniques involved for the participants are outlined in the grant proposal Connie will provide for you.

"I see my calls are starting to test the capacity of my secretary's patience. I'd better let you go, Dr. Ozelts. It has been a pleasure to discuss the program with you, and Dr. Leonard will take it from here. Good luck with the staff and the other participants. Give this your best effort, Dr. Ozelts. I think we can help each other. Connie and the staff will show you to your accommodations."

Dr. Benedict stood up and shook Ozzie's hand firmly. Ozzie hadn't felt so good since the birth of his son. Someone believed he had something left to give.

Ozzie and Dr. Benedict left the office, and Connie gave him a copy of the grant proposal and a map of the facilities at Cedar Point. The building housing the UDISI Project personnel was on the other side of the campus and was called Henley Hall.

He had a pleasant walk across the campus and observed the rich variety of flora and fauna along the paths he took. He could smell the ocean.

The Henley building in fact was only a few yards from the bay. It had a lot of floor space but only three floors, kind of like a mini-Pentagon built like a triangle. The first floor was administrative with offices, and very busy people. He entered through a large glass door and saw a sign with an arrow: "UDISI Personnel Only." There was a pretty secretary, short with light brown hair and a sweet smile, who knew he was coming and explained to him the logistics of the project, living accommodations, and various "house rules." He would be living and working on the second floor. There was no public elevator to the second floor, and he took the stairs. When he opened the stair doors to the second floor there was a lobby and a set of double doors ahead. He knocked on the double doors and was allowed entrance by a large man in a white hospital suit with blue eyes and blond hair combed straight back into a short tail tied tight by an elastic. He had a business-like manner, and "Don" was on his nametag. To Ozzie, this character was the first indication since arriving at Cedar Point that this was indeed a mental health facility.

"I'm here just for the changeover," Don said, "getting people situated. I'm usually on the other side of the campus. You might never see me again, unless you try to hurt somebody."

"What if they try to hurt me?" Ozzie asked.

"I'm not a therapist, sir. I'm more like a bouncer."

There was a large central area, like a large ballroom with dorm-type rooms at the periphery. The central area looked like the world's largest living room, with sofas, chairs, round tables, and a recreation corner. There was also a library room and a computer room. Ozzie noted that the architecture was designed in such a manner as to make contact with the participants coming out of their dorm rooms unavoidable. People were walking diligently about; there were small groups in discussion, and some were writing or filling out what appeared to be forms, at tables. And there were windows, a lot of picture windows with beautiful views of cedars, pine trees, and the bay. The whole floor was a small, "live-in" convention center.

Ozzie was assigned to a dorm room that had a small desk, a kitchenette, shower, and toilet. He was starting to feel strangely comfortable here. "A few weeks of wisdom and interpersonal understanding, and I might actually learn something useful," Ozzie told himself. "Besides which, I'm getting paid for this, and I bet the food is good."

That night Ozzie checked out the library. His favorite reading topics were non-fiction documentaries, history, and biographies. Checking out books was based on the honor system, and he took out three volumes: one on Lord Byron, one on Galileo Galilei, and another on Josef Stalin. There were also some music cubicles. He was too pumped up to listen to music right now, but Ozzie was particular about his music and knew that he was going to listen here.

Later that night after a long, hot shower he felt deliciously free from the ambitious, the aggressive, the competitive, the angry, and the indifferent in his career. He felt somewhat like he had boarded a jet plane and his fate was now in someone else's hands. In bed, he crossed his arms under the back of his head and visualized strings of vibrating energy.

Then he slept.

There was a knock on the door. Like with most doors in his dreams, Ozzie wanted to open it immediately; he liked threats even less than confrontations—"Let's get it over with." But he couldn't get to the door with the super-speed required in dream-space. Yet he was determined to open the damn thing. He knew who it was, anyway: it was Jesus, the face of Turin, the bloodied shroud. Pretty scary.

Ozzie charged, but Jesus said, "Hold on. I'm not here to hurt you. I had nothing to do with this, I voted for Kucinich."

Ozzie said, "Why Kucinich?"

"He's a vegetarian."

"Oh, OK. You mean it's all right to kill live veggies just because they're immobile?" Ozzie challenged Jesus.

"They don't feel any pain," Jesus said.

"Neither do stem cells or the millions of sperm cells I stranded last week," Ozzie retorted.

"Knock thyself out… Hey, don't get smart with me, fella, aren't you in enough trouble?" Jesus warned.

"And what about the fish and bread?" Ozzie asked. "When you made all that extra fish."

"The fish? THEY ate the fish. It's OK to eat other animals alive if it's to save creatures created in my image: Deity privilege."

Ozzie was getting confused and didn't want to wrangle with deity any further. "Can we continue this later? Because I'm trying out a new way to understand the human experience, and this is my first day."

"Yes, I know. I set it up… Just one more thing, Dr. Ozelts."

"What?"

Jesus' presence and voice… were… fading… now…

"When you regret the impossibility of being Wellington, remember the impossibility of being Jesus…"

Ozzie was startled out of his dream by another knock on the door, this one in real time, 3-D space: he was back in his room at the institute. It was the early morning and time to go to work.

CHAPTER 4

The First Session

O zzie got out of bed slowly, checked his watch, and donned his favorite short-sleeved shirt. He brushed his teeth and looked into the mirror.

"I hope I'm doing the right thing," he said to the mirror. "...me too, speaking for myself, of course."

He opened his dorm room door, and everyone he saw was hustling and bustling about, except for a stocky fellow passing by, with the barreled back of a bosun's mate, who was quietly sauntering and appeared to be enjoying the fact that everyone was generally ignoring him. Ozzie noticed a pair of small dimples that complemented the faint smile on his face. With his shaved head he resembled the actor Telly Savalas ("Kojak") but with light blue, penetrating eyes. He was holding a book in his left hand like a preacher, and responded to Ozzie's curiosity in a clear and emphatic voice,

"Can I help you, sir?"

"Yes, I'm a UDISI participant, and I don't know where to go or how to start."

"Well, it's too late for breakfast. But I've been told our first meeting is in the conference room just past the last dorm room on the left."

"Thanks... Oh, I'm Wellington Ozelts?"

"Yes, the one with the doctorate in physics. I'm Dr. Myles Leonard. I suppose I have to admit that I'm your group leader. Follow me, Wellington, let's meet the others."

"OK, but most people call me Ozzie, Dr. Leonard."

"May I suggest for a mutual benefit experiment with the group we try 'Dr. Ozelts' for a while? The change may do you some good, but if it still bothers you we'll have to go with 'Ozzie.'"

"Call me 'Leonard.' 'Myles' is a long story."

The conference room had a long, oval table, and when Leonard and Ozzie entered, most chairs around the table were occupied with people having conversations or staring out through the tall windows toward the water. Leonard made a quick announcement: "OK, everyone, let's get seated."

Leonard took a chair at the midpoint of the long side of the table with his back to the window—*Probably for strategic purposes*, Ozzie thought, *but who knows*. Ozzie found a seat on the opposite side and to the right of Leonard, who glanced around and said, "All right, let's get started; if I did my math correctly, there should be nine participants, yours truly, and two empty chairs. I'm Professor Myles Leonard, and I've been called many other things, but for the purposes of this group, I'm a counselor, facilitator and group leader. You are all here, I presume, because you want to be."

Then Leonard paused, folded his arms and continued emphatically, "..and we want you to be here."

He then dutifully pulled out a folded prepared text from his book. "And now I guess I have to read this...

"You have all been chosen for the program for your intelligence, education, talents, and abilities; and the fact that your upward mobility and advancement have not been, shall we say, what would have been expected by peers and competitors in your chosen fields. You are in that sense all definitive under-achievers. The purpose of the UDISI program is to extract and understand the specific correlates and causal factors involved in such under-achievement. Our techniques will involve group dynamics, interpersonal interactions, mutual and leader-facilitated learning processes."

Then Leonard looked up from his prepared text, smiled, threw his hands up in mock disgust and said, "Well, that's enough of that."

Ozzie noted that Leonard had rather small hands for his body size but that he liked to gesture and delineate when he talked. *A word merchant*, Ozzie thought to himself, *...but a charismatic one; he loves his work.*

Leonard folded his arms again and leaned forward.

"Well, let's go around the table, introduce yourself. Try not to contain something called social pressure." Leonard formed a box with his hands. "Put that in a box to the side."

Ozzie thought Leonard purposely verbose—his M.O.; he was trying to comfort his audience, buy time with words.

"You might try giving us your name or any handle we can use to communicate toward you and go ahead with anything else you want us to understand; this is a table of social awareness."

Leonard then looked at the participant to his immediate right, smiled and said, "Please."

To Leonard's right was a woman in her late forties or early fifties, and the first thing Ozzie noted was the wistful look about her. Her hair was a very light brown or sandy. Some strands of it seemed to separate and lift away as if charged with static electricity. She had a fair complexion and perfectly placed cheekbones. Her nose was long but not disturbingly so. Her eyes were hazel and penetrating. Although there was no doubt some fading of her beauty with age, Ozzie was convinced that more than a few amateur poets had been spawned by the effects of her physical beauty and charm.

"My name is Linda Bell and I am originally from Mitchell, South Dakota. OK? I came from a large Catholic Family. My father was very strict and I left the family to marry a German named Rolfe. We had two children, a girl and then a boy. But I left the marriage after five years because I was being crushed by my husband's domination.

"After a couple of affairs I entered the State University and obtained a Masters in Pharmacy, OK? My children grew up in New York City. I visit them, and they are doing fine. I am a grandmother now. I work part time in a local pharmacy, but I suffer from occasional bouts of depression which I can control by prescription drugs, but like, right now, they make me feel a little spacey. Or maybe I'm nervous."

Linda giggled a little, drew a long breath, sighed, glanced down at her hands in almost a coy gesture, then looked at Leonard with those eyes.

Appreciative but unperturbed, Leonard said. "Thank you, Linda."

Leonard then folded his arms and leaned over to look on the other side of Linda, at a rather plump blond woman with a round, pretty face with chubby cheeks, in her late forties, who introduced herself assertively.

"I'm Debbie Storm. I'm, like, in real estate now but I also have, like, a website which I use to sell entertainment and communications equipment. I was an orphan and I was adopted by my stepmother Dorothy Green and her husband Albert, from Paramus, New Jersey. They were very good to me and set up, like, a trust fund. I was, like, super on IQ tests but my grades were low because I have, like, some kind of ADD or bi-polar thing or something. Although I've gained weight since my pregnancies I am reasonably good-looking, right? But the thing is… men have a tough time making eye contact due to my large breasts. I once arranged a confrontation at a restaurant when a man sitting with his wife was staring at me. The wife came over and, like, bitched at me like it was my fault to be born with big ones. Can you believe that?

"I met my husband Roger at a bar, and we moved to Rochester, New York, where he got a job as a garage mechanic. Roger drank a lot and although he was a good father could not deal with my sexuality. I left with my kids, a daughter, eleven, and a son, thirteen, for Portland, Oregon, where I moved in with my biological father, Bill, whom I found through a lost persons website, or was it at a strip club…kidding!

"Dorothy and Albert created a trust fund for me which I will be able to draw on when my kids are college age. I need men to pay for my living expenses, but I can't say that I've ever been in love. It's like I don't want to be in charge of relationships, but that's the way it always turns out. When you fall for someone there'll be a power shift. Is that enough right now, Dr. Leonard?"

Leonard took a deep breath, looked Debbie straight into her eyes and paused; there was some ripple effect of shifting around the table.

"I think we have enough to go on, Ms. Storm. Thank you for your frankness."

All eyes at the table turned to the next participant, a woman perhaps approaching the eighth decade of life, with a pleasant face, apple-like cheeks, a freckled button nose, and well kept hair, colored brown. She had a smile accompanied by a twinkle in her eyes that suggested trust and faith. She had a small pile of neat folders placed in front of her on the table.

"Hello, my name is Margaret Worthington. I have a master's from Boston University in English. I taught high school English until the late nineteen seventies. I had always thought of myself as a career English teacher. I gave my students their final foundation in grammar for a lifetime of writing. The key to success that I emphasized in writing and studying was organization: organizing ideas; organizing time.

"The seventies and eighties were times of great changes in our school system; too difficult for me, I'm afraid. I lost control over my classes and my teaching methods appeared to become unappreciated. I'm of the old school, and I'll always be of the old school. If you want to talk or leave my classroom you need to raise your hand and ask permission, period. No spontaneous comments or insults. Raise your hand to seek my permission if you wish to speak. Am I starting to rant?

"After a year's sabbatical and reflection, and with the inspiration of my favorite historical role models, Abigail Adams and Ralph Waldo Emerson, I decided to become more active as an environmentalist. I succeeded to an extent by halting the construction of a couple of environmentally unfriendly incinerators during the nineties. But I wish I could have done more; I am hampered by my lack of training in chemistry and biology. I was and still am, in spirit, a teacher of English, I mean 'good English.' I have never been married, but I won't lie to say that I have never been in love. Mr. Grayson in physics and chairman of the sciences at our school was a very special person in my life. When I love someone it's forever… except for the Red Sox.

"But they don't need me. I now live with my sister and two spoiled cats and we divide our time between Florida and Massachusetts. Once I overheard one of my students say I should have been a nun. That doesn't bother me. I believe in the savior, our Lord Jesus Christ, and that everything happens under his watchful eye for a purpose. I'm sure we can discuss these and other matters under the watchful eyes and sagacious ears of Dr. Leonard." Margaret looked over to Leonard and smiled. Margaret had excellent locution.

Myles Leonard leaned back and laughed almost affectionately with an acceptance of Margaret's respect and then said, "We are delighted that you are with us, Margaret, and thank you for your initial presentation. I don't know what would happen to English usage without English teachers; they're our last line of defense…

"Dr. Ozelts?"

"Hello, I'm Wellington Ozelts. I'm a Ph.D. in string theory physics who can pack a perfect bag of groceries at your local supermarket. I've spiraled down from the highest echelons of academia to basically minimum wage jobs. And if you drive the interstates you might even find a license plate or two I have designed. If this precipitous unraveling of my career has Ms. Worthington's purpose behind it, I'm willing to listen. I enjoy the arts, especially reading and music. I have two children, and I was a good father and still am. My wife ran away with a pesticide salesman. I guess the sterilization of insects was more attractive than String Theory."

Ozzie laughed nervously and looked around to see if people got his self-effacing humor. Debbie Storm was busy checking her polished fingernails, but Linda Bell giggled appreciatively. Ozzie continued, contrasting himself with Margaret Worthington yet again, "I'm not a believer in Jesus as my Lord and Savior but I do believe in the people around this table, and I believe Drs. Benedict and Leonard are running an important research project. The participants here are in a unique position to help each other. This may be the best job I'll ever have."

"Thank you, Dr. Ozelts," Leonard said and nodded over to a fellow sitting next to Ozzie.

"Willy, do you want to say something today?"

Wilbur Hanson was a small, wiry figure of a man, in his sixties with gray but naturally wavy hair. Ozzie has noticed that some people, usually women, have eyes with a perpetual gleam, as if a life force were emanating from them. Willy's eyes were like that. His brow was constitutively furrowed, and the corner of his eyes had deep crow's-feet. Ozzie noticed Willy's hands, like old briar wood, hard and twisted but somehow sculptured.

"I'm Wilbur Hanson. I don't have all this high and mighty education. I was a millman at Corrigan's Lumber Yard, and before that I had my own cabinet making company.

"I didn't handle the finances and taxes right, and my partner stuck me with debts; I've been in the hole ever since. Now I work in the area doing odd jobs for rich people in their big houses. They have money but most of them don't know how things work.

"I was married to Joyce, a third grade teacher, and we had one kid, Billy. She threw me out of the house when I lost my cabinet business. I don't know where they are now. I'll never understand that; maybe I didn't show it much, but I loved them both.

"I've been hitting the sauce pretty hard lately. Like I say, I'm not much in the way of a thinker; maybe my hands think for me. Sure, I've screwed around, but I never got married again. That's water under the bridge. I hang around bars now, but I miss the wood; it's part of me."

Leonard saw that Margaret was almost pale with an empathetic urge to say something to Willy, but he interrupted that process purposely; it was too early. "Thanks, Willy. Let's do a break now before we continue initial presentations. Part of the sense of being alive is the need to go to the bathroom. There's also a table over by the couches in the near side of the central area that should have coffee. Try to be back by eleven if you want to get paid."

During the break Ozzie walked out of the conference room and passed his dorm room, continuing to the tall windows, and looked out at the cedars. He asked himself whether he could remember a tree that hurt anybody intentionally, particularly a cedar, and the answer to his own question was "No." His whimsical self-quiz was interrupted by a soft voice coming from his left; it was Linda Bell.

"Hi... I liked your joke about the pesticide salesman and the strings. You're funny."

"Thank you," Ozzie replied. "I need people to appreciate my humor. You're Linda... right?"

"No, I'm Linda Bell."

Ozzie was slightly surprised by the retort, and Linda Bell appreciated herself with a long, soft, downward sigh. They both walked back to the conference room with their polystyrene cups of coffee, making small talk, and Ozzie was content that he was already starting to make friends among the participants.

All had returned to their seats in the conference room, and Myles Leonard took his seat with a slightly rocking gesture of the head that was body language for "Let's get rolling."

"Now, if memory serves, Willy was the last one to speak in our initial presentation series, and that would make Mr. Brader next... if he would."

Billy Brader was well built, just over six feet with broad shoulders. He was balding but handsome in a way you might see in a safety razor commercial. He had a Midwestern "comfortability" to his body language. He had a deep, clear voice with an effortless enunciation and frequently adjusted his glasses with the thumb and index finger of his left hand as he spoke.

"Billy Brader... I'm from Youngstown, Ohio. I was taught at an early age that if I did not excel in academics or athletics I would end up in 'the valley': the steel mills where my father worked all his life. I don't know if this was the reason I was one of the best scholar/athletes in Ferris High School history, but it might have had something to do with the motivation.

"I signed a professional baseball contract with the St. Louis Cardinals, but I exercised the option of using the bonus money to pay for my education during the off season, at a small college in Northeastern Ohio. I married my high school sweetheart. Even though she wasn't Catholic... she was my girl. One night in my second year with Rock Hill in the Class A Carolina league, the general manager came by my locker, as I was dressing for a game and asked me how long I had been wearing glasses. I told him, 'since I started college classes.' The next day I was released. I was a math major; maybe reading all those small digits got to my eyes. It was more heartbreaking for my dad than for me. He wanted me to be a ball player. It was a dream that most all dads in the steel mills had. He still calls me occasionally to inform me that the Milwaukee Brewers or the Seattle Mariners need a first baseman. I tell him, 'Dad, I'm fifty-eight years old.' He says, 'That's all right, son, tell them you can be a designated hitter against right-handed pitching.'

"After my release from the baseball contract, I couldn't play college sports because I was considered a professional athlete, but I got my bachelor's degree in math and got a job for GE as an estimator; I moved up in the company over twenty-five years, but I was laid off in the nineties during an economy drive. I then moved over to Rubber Maid in the sales department. I was laid off there too when the company was taken over by a conglomerate. Now I'm on the road a lot as roving consultant and troubleshooter for small businesses… and a ten-handicapper in golf. My wife Jennie and I have two adopted children that we dote over. My daughter is married to a bricklayer. He doesn't say much, but he makes more money than I'll ever make and he takes good care of Susan. My son is a sixth-year senior at the State University and has yet to learn that skateboarding trophies won't get him a job. His mother and I keep trying to understand him."

Billy spread his big, strong hands to make a point. You could almost see them around the handle of an ash wood Louisville Slugger. "Would I do everything the same if I had to do it over again? I don't know. The Cardinals should have given me more of a chance. Reggie Jackson was a left-handed hitter who probably hit a lot of home runs *because* he wore glasses. I saw the fork on the road, and I took it.

"Anyhow 'there's no crying in baseball'. It was a long drive down here, but thanks for including me in the program."

Leonard leaned back and reacted as if experiencing a revelation through Billy's presentation:

"Aaaaah … Americana… there it is. Thank you, Billy!"

CHAPTER 5

Surviving the Age of Aquarius

"Carolyn, should we look forward to your introduction after lunch or…?"

"That's all right, Dr. Leonard. I love to talk and you can't stop me now."

Carolyn Mayfield was wearing a bright orange dress with red, light green, and purple flower designs. Her hair was up in a tight, perfectly set bun. She wore a silver necklace and several bracelets that complemented her brown skin. She had a unique timbre in her voice, telling of singing ability. Ozzie was thinking "Sunshine" as his private nickname, for her dimples, large brown eyes, her beautiful teeth, and lovely complexion. She was attractive and sensual in her movements and phrasing.

"I'm from Baltimore, Maryland, originally, not to be confused with 'Balmer, Murrlen.' As a child I loved to dance for the family and sing my versions of hit songs from the Supremes.

'Baby, baby where did our love go,
All your promises, all the love I've ever known...'

"And,

'When will I see you again...
When will our hearts be together?'

"In high school I sang the national anthem at the graduation...
my version of it, that is...like, wow... I thought the national anthem
police were going to arrest me, but everybody actually liked it. A
few years later, in the seventies, at Towson State, when I learned
they were auditioning for an off-Broadway cast of the musical *Hair*
in Chicago, I left home. I am a child of the age of Aquarius. I got
the part and moved to the North Side of Chicago. Those were wild
and crazy times. Like, I kept meeting strange dudes. I also got into
'speed'—you know, amphetamines. It kind of happened with the
hectic schedule of shows, rehearsals, and parties. And at that time
everybody was doing something; you know... dope, coke, speed.
Something happened, though, to change everything. A gray dude
named Walter moved into our apartment complex; he was a tall,
skinny cabby with long brown hair who had been, like, a med student
or something like that, you know... a real bright dude, but lonely and
'looking'... looking for something, you know.

"We used to call 'cool' white guys 'gray dudes,' because they
accepted our music, our style, and you could talk to them. Well I can't
tell you the whole story about this dude, but he fell like blood, sweat,
and tears for me. He would sit by my door reciting poetry. I couldn't
handle that. One night when we were, like, sitting and talking about,
probably music, I showed him a sample bottle of amphetamine I
had on the window ledge. 'There it is,' I said, 'Instead of staring at
me, take a hit of that, baby, and I promise you you'll feel like, wow,
a whole lot better.' He took the bottle and the plastic syringe next
to it and went to his room. I figured he knew what he was doing.
That night he never came back. I went next to his door and heard
crying; I don't like to see men crying so I went back to my pad. I
fell asleep on my sofa and woke up about 3 a.m.; still no Walter. I

31

knocked on his door…nothin'. Now I started to worry. I called my boyfriend who was the bass player in the show, André. He came over in his motorcycle, and he climbed into Walter's apartment through the street-level window. André wouldn't let me in. He kept saying, 'This is not for you to see, baby.' He climbed out the window and took my hand. We walked back to my apartment. André locked the door and told me Walter was dead and that I should get my stuff and move out. I didn't ask André what he did in Walter's apartment, but he must have gotten rid of the bottle of speed and the syringe. The police must have concluded that it was just another freak 'OD.' After that I kept like getting anxiety attacks and lost my part in the show when I called in sick too many times. I moved to LA with André, who got me into therapy, and I even got some bit parts in TV shows like *Good Times* and *The Jeffersons*.

"But I started gaining weight like crazy and couldn't get work anymore, or I was always an understudy. It was tough then for black women to get parts except in ethnic plays or shows, you know what I mean? I was losing money, and I couldn't support myself. I had to get real. I was not going to make it big in LA.

"Anyway, I moved to Indianapolis, where I had a younger cousin. Somebody told me there was an active black theatre company there. Now, I sing and act, like, in community theaters and teach drama at a local community college, and I'm married to a house painter.

"When Walter died that night I guess part of me died with him: the naïve, flower-child part, maybe. Sometimes I feel like I loved Walter. Maybe I did; he just never gave me the freedom to understand my feelings for him; it was like I *had* to love him; he was too heavy for me. He didn't give me the time to understand him. I know I did wrong, but it was all too quick then… you know what I'm sayin'… too quick."

Carolyn broke into tears; Leonard pushed a box of napkins in her direction. She wiped tears from both sides of her face and blew her nose. Everyone was silent around the table and didn't know what to say. All eyes turned to Leonard as he broke the silence.

"Let it hurt, Carolyn, and let yourself come down; then think about the importance of your presence here and our capacity to help and, incidentally, eating well. Yes… let's break for lunch. We have the original greatest cafeteria in the civilized world… Carolyn, eat something, bon appetit.

"Let's all be back here by 14:00 hours"

The cafeteria was upstairs, but Ozzie was tired. He used the lunch break to take a nap in his room. He awakened at about 1:00 p.m. and then went upstairs, where he bought a coffee and garden salad with the most delicious vinaigrette-type dressing he'd remembered tasting since his post-doctoral in Houston. It had little bits of spices and red wine in it. Ozzie was always looking for the ideal salad dressing, and this Arthurian quest occupied his mind disproportionately when he entered the cafeteria. When he thought about food like this, it was a symptom of enjoying life again.

When he had finished chomping on his salad and soaking up the last drops of his dressing with fresh French bread it was almost 2:00 p.m., and the cafeteria was closing. He left his tray and ran down the stairs to the study center.

CHAPTER 6

Creativity: Keeping an Open Mind

As he entered the conference room he saw that he was the last participant to return from lunch; Leonard gave him a sideways glance. Sitting next to Carolyn Mayfield was a gaunt man with a reddish gray beard and larger ears than his oblong-shaped head required. He had fidgety, thin fingers that were constantly tapping the table. Leonard addressed him as soon as Ozzie hurriedly sat down.

"Dr. Kiley, I presume."

"Yes, my name is Scott Kiley, and I have a doctorate in medicine as well as an internship and residency from a major Midwestern university. My residency was in neuropathology where I studied and participated in surgical procedures to diagnose, remove, and study malignant and benign tumors of the human brain. In my research on glial and neuronal cells I was struck by the special complexity and coordinated function of cells in the nervous system. But over time the practice of almost arbitrary resection and disposal of these tissues by ambitious fate-deciders became problematic for me and I accepted a position in Mechanicsburg, Iowa, as the only physician in town and one of the few general practitioners in the county. My wife, who was an anesthesiologist, was originally from Iowa and had supported me through medical school. Not long after we settled in Iowa, she ran off with an Italian anatomy professor who later became the head of research and development for a drug company even though he'd never done an original piece of research in his life. I had thus inadvertently expelled myself from the mainstream of upwardly mobile professionals.

"It was too much about the money.

"But the rural people are the people I wanted to be with; these are the people I wanted to help, these are the true people of the land. Most of my services are routine: I remove warts, repair intestinal hernias, give flu shots, and listen to hopelessly hypochondriacal librarians and schoolteachers expound on symptoms for exotic ailments they've discovered on the *New England Journal of Medicine* website.

"I am here in the UDISI program because I am not a successful man. I am unable to hold a conversation with anyone for any extensive amount of time. I have no interests other than maintaining the physiological functions of my patients. I try to read books on other subjects, but I inevitably fall asleep. I bought a guitar, but I'm afraid I have no musical talent and I can't get past 'Red Sails in the Sunset.' I might have tried to include myself in the cultural and artistic events and trends during my pre-med and medical education, but there was never any time. It seems as if there has been a gradual deterioration of the functions of the abstracting or romantic side of my brain tissue during my professional development. Ironic, isn't it for a former brain surgeon to admit high-end dysfunctions of his own nervous system? That's about it for now, Dr. Leonard, Thanks."

"Thank you, Dr. Kiley. Your romantic side is not dead, doctor, it's hibernating—there's a difference...I believe Rolland Balis is next. Rolland?"

Rolland Balis had a cube-like head topped with red curly hair that Brader concluded was a perfect lie for a six iron. He wore rimless glasses and squinted like a man uncomfortable with light. He smiled while speaking—not the kind of smile to make people happy or even comfortable, it was a suggestion that he knew something other people didn't. In the boondocks they call it a "shit-eatin' grin." He spoke in terraced dynamics not through calmness but through passive aggressiveness. His eyes roamed the room, not for the reactions of men but for the acceptance of women.

"I'm Rolland Balis. I'm from California, and I have a doctorate from Stanford in physical chemistry. My first junior faculty job was in the basement of a science building of one of the top-ranked private universities in the country. There, I was in charge of maintaining and using the nuclear magnetic resonance instrument. Nuclear magnetic resonance is the principle which is used today in medical MRI scans. We were using it then in the seventies for basic studies on the mobility of molecules and parts of molecules. Paul C. Lauterbur had the imagination and creativity to convert nuclear magnetic principles for medical diagnostic purposes; today we call this application 'MRI scanning.' In contrast, I lost tenure at the university and became an analyst for a chemical company. I hate Lauterbur.

"In those days I had the top-of-the-line NMR machine, and I had the medical school, a virtually inexhaustible source of pathological tissue, right across the street. All I had to do was put two and two together; but I was too busy being clever and getting graduate students to increase my chances for tenure.

"When everything was laid out for you on a silver platter and then you still missed the boat on a great idea, a great simple idea… just using common sense to take the next step, it's devastating. And the regret gnaws at you everyday. My wife left me, I drink like a fish, and my life doesn't fit my erudition. I have an IQ of one hundred forty-seven, and I'm an idiot. Thank you Dr. Leonard."

"Thank you, Rolland. You're here precisely because you're not an idiot, Doc."

CHAPTER 7

Regenerating the Learning Experience

"And now, the tenth and last presenter of this group…"

The participants looked around the table wondering whom Leonard was referring to.

'Hello. My name is Myles Leonard, and I'm the tenth participant.'

All participants at the table reacted in different ways to this surprise announcement. Margaret Worthington whispered something to Billy Brader. Wilbur Hanson laughed. Carolyn Mayfield predictably said, "Oh, Wow." Debbie Storm was again checking her nail polish, but this time while shaking her head. Linda Bell giggled. Dr. Kiley stopped tapping on the table, folded his hands, and looked at Leonard with professional appreciation. And Ozzie was glad too; this was going to be good.

"I was born and raised in Sioux City, Iowa, by parents of Serbian descent. I wasn't into 'the old country' thing, to the disappointment of my mother, and as soon as I could, I changed my name to Myles Leonard. My brother and I keep trying to talk to each other, but our sense of self keeps getting in the way. I was a tough kid in high school but not much good at anything that you might interpret as constructive. I enlisted and served in the marines in Vietnam, where I found out everybody has some kind of foxhole. After my tour I used the government's appreciation for my capacity to kill in its name to apply to a Big Ten University and there I slogged my way to a Ph.D. in counseling. When I received my congratulatory letter from the dean for my promotion to full professor at the age of forty, I finally understood the importance of words. I had two sons by my wife, June. We are now separated, but she was a tiger. For almost seven years now I have had a continually draining and mutually destructive relationship with a bisexual woman who was my student. Possession hurts either way, and she might be part of the process that kills me. I have had at least one minor heart attack, and 'the first team' at the University Cardiovascular Center expects another if I don't stop eating steaks and drinking beer—two unlikely conversions for an old soldier from Sioux City. I believe as Socrates that an unexamined life, regardless of how seemingly comfortable, is not worth living. Until this opportunity I couldn't seem to find the time to examine my own. The way in which we interpret our lives together will help lend meaning to our experiences. I'll stop here for my initial presentation. Thank you."

There was scattered applause around the table; Leonard had established himself as the leader, even as he integrated himself as a participant.

Leonard continued. "The next phase of our program will be the primary response series. Think of yourselves as first responders to your own fears. I'll make a prediction based on pre-conceived academic notions. Here it is. There are participants here who are anxious, even enthusiastic, about your set of feelings and emotions. All of you have heard, thought, and felt some level of awareness in your continuing process of projecting, and denying. I'll start..."

Leonard folded his arms, looked directly at Margaret Worthington, and took a deep breath, like he was taking a chance, early on. Then he said clearly and deliberately, "Margaret Worthington, I respect you."

Margaret reacted by shooting straight from the shoulder. "I hope you mean that you respect me through the presentation of my character up to this point, Dr. Leonard. Respect has many definitions. Please explain yourself."

"I also respect crystals. If I hadn't become a word merchant I would have gone into something concerning the formation of crystals. There it is, Dr. Ozelts and Dr. Balis, this miniscule center of 'becoming'; beginning in this huge liquid universe; and through persistent and perfect contact and communication it grows into perfected angles and clarity. There are jagged edges to be sure and depending on the elements and structure, light is bent and transformed, giving impressions of—"

Willy Hanson broke in. "Dr. Leonard, I don't know what the hell you're talking about."

Myles Leonard leaned back and laughed; he was using his wordy metaphor like a drum roll to get a discussion started.

Carolyn Mayfield looked at Willy and said, "He's trying to explain his feelings about respect. I think it's a good try. Most people's feelings, the first time they meet someone, are like that. Simple and hopeful."

"Or if they're fops, simple-minded and cynical," Billy Brader added.

Ozzie gestured slightly as if wanting to say something, then went ahead. "Balis, is it?"

"Rolland."

"OK, Rolland. I think I understand or empathize with Rolland's regret. He's trying to relive it, but he can't. The MRI discovery has been made; Lauterbur has won, and that's the end of it. But he can't go back and reinvent the MRI. And he can't move on. It wasn't that he was an idiot as he says; it was that he lacked imagination. The contradiction in creative science or any creative act for that matter, is that you may have to imagine breaking the rules, altering, or even changing, expanding or even contradicting hallowed classical truths, in order to discover...anything. Then again, for every Rolland Balis there may have been hundreds of enthusiasts who did try Lauterbur's type of initiative. It didn't work the first time for one reason or another, and they were laughed out of the workplace, or they quit on the idea and returned to the routine of keeping their job, of 'thinking inside their box.' Imagination by its nature is something that just pops up. And how far do you want to go with it? It almost got Galileo burned at the stake. You can't always control its timing. That's why I'm in the position I'm in today."

"What position is that, pray tell?" asked Scott Kiley.

"I'm a wimp and a dreamer. As a graduate student I was fascinated by the equivalence of matter with energy or transmutation of matter to energy. Just the idea that if you think to a small enough level, matter dissolves conceptually into energy and space, drove me nuts; but you can't make any money with that kind of obsession. Strings of energy, for example; string theory was at the fringes of acceptance at the time of my thesis, and in fact I almost flunked my thesis defense. Today string theory and its corollaries are under serious mainstream academic study; and *it is I, on the fringes of society*. At least Rolland has some practical application to the principles of his specialty."

Dr. Kiley interceded.

"Rolland could have gone with flow..."

"What do you mean, Dr. Kiley?" Leonard asked.

"Once you heard that Lauterbur had made the initial application of... what was it, nuclear magnetic something or other..."

"Resonance..."

"OK, resonance...you could have jumped on the bandwagon... worked with him... or improved his 'eureka' ...Instead you just kept flaying yourself that you didn't get the glory."

"Why are you jumping on my back? I'm just telling you what happened in my career and how I felt about it. I don't think it's fair for Dr. Kiley to make me into some kind of wannabe."

Leonard saw this going off track. "OK, OK, we're straying from the empathy here, the discussion has indicated that Dr. Ozelts' case is different in one very important aspect from Dr. Balis'… How can we express that in order to learn something today, Carolyn?"

"Wellington is a scientist with a philosopher's mentality. Rolland is a scientist with a hunter's mentality."

Margaret Worthington gasped and looked at Billy Brader in a kind of *wow* expression in appreciation of Carolyn's insight.

Leonard, almost pale, looked at Carolyn so affectionately that it froze most of the participants at the table—all except Carolyn, who looked back at Leonard with her big brown eyes like a teacher's pet.

Leonard had gotten what he wanted out of this session, but then asked her rhetorically, "Is there room in our perceptions for both? We need to look at ourselves and how we perceive success, how others perceive *our* success. This is civility taken to another level."

Leonard then folded his hands. "Thank you all, good work today; we began at the beginning. Tomorrow is a day off. Transcripts or tapes of our discussions will be available in the library as are literature and art for study and relaxation, especially relaxation. See you all Wednesday at 11:00 a.m. sharp… right, Dr. Ozelts?"

"Right, Dr. Leonard."

CHAPTER 8

People Who Need People

O zzie left the room smiling and waved to Carolyn and anyone else from whom he might get the wave back. He wasn't sure, but the reason for his contentment may have had something to do with the communication in the conference room. He was interested in these people, and that was therapeutic already.

He had a schedule. He would test the library's music collection tonight, and tomorrow he would go to the beach. Ozzie wasn't aquatic particularly, but water is the medium of life, two thirds of the world's surface area, and he felt he should at least occasionally respect that. He went back to his room and shaved. He had forgotten to shave in the morning, and when he saw himself in the mirror he thought about growing a beard again. Maybe it was a sense of adventure with this new experience. He had had a beard when he was working in Chicago, but it colored first impressions of him so dramatically, and often, that it was more trouble than he had bargained for. Besides which, it was too crunchy against the pillow; he wondered if Melville, Brahms, Lincoln, and the rest of those guys with beards could sleep sideways. His shave completed, he added a dash of aftershave lotion; who knows, he might meet Carolyn in the cafeteria.

He went upstairs to the cafeteria, and the smell of home-cooked food made him hungry again. There wasn't a long line. He saw Balis and Kiley sitting at a table in the far corner near a window but decided he would avoid them for the time being because his impression was that they were strong personalities and he needed a break.

Myles Leonard was right. This was a great cafeteria. Mounds of food and much of it fresh. Ozzie took a chunk of broiled swordfish, garden salad, and fresh Vienna bread with a peach cobbler for dessert. He went with his tray to an empty table and looked back up at the line. Carolyn Mayfield, Debbie Storm, and Linda Bell were in the queue now. Ozzie noted that Carolyn Mayfield had changed dresses. She was wearing a dress with what looked like large, drop-shaped patterns of blue, red, green, and white. Her hair was still up in a bun but held in place by a white hairpin. Her earrings were round, probably gold-plated, and a bit too large, Ozzie thought. She was talking to Linda Bell, and they were both laughing. Debbie Storm was tasting pieces of her entrée and licking her fingers as she moved toward the cashier. Participants didn't have to pay for food, but their fare was noted and billed to the program's funding. All three women went to a table not far from Ozzie, and Ozzie thought about joining them. He decided that if anyone of them waved he would take his tray and switch tables. When Carolyn waved for him to come over and join the group, Ozzie picked up his tray. A fork dropped to the ground with a resounding tinkle, but he continued to the table and joined the three women.

"Hi, Dr. Ozelts…. hello, hello." The girls echoed each other as he sat down. Ozzie had half a mind to call over Balis and Kiley now that he had help.

"Why don't we call over Doctors Balis and Kiley?"

"Why not?" Debbie Storm agreed.

Balis and Kiley brought their trays over even though they were almost done.

"This must be the first day's summation subcommittee meeting," Kiley said, starting the conversation.

"Or the executive meeting of the Loser's Club," Balis said.

Ozzie was slightly miffed. "I never liked that term; losing with respect to what, and winning with respect to whom?"

"I'm getting a paid vacation in Florida; partial payment for screwing up my life," quipped Debbie.

There was chuckling around the table, but Dr. Kiley wanted to make a point. "I, for one, think we made progress today, and I'm pleased to be among us. How's the chicken Kiev, Linda?"

"It's so tasty, the juices just flow; perfect with the little green peas. What does Kiev mean?"

"It's the capital of the Ukraine. When I was a kid we used to quiz each other on capitals of countries, the states too," Ozzie said.

"Never heard of it, is it anywhere near Timbuktu?" asked Linda.

"Timbuktu is in Africa in the Sahara; Kiev is more like in Eastern Europe near the Black Sea I think; it's weird how people bring up Timbuktu like a metaphor for a far-out, exotic place, and they don't even know where it is."

"It's in Africa... Mali," Carolyn interjected.

"I wonder if there's a Chicken Timbuktu?" Linda Bell asked, keeping a straight face.

"The KFC there probably features it," Dr. Balis said smiling.

Everybody laughed, and Ozzie started to look down on his plate again.

Linda Bell changed the subject.

"Wasn't it great how Dr. Leonard volunteered to be the tenth participant?"

"There was something special about that," Carolyn said.

"He certainly has a flair for the dramatic," Balis added.

"I agree." Kiley joined in. "He figures we're in this together, and he's facilitating by integrating. I can hazard a guess from what I've heard already: that we were all carrying too much baggage before we even tried to succeed. Leonard's going to try to get at some of it, so we can move on, maybe in a different way, in a different light."

"Then this ought to be a hell of a ride then; I hope he stays with the project; doesn't he eat in the cafeteria?" Ozzie asked, looking around.

The group was almost finished eating except for Ozzie, who had not kept up with their rate of consumption because he was alternately distracted by their company and looking for his fork.

Eventually, most eyes turned impatiently toward Ozzie and his crumbling block of swordfish, mountainous salad, and generous portion of peach cobbler. Balis glanced at Ozzie's plate, wiped his mouth with a paper napkin, folded it, placed it on his tray, and took a deep breath. Then, as if driven by the possible social entrapment of having to watch Ozzie eat, the rest of the group rose with their trays, leaving Ozzie to meekly wave and say, "Bye, bye now."

Carolyn Mayfield turned around though. "I guess your eyes were hungrier than your stomach, Dr. Ozelts."

"I was distracted," Ozzie responded.

"You might need a fork for your swordfish."

Carolyn gave Ozzie a clean fork and smiled. Somewhere between her brown eyes, dimples, and all those colors, he felt an expression of life he had never encountered before.

Later that afternoon Ozzie walked down the hall to the departmental library. The library was actually a converted conference room with volumes of textbooks and journals on one side and reading literature on the other side. The literature seemed to be more in the line of psychological and character studies. He noticed *Lord Jim*, *Moby Dick*, *The Wreck of the Mary Deare*, *To Kill a Mocking Bird*, *1984*, *The Three Faces of Eve*, *A Separate Peace*, *The Gulag Archipelago*, *Slaughterhouse Five*, *Profiles in Courage*, *One Flew Over the Cuckoo's Nest* and *The End of the Road*. Toward the back and the far left of the room, past the windows, were two cubicles for listening to music. There was a setup much like you see in bookstores, and the albums were programmed into the system. You called up the titles and chose your album on the screen readout. Ozzie chose Mozart's Great Mass in C Minor with Kiri Te Kenawa and the London Symphony directed by Colin Davis, and closed his eyes.

His mother had been a soloist for the church choir, and when she was preparing to sing for the following Sunday she would walk around the house doing her chores and practicing her assignment: "Jerusalem, Jerusalem, lift up your hearts and sing," she'd sing while scrubbing clothes on the washboard. By Thursday little Wellington was already nervous for his mother, and she would ask him sometimes to accompany her rehearsals on their ancient mahogany piano. The piano was so aged most of the keys in the middle register had matured to different off-white colors which little Wellington associated with the written note; that's how he had learned to read notes. On Sunday morning Wellington would dutifully get dressed in his best polyester blue suit, his hair slicked down with Wildroot plus a touch of his mother's saliva, and they walked down Lincoln Avenue for the service.

The church was built from New England granite and appeared to little Wellington to rise out of the earth's bedrock. The pews were made of behind-numbing, densely grained solid oak wood. The choir seats and organ pipes were situated to the sides of the altar and would resonate their sounds against and through the oak so powerfully that Wellington could feel the vibration if he put his palms onto the wood. Usually Wellington sat in the last pew because he wanted to be nervous for his mother by himself. After the introductory parts of the service, a hush would fall over the congregation, the lights would dim, and he knew it was time. The choir arose with the accompaniment of the organ to sing a prelude to the solo. And then, an intimately familiar, mellifluous voice soared like a lark ascending from the darkness, high and around the nave of the church… *"Kyrie eleison…"*

"Dr. Ozelts… Dr. Ozelts." Ozzie had dozed off; Carolyn Mayfield had lifted the earphone off Ozzie's right ear and was calling him gently back from his reverie.

Ozzie removed his earphones. "Hi, Carolyn, what are you doing here?"

"I was listening to some blues over there and I saw you kind of passed out. I wondered if you were OK."

"Maybe I'm still dreaming," Ozzie said. He checked the earphones, and the Mass was in its *Sanctus*. Carolyn threw her eyes to the ceiling, in a *"whatever"* resignation, and returned to her cubicle.

But Ozzie, now fully aware, took off his earphones and walked around to Carolyn's cubicle to ask her if she would be interested in a walk along the beach to watch the sunset. She said, "Not tonight," but that tomorrow would be a better day. They made a date to have breakfast and then explore the shoreline together.

CHAPTER 9

Willy and the Boys at the Yard

The sun was setting now, and Ozzie wanted to get outside, breathe some fresh air, and maybe also scout the area in preparation for tomorrow's walk with Carolyn. He went downstairs into the lobby and told the security guard he wanted to go out for a walk. He got a card key that identified him as part of the program at the institute, opened the large glass doors, and walked toward the sea breeze and the scent of salt water. He walked past the parking lots and then diagonally across a green lawn padded with needles and cones and dotted with cedars and pines, to a small footbridge that crossed a tidal stream. The path after the bridge led through low brush and marsh grass to an expanse of beach on both sides. It was low tide, and dunes of sand were visible for a mile or more before the blue line of water. It was an evening in September, and the sky was streaked with stretches of cotton candy clouds. The sun wasn't red yet, and there was time to wander. He saw a figure sitting on the bench of a picnic table to the right up toward the marsh grass about fifty yards downwind. It looked like Willy Hanson. He was smoking a cigarette, and a brown bag was sitting on the picnic table. Ozzie wanted to talk to Willy because he felt that Willy might be feeling out of place in the group, and he hadn't seen Willy in the cafeteria or library. He waved to Willy, and Willy waved back. That was at least a good sign. Ozzie slogged his way through the soft sand with his tennis shoes to the picnic table. He offered his hand to Willy. "Hi, Mr. Hanson, We didn't see you in the cafeteria and wondered if you had eaten at all. How are you doing?"

Willy offered Ozzie a beer.

"This is crazy. I don't know what I'm doing here. I'm a cabinetmaker. This kind of bullshit is for you professors. How do I get the hell out of here?"

Ozzie answered, "Obviously someone assigned you here or offered you this group session because they thought it could do you some good. Of course, it's not about cabinet making or lumber tallies. It's about you and your life. Try to stick it out for at least another week. The program pays well. You'll make some money, and you might learn something about people that might help you."

"Help me, how?"

"I don't know…to be happier, to be stronger, to communicate better, so we can learn from each other, and whatever else Dr. Leonard and the rest of us have in mind for each other. He's a conscientious worker and a charismatic group leader. Let him try this… this experiment, relax."

"You make it sound as if we're guinea pigs or something."

"We're not guinea pigs. We're more like participants. Guinea pigs don't get paid fifty bucks an hour," Ozzie pointed out, raising his eyebrows.

Ozzie had made his pitch, but he didn't want to turn this discussion on the beach into an argument about the program. So he tried changing the subject.

"So tell me where you're from, Willy. You miss working with the wood?"

49

"It's not just the wood. It's the guys, Al McGiver, Victor Saxon, John Small, Bill Colson, and Harry Browne. They don't make them like that anymore. We lost Brownie at the yard. That's when I cracked, lost it. He was my closest at the yard. My family had left me, you know.

"I loved the guy. Died of lung cancer. We played cards together. Went to ball games together. Snuck out at night to the clubs together. I'd go over and panel his basement for him for a tall cool one or two. He had a family so, I didn't charge him; he just kept those fresh high balls coming on the stairs.

"Brownie was a chain smoker, and he was coughing a lot, you know. And he kept tellin' me, 'I don't feel right, I don't feel right.' I'm not like one of you guys so I didn't know what to tell him but, 'Brownie, go see somebody, if it's somethin' it's somethin', if it's nothin', it's nothin'… But you can't force the guy at gunpoint, you know. I still felt if he'd have a gone in earlier…"

Willy paused and looked out at the water.

"Anyhow, one beautiful, bright New England day at the yard a call came over the loudspeaker at the yard: 'Brownie, please report to the office immediately.'

"It was a call from the hospital that they had seen something on the X-rays and Brownie was supposed to come in. The X-rays showed a spot in the lungs that shouldn't have been there, and they put Harry into the hospital.

"I'll never forget how we all got together to see him after work, a little caravan of his friends, real friends, going to Memorial Hospital. We found out what room he was in at the lobby and then, pouring sweat from being nervous and with hats in our hands looked in on Brownie. He was sleeping, or making out like he was sleeping, because suddenly he opened his eyes and said to the nurse, 'throw the bums out.' He was always making wisecracks, you know. The nurse left when Brownie gave her that look, and Brownie quickly popped a cigarette out from under his sheets. Earl asked him, 'Are you sure you're supposed to?' Brownie said, 'Just light me up the goddamn cigarette, Earl!' He took a puff and in a hoarse voice poked his finger like in somebody's face, and he said, 'Me and that kid doctor they got here… we're going to have a little talk.' I thought to myself, Harry's not going to win this argument.

"While making small talk with him about what's going on at the yard, we all hustled to fan away the cigarette smoke before the nurse came back, but the nurse was on to us and told us to leave.

"On the way out Brownie and I did together, for the last time, the old joke we used to tell at the yard: Brownie asked me,

"'Hey, Willy, what'd the giraffe say to the monkey?'

"I said, 'high balls are on me, Harry.'

"'You got that right, Willy,' and we laughed until he started to cough again. He wanted to leave us laughing. He was fighter. God love him."

Willy's eyes were red and moist, either from the salt wind or thinking about the loss of his friend. The sun was halfway set, and Ozzie felt that was enough gut-wrenching recall for Willy.

Ozzie grabbed the brown bag from the table as they both got up to walk back and said, "You ought to tell this story to the group, Willy."

"You really think so, Dr. Ozelts?"

"I think it's an important story. Some of us have no idea about the lives 'working men and women'; just tell it the way you told it to me."

The sun had set, and there were only diaphanous patterns of red and violet hues emanating from the horizon as they both made their way back together, down the beach to the footbridge, accompanied by swooping sea-gulls and busy sand pipers.

CHAPTER 10

The Nun Within

Margaret Worthington returned to her room after the conference session of Myles Leonard's group and began to arrange her affairs. Most important to her right now was her work as a participant in the program, so she began with the desk. The papers were arranged in a cardboard paper file cabinet she had brought with her. She didn't like the lamp on the desk and thought about getting another, perhaps tomorrow; she noted that down on a sketchpad. She took out the notes from her session and began outlining her sources of conflict and under-achievement toward a strategy for contribution to the program.

As she had explained to the group, her general reason for leaving teaching was the breakdown in authority in the classroom. The specific reason for leaving teaching was the effects on her health as a consequence of the stressors accumulating in the classroom. She was trapped in the ambivalence of her love of teaching, on the one hand, and her frustration with the disrespect and indifference to her dedication shown by students and administration, on the other. She didn't like to hate and never expressed it; she always repressed it. Margaret had deeper and more personal conflicts, however, which eventually led to her therapy and may have led to her inclusion in the program. She'd had two men in her life toward whom, one might say, she had feelings of physical love, feelings which were forbidden by her system of moral values. She therefore conceived of herself being in a state of constant forgiveness by Jesus Christ, whose Da Vincian image she kept over the headboard of her bed. She loved Mr. Grayson the physics teacher and head of the science department during her tenure as an award-winning English teacher. Mr. Grayson was a father of three boys and an associate fellow at Harvard University—and as far as anyone knew, happily married. He was a very serious and conscientious teacher, but the aspect of him that invited Margaret's affections was his gentleness. He never raised his voice, and even the most retributive comment to students was delivered with a certain grace. The affair was never consummated, but the idea of wanting Mr. Grayson was at once a source of unrelenting warmth and unrelenting guilt to Margaret. She prayed for him every day and still does.

Margaret's other conflict, perhaps more complex in its effects on her, stemmed from her affection for a student. The boy was an immigrant from Europe whom she sort of adopted. He was an abused child who had a way with the written word, and Margaret was determined to convert him to be a writer. She would assign him poetry topics, and the boy even wrote an epic poem about the complexities of a lifetime friendship between two ancient Romans. She took him to a writers' conference at Boston College, where he met Lillian Hellman, and to a poetry reading at Harvard's Sanders Theatre, where he heard Robert Frost read. Margaret and the boy had frequent meetings after school, and she would invite him to her home for meals and ice cream. He would occasionally play piano for her, and she would rave adoringly about his performances. But her most direct expression of love for the student was a curious ritual whenever the boy visited her home. At the end of a tutoring session at her home she would take him on a tour of her bedroom, usually explaining how she had redecorated it from the last time he had seen the same white bed, white walls, and the portrait of Jesus over her headboard. To Margaret, bringing the boy into her private bedroom was an experience of intimacy and, in a sense, a consummation, albeit symbolic, of her affection.

She had lived with her sister, her mother and Jesus as long as she could remember. Toward the end of her teaching career, they all noticed she had stopped eating, became obsessed with cleanliness, and prayed constantly. She was a good patient in therapy, had a great respect for physicians, and responded well to care; her treatment did not resolve her conflicts but at least helped her concentrate on practical matters and a second career. She took early retirement and educated herself on environmental issues. In this, her second career, she even succeeded in saving a river mouth from irreversible pollution and then later in creating a town park named after Ruth Gordon, the actress she admired.

After completing the revision of her notes, Margaret continued arranging and rearranging her room well into the night until she was comfortable enough for her prayers. This was her first extended hiatus away from her sister since her teachers' reunion retreat in the Berkshires in a summer twenty years ago. At that retreat she received an award for her contributions to teaching and the environment, from former students. She pulled that plaque out of her carrying case and placed it above her desk, across from the benevolent gaze of Da Vinci's Jesus.

CHAPTER 11

A Visitation of the Unconscious Mind

Ozzie awoke very early the next morning; as far as he could tell through the fog in his eyes and the darkness in the room it was 5:00 a.m. He had been thinking about the participants for whom he had generated affection and interest and had not slept well. For this reason he also thought this would be a good time for a shower, as a wake-me-up—and there was nothing wrong with showing up clean for the beach walk with Carolyn Mayfield. He stepped with his flip-flops onto the tiled floor.

Ozzie was generally prepared for all the booby trappings of the modern bathroom—cold, hard tiles, metallic edges of sliding doors, hard ceramic ledges—but not for the spot of soap or shampoo that almost flipped him out of his flip-flops. This was a new bathroom and a new challenge. He recalled John Glenn, who had slipped in his bathroom and knocked himself out cold, and out of the Presidential election. Glenn was a marine pilot, an astronaut, a war machine, and he hadn't stood a chance against his bathroom.

He opened the shower sliding door and closed it behind him, trying to hold on to the soap dish but noticing that he had forgotten the soap; there was no handle engineered into the shower wall as there was in most showers. He spread his feet and reached for the soap outside the shower curtain near the sink and couldn't quite get to it. He turned on the shower water, and the walls began to fog up as the water heated. He was beginning to get that relaxation that comes from thousands of hot water droplets massaging his tense muscles, and he tried for the soap again, and… *Hold on…. what's that?* Two lights like small headlights shone through the fog and mist; he thought it was his retina detaching again, and then came an unmistakable voice. "Hi, Wellington."

"Daddy, what are you doing here? I'm taking a shower… Can you respect that for God sakes? …anyway, I thought you were gone."

"That's why I showed up to talk to you here; when you were a kid, anytime I tried to talk you'd just walk away. Now you're stuck and have to listen."

"OK, the hell with the shower, I'm out of here."

"I wouldn't try that if I were you. My two little lights will zap you back faster than you can say 'woulda, coulda, shoulda.'"

Now that his natural father's presence had Ozzie's full attention, the voice from the lights continued.

"I understand that you have certain repressed ongoing regrets, recriminations, and conflicts regarding the performance of your parents during your childhood in relation to your performance in adulthood."

"You sound like Von Ehrenstein… Well you left early, that was tough on a mother who had deep insecurities already from her orphan childhood, deserted again this time with a child…you know what I mean. And I got stuck with an abusive stepfather. Hey, I have to be ready for a meeting tomorrow, and I'm going to the beach with an interesting woman this morning, so get to the point."

"OK, my presence here is to tell you, before you waste anymore time, that none of that grist for the regret mill was anyone's fault; you need to separate the past from the present.

"It's like charged intra-atomic particles; you have to keep them separate. When they collide, that's when you get into problems. Boom."

"That's what you came to tell me behind those little lights… 'boom'?"

"Don't make fun of my visual and my metaphors; that's all they gave me to work with here."

"OK. OK. Dad. I'll think about it. I don't mean to belittle your cameo appearance in my shower. Thanks for showing up. But while I have you here, can I ask you a question?"

"Go ahead, son."

"What happens when you're, you know, over there, on the other side of life?'"

"The best way to answer that, son, is for you to try an experiment. Look into a mirror, which is really your visualization at approximately the speed of light. Then be aware that you are looking into the mirror: now your visualization is at the speed of consciousness. Then continue and try to be aware that you are aware, and so on. If you continue this process, is there a final awareness to which you can expand: an all-encompassing awareness? If you follow me… the transition from life to non-life, from matter to energy to space, from finite time to the infinitesimal instant, is not an occurrence: it is a continuum. The human mind, generally through its limitations, imposes frontiers and borders, beginnings, and ends, on all transitions empirically. Here, on other side we don't do that."

"Dad, they didn't tell me that you were on the cutting edge between physics and metaphysics."

"That's all we do over here, kid."

The two lights began to glimmer and fade back. Ozzie tried to reach into the fog, but then instead grabbed a little bump where there used to be a relatively smooth forehead. He had fallen in the shower and knocked himself out; he concluded he had slipped out of his flip-flops, probably while reaching for his soap. The shower had turned colder during "his indisposition" and that perhaps had recalled him to consciousness. He did his best now to dry himself and brush his teeth. He made his way to his little breakfast table and sat down. Then, sipping yesterday's take-out coffee in his shorts, he held some ice cubes in a hand towel to his forehead; he wasn't in the best shape to find his companion for the walk on the beach.

CHAPTER 12

The Walk on the Beach

Ozzie checked his watch; it was almost 8 o'clock. He wondered what time Carolyn ate breakfast, or if she ate breakfast at all. He decided that he'd better spruce up and go up the stairs and check. Maybe she hadn't even taken him seriously or had just acquiesced out of a social mantra, kind of like "we should have lunch sometime"— which translates into "I like you but not enough to set a specific time for doing anything."

Enough, he said to himself. *Stop theorizing, go upstairs, get a cup of coffee and if she's not there, wait until just before you begin to look like you're desperate for company, and come back downstairs.* In any case there was plenty of material to read for Wednesday's meeting of the UDISI project, and he could do that if this beach walk idea fizzled. As he opened the door to the third floor, there she was in front of the cafeteria entrance. All his theorizing was for naught.

"I didn't know if you remembered, or if you were afraid of me, Dr. Ozelts, but I waited."

"Afraid of you, why would I be afraid? I'm glad you're here, Carolyn, wow."

"What about your breakfast, Dr. Ozelts…hey, what's that bump on your head?"

"Two tough questions already. I'm not hungry… and I got decked in the shower, maybe I'm not hungry *because* I got decked in the shower."

She smiled, and that made him comfortable but excited.

They walked down the stairs and out of the tall front glass doors, and he pointed toward the direction he had taken yesterday for his evening walk. They crossed the little tidewater bridge, and the shoreline was open to them on a beautiful morning with only a few bundles of soft cotton meandering in the azure sky. He automatically turned to the right because that was the direction he took last night and he still had lingering thoughts about the talk with Willy as they passed the picnic table.

Carolyn was dressed in dark blue Capri pants with a white top and a spotless linen scarf tied in front. She walked through the sand placing her feet, rather than pushing or slogging her way. She looked ahead and pointed to a breakwater about a quarter mile up ahead and said, "Let's go out on the rocks and see if the fishermen have caught anything. Do you like to fish, Dr. Ozelts?"

"Well, I never really understood it. For example, I wouldn't enjoy being pulled out of the water by a hook in my throat. It's amazing… how nonchalant man is about inflicting random acts of pain on other species as if it's some kind of inherent birthright."

"Random acts of violence on his own species, as well," Carolyn added almost under her breath.

The sun was now a little more intense to Ozzie, and he noticed an ever so thin veneer of sweat forming on Carolyn's hairline, so he slowed his walking pace to her rhythm. He looked at her; she returned the glance and favored him with a smile and that dimple but didn't say anything. Ozzie felt inclined to speak.

"I liked the way you picked up on Dr. Leonard's style at yesterday's meeting."

"You mean about Dr. Balis and you, being scientists but with different perspectives? I'm glad you remembered that."

"How could I forget? That's the first time anyone has called me a philosopher even though I'm a doctor of philosophy."

"I meant that you had a philosopher's perspective. Anyway, that's what Ph.D. means, doesn't it, it's a recognition of creative thinking? …Look, there's a heron! Aren't they magnificent!"

They walked in silence for a while.

They looked up from their footsteps, and they were getting closer to the breakwater; they could see the fishermen way out, almost to the end of the long breakwater of boulders.

Ozzie felt adventurous. "Let's go out to the end."

"OK, but I hope you can swim."

"This isn't swimming, this is walking on wet rocks."

Ozzie was glad he was wearing his new tennis shoes as he led the way, sometimes holding her hand across a precipitous gap. There was seawater sloshing on both sides, and when the waves splattered drops onto their clothes Carolyn let out a little gasp and Ozzie laughed.

When they started to approach the fishermen there was a decision to be made, as Ozzie saw it: pass them to go to "land's end," or find a comfortable, flat boulder to sit on and take in the atmosphere. Ozzie helped Carolyn find a relatively comfortable perch where the waves couldn't get at her, and he took a Roman chair–shaped boulder for a seat right next to the sloshing saltwater.

Carolyn put her arms around her folded knees. She looked out at the water and then turned to Ozzie, almost reaching for him.

"What is this all about; how did the ten of us end up here?" she asked.

"If you want to know my opinion, Carolyn, I think we're a highly select group. From what I understand there were thousands of candidates. Leonard and the program directors have chosen us with a goal."

"Goal?" Carolyn asked.

"I think what I mean, is that he wants us to reach a point where each of us senses the help of the other nine. It's an interesting experiment and a hell of an accomplishment if he can pull it off."

"And 'a Gift For Life,'" Carolyn added.

"You put it well. It's to be an experience gathered from all our experiences. And Leonard has to engineer, 'facilitate' is a better word, until we are 'the power of ten in one.'"

"Including himself."

"Yes, including himself. I bet he's the only group leader that's had the guts to do that. It's almost like he's doubled the ante, and put himself on the line for the program and the group."

"How did you conclude all this?"

"In the French language the verb for 'like' and 'love' are the same. It's a language that incorporates the escalating consequences of profound human communication."

"Now you lost me." Carolyn let out a little scream…a long splash of seawater lunged at Ozzie like a snake, and he jumped up, supporting himself with one arm. "Whoa! It's a crotch-slosher!"

They both stood up, and Ozzie tried to dry out the wetness with some Kleenex Carolyn drew from her pants' pocket. Metaphors did not escape Ozzie easily, but for some reason he was not uncomfortable cleaning the seawater in her presence. The act dismissed any formality left in their rendezvous.

And just then a fisherman with his gear started to pass them along the boulders, hardly noticing Ozzie's predicament; seawater splashing on people is not an earthshaking occurrence for veteran fishermen.

Ozzie, still a napkin in one hand, trying to show reserve, asked, "Catch any fish?"

The fisherman was dressed in a faded red baseball cap, a worn, polyester, charcoal plaid jacket, and old, torn jeans. He had a white, unkempt, short beard and green sunglasses.

"Naw! …Nothin' out there."

"That's too bad," Ozzie said.

"Why?"

"You know… all that effort, preparation, you walk all the way out here…"

The fisherman smiled and said, "It's a great day though; that's the important thing."

Carolyn and Ozzie watched the fisherman negotiate the boulders of the breakwater with the facility of someone who'd done it a thousand times.

"Now there's a man with a great attitude," Carolyn said, and they both forgot about the sneaky splashes and started their walk back to shore.

They jumped to the sand when they got to the end of the breakwater and turned right, back toward whence they came. The beach now had more diversity: anorexic joggers with headphones, fast pacers with small weights in their hands, young parents with their busy toddlers and dogs, older couples in their forced-march mode, and scurrying sand pipers. They walked for a while on that packed sand between the advancing waves and the bone-dry, soft beach sand. Then Carolyn turned toward the sea and Ozzie turned with her. She took his hand gently, and they both looked out at the sea. Their feet were right at the point where the seawater seeped into the dehydrated sand. The reflections off the water were stronger the further they looked out, on up to the horizon. And to Ozzie, the iridescence, the sea breeze, and the sun seemed to envelop both of them.

For one, brief instant it was like a "high," like he was being lifted. After that timeless moment, they turned toward each other, smiled, and breathed normally again.

As they approached the footbridge toward the institute they stopped holding hands and crossed the wooden bridge in single file, passing sunbathers and picnickers. Ozzie picked up the pace heading back. He'd had a "reality check," and he was in need of another shower since the breakwater sloshing. The sea salt had penetrated his clothes and was destabilizing the proximal region.

CHAPTER 13

Catcher in the Cornfield

Ozzie woke up Wednesday morning to the sound of rolling thunder. The skies were overcast as he looked out upon the cedars that were swaying to strong gusts of wind. He had spent yesterday afternoon recovering from the beach walk and preparing for today's session.

"I hope the others worked as hard as I did," he said to himself.

The syllabus for Wednesday's session asked that each participant present an important experience or occurrence in their lives to the group, "...one that affected or changed you. It could be a childhood experience, a personal experience, a professional experience, a social experience or 'an inner experience.' By a 'change' is meant a change in the way in which you relate to, think about, or generate your emotions for other members of the human race."

Ozzie spent most of the night choosing and preparing his presentation.

These people are deep, he thought. *I hope this doesn't get scary.*

He ran upstairs for a blueberry doughnut and a large coffee and snuck it through customs and back down to his room. It was 9 o'clock, and he was late again. He gulped his last draw of coffee, grabbed his papers and notes, closed and locked his dorm door, and sped down the hall to the conference room. Leonard wasn't there yet, and the participants, seated in about the same seats as last time, were engaged in either active conversation or active tolerance. The two empty seats to the left of Leonard's seat were still there and still empty. And then Dr. Leonard sauntered in.

Although he had served in the military, Leonard never marched, or power-walked, into a room; he sauntered. But Ozzie noted that he had a business-like presence today. Leonard had also done his homework. He was carrying his "usual book" but today also had some notes. He moved his chair so he sat with his back to the tall windows and looked back as he sat down acknowledging the stormy weather.

"Good to see all of you back again. This morning may not be fun for some of you. But life isn't always fun. If you read your syllabus you should have prepared a story for us about an important occurrence in your life; or about someone close to you... as long as it's important to you. Of course, that leads to all kinds of taffy-pulling about what's important and what defines a change in your lives, but the hell with that. Use this occasion to find something you can't shake loose. Remember that we are using memories and words to express something that may or may not be descriptive of the real event; notwithstanding that, most us in this room would not be able to agree on the definition of a real event. We may however find more agreement on words such as 'trust,' 'caring,' and 'love.'

"We'd better hold on about that last one. I don't know about you but I'm still trying to understand the human experience. For example, is loving someone a revolution, an evolution or a realization?"

Leonard answered his own question with a smile. "Well, I couldn't define it but I sure know it when I feel it. But then the words to explain it don't matter anymore." He laughed but then leaned forward again, arms folded.

"Sometimes feelings have more of a sense of reality than the events which spawned them. James Baldwin wrote somewhere that:

"'The artist cannot allow any consideration to supersede his responsibility to reveal all that he can possibly discover about mystery of the human being.'"

Thunder blasted outside, and Leonard looked behind him at the sky and exclaimed, "Now that I have your attention…"

There were nervous laughter and smiles around the room and a palpable augmentation in the drama level. Ozzie was enjoying the show already.

Leonard checked his notes, scratched his earlobe with his left hand (body language for "I'm ready to listen"), and gestured toward Linda Bell with his palm. Linda was dressed in a colorful red and white blouse with a high white collar. Small pearl earrings hung from under her strands of light brown hair. She was very attractive this morning. Leonard addressed her formally:

"It looks as if I might call again on the courageous Ms. Bell to start things off today. Tell us a story, and think of your sense of trust being as large as this conference room."

Linda Bell went into her story.

"See like… you've got to understand we had a large family, OK? And South Dakota is a farming state, and the winters are long. A farm like that is almost a world of its own: a dominion, with its own dictator and little people. I think I had problems early on when I was a little girl because I was trying to understand things that didn't make sense. One day my daddy would be affectionate and talk to me and the next day he would slap me for nothing… or I thought it was nothing. I think he had too many children, or the farm and the family were too much for him or something. Especially in the wintertime he would just sit at the breakfast table sometimes, and sit and sit. Once when he was like this, I think I was about five years old, my mother left the house and he was sitting there like that and called me into the kitchen and grabbed me. He stunk of sweat and like an old barn and he was wet with tears, and held me and wouldn't let go until I screamed and my sister came into the kitchen and screamed too. We began to see when he was… like… weird like this, and we stayed away. He seemed so powerful; his moods would set the mood of the house, you know what I mean?

"There was one happening then that made me feel important to someone. It was in the third grade in school. A boy kept staring at me. I made fun of him, but he wouldn't stop. He would follow me home after school. I told my mother but she just laughed and said, 'He has a crush on you.' I asked my mother what a crush was and she said it's when a boy likes you so much he thinks about you all the time.

"I said, 'Mamma, why does somebody want to think about me all the time?'

"'Because he thinks you're so special.'

"'Mamma, do you think I'm special?' I asked.

"'I think all my children are special, especially when they obey their parents and go to mass every Sunday.'

"You see, now that wasn't the exact answer that I wanted. Maybe a simple, 'Yes' would have been better. But I began to have some sense of worth, and that it would be in my physical appearance. All I'd have to do was to attract boys and I was going to be special—I would have power. Maybe not a whole lot, but if someone thought that I was the most special person in the whole world... well, from a Catholic family of eleven children where I came in tenth, that was much better. I developed the art of flirting and encouraged boys to have crushes, and I loved it.

"But I want to tell another quick story about life on the farm. Can I, Dr. Leonard?"

Leonard nodded supportively.

"We had a huge cornfield, a thousand acres maybe. During the harvest season everyone was busy, and my older brothers and sisters were expected to help out. Sometimes even the neighboring farmers were recruited and came over. While the men were out in the fields the women prepared meals and took care of the house and watched us little ones, that we wouldn't get into trouble. On farms there's all kinds of places to get into trouble and accidents. Once when I was six or seven, it was during the harvest season and everybody was busy running around while Jan, my sister, and I were playing by the swing in our huge front yard. My mother must have been called into the house, and I saw a jackrabbit hopping zigzag all over the place and I decided to chase it. I chased it across the street and into the cornfield and down the rows of cornstalks. Sometimes it stopped and I felt like I could catch it almost and I ran and fell to me knees and tried to grab it with both arms. But it hopped away again just as I almost reached it. It was like the critter was taunting me. I don't know how long that went on but it was like a funny game to me. You know little kids are like that. Anyway, I eventually lost the trail of the rabbit. I looked all around. No rabbit. It was like I had lost a new friend. But I then realized that I was in the midst of corn, corn everywhere, totally lost. I could hear distant sounds but I had no idea where the house was. I just started walking but I was too small to see above the corn. I began to be afraid. It was a new kind of fear for me, the fear that comes from isolation, being totally alone. I got so tired of walking, and even tired of the fear, that I sat down and I must have fallen asleep. I eventually awoke to the sound of human voices. It was night, and I remember flashing lights and stars everywhere like large fireflies. The fear rose up again, and I started to cry and screamed for my mother over and over…

"…until a large silhouette behind a blinding light came through the corn. It was my oldest brother, Michael. I adored Michael. He dropped his flashlight and grabbed me by his strong arms and yelled out, 'I've got her!' and so loud it rang my ears. I guess Jan must have told my mother that I had disappeared and then the harvest came to full stop; a family search party was sent out after me.

"But as I grew older and on into high school I began to have these scary moments of recall about isolation. It was like I wasn't just alone but really, really alone. The consciousness of being alone became almost unbearable, like a snowballing awareness at times. The other funny thing is that you'd expect anyone feeling like that to cry. But it's not the pain, it's the intensity that is overwhelming.

"These were, like, the beginnings of my depressions, and today they have drugs that help me forget about that feeling. I know that wasn't a great story, and I kind of rambled but it's what I felt I should talk about this morning, Dr. Leonard."

"That was outstanding, dear heart." Leonard paused and then, performing what was beginning to be signature body language, leaned over, his huge forearms folded, and made full eye contact with Linda.

He spoke clearly.

"And in a deeper sense, you are special; special to us and to yourself. Michael reminded you then, and he reminds us now."

The thunder was roaring now intermittently, and drops of rain were pounding the windows, twisting scurrying down the panes.

But Ozzie noticed that a transparent teardrop was resting on Linda's cheek as she looked up.

CHAPTER 14

The Defiant Child

Debbie Storm was "all business" in anticipation of her turn to present. And Ozzie across the table wondered how she could be unaffected by Linda Bell's story or by the attention Linda had received. The honesty of a child's story would put pressure on the others to be forthcoming.

"Ms. Storm, how are you today. As unpredictable as the weather?"

"I'm fifty percent predictable, Dr. Leonard, just like the weatherman."

"OK, does that mean we have something in the way of a story for us this morning?"

Ozzie and the others noticed Debbie's voice became more delicate, almost childlike.

"I don't know where to start. It's like… My earliest recollections are so like, vague, that… well, I remember being moved from house to house. Everything was like, always new and different. And just when I began to get used to where the bathroom was, I'd be in a different house the next day. You know, for a little kid most situations aren't correctable. And I got to where I thought this is the way it's supposed to be. I guess my aunt's 'house,' which, now that I think back, was more like a trailer or mobile home, was where I remember being most when I was little. Sometimes it was tough to sleep though with some weird 'uncle' in a grungy undershirt rubbing your stomach and your butt all night. His breath stunk like tobacco and cough syrup, and he had prickly hair. I would get out of bed from this guy and go sleep on the couch. The dog, a small furry thing, liked me because we kept each other warm on the couch, and he would growl if the uncle came after me after going to the can; like five times a night.

"Good dog.

"I think the aunt got wise to her two-timing bastard although she didn't want to flat-out admit it. Then I remember a lady came over one day, a lady with a big stack of papers. I remember her glasses; they were thick and too big for her face. She looked serious all the time. They all talked and I was told to sit still on the couch with the dog. My aunt started to cry and I was told to get my toys and things, that I was going to a new house.

"It's funny, when I left my aunt's I don't remember feeling anything, except for the dog. I asked if the dog could come with me but the boss-lady said 'not right now' but she would try. Actually, I felt like this was just a move, another adventure; maybe another house, more food… you know how kids think…!

"And it sure was a big house…. run by ladies dolled up like batman. With a lot of kids and bunks and an all-you-could-eat-in-a-half-hour cafeteria. I think that was an orphanage of some kind in New Jersey. Except for the yelling, screaming, and crying by some of the kids, I liked it there. We were taught how to pray every night by the Big Mamma Batlady. I really didn't know what we were praying about, but that stopped the yelling and screaming but not all of the crying. At least there were no greasers rubbing my booty in the middle of the night.

71

"Soon after that, though, I was called to a room by that lady in the thick glasses again. There were some chairs and a large table, and I sat myself down at the end of it. I was introduced to this couple; they were all dressed up in clothes I had never seen before. I'd never seen such clean people before, and they smelled good, like fruit salad. The guy was bald but very nice; the woman was little, with reading glasses and did all of the talking to me. She told me how cute I was and how would I like it if they would be my mom and dad. I said sure... if I can have my own bed. They said, 'That's not going to be a problem.'

"The house they took me to was huge. It was like a new world. They took me up some stairs which were so tall to me I had to use my stronger left leg all the way up. The room had pink wallpaper; I don't really like pink, but it was also full of toys so I could live with that. I thought to myself that batman and big mamma were right: there was a heaven. The tough part was going to school though, I hated it; but that's another long story.

"Well, abbadee, abbadee, abbadee that's all, folks!"

"Thank you, Debbie." Leonard looked at Debbie with a furrowed brow, like he wanted more, but Debbie did not look back. Debbie's defiance could be useful to Leonard's group dynamics as an assertive feminine force, a protagonist.

It was obvious to Leonard's trained ear that Debbie had spared the group the gory details of her sexual abuse. Leonard respected anyone who could intellectualize or attenuate stress in order to survive, regardless of style. There wasn't a tiger presented yet that Leonard couldn't ride and integrate into a group's growth. But Debbie was different. There was something there that was almost scary. If the source of Debbie Storm's defiance and attenuation were pathological adaptations—shallowness, cunning and manipulation, contra-indications—then Leonard foresaw them as constant distractions for his goals. He always had the option of shifting her to Dr. Benedict's clinical group. Benedict was a psychiatrist with expertise in anti-social personality disorders.

CHAPTER 15

The Teacher Within

"Margaret Worthington! …sunshine on a cloudy day. Knowing your background as a great educator, I know you have something special for us. If you will, please."

"Dr. Leonard, and my fellow participants, this morning I have heard already horrendous stories of abuse and difficult childhoods. My heart goes out to these young ladies, and I pray from my heart for their recovery and happiness despite what they have been through. I have searched my own memories and my past for this presentation today. But I have no stories of parental abuse and even cruelty. Most of my childhood was spent in an upper-middle-class environment where my sister and I took care of each other and our parents cultivated what are called traditional values and also Catholic religious beliefs. But I do confess to the presence from, time to time… of anxiety and even fear: fear of losing a parent, fear of losing love and affection, and fear of losing life itself. Those fears were in part realized when my father left the family when I was a child of thirteen. We never knew why he left, and I was told by my mother never to talk about it. That night, on the day my mother told us that father was not coming back, I knelt before my bed and folded my hands and prayed to our Lord and Savior, Jesus Christ, to take care of Daddy wherever he is… that I don't blame him for leaving… that I don't blame him for anything, and that I will always love him. I also prayed for the strength to help my mother and my sister survive as a family; that with the Lord's help and our mutual love and trust all would turnout for the best in the end.

"But my experience has evolved in my mind, and I learned from it. It taught me to be stronger, that the alternative to becoming stronger as a child was to give in to fear and loneliness. Ms. Storm has shown great strength even by her presentation today.

"I also learned the importance of education; I would get lost in books. Still do. They were like friends to me. Much of what we fear is simply what we don't know. And I would like to add another thought here, if I may. I know that there's a small generation gap here between some of us. I cast no aspersions through that awareness, as Dr. Leonard might say. But I don' t think that, because some custom or style is newer than another, it is better. I see what couples are doing to each other today; I see the institutions and traditions being cast aside, and I have a fiduciary fearfulness arising. I fear for the children whose parents are so absorbed with their own gratification that they at times forget their primary parental responsibilities and their obedience of God's Laws, as Thomas More would put it. I fear the bitterness, vengeance, and ruthlessness generated by the pursuit of the almighty dollar.

"And, yes, some of this cynicism arises out of what some see has happened to the Church. I fear for my Church, a massive edifice of hierarchical bureaucracy, where ambition, business, and politics are as important as faith. Where men are bowing to each other for favors like they themselves are the chosen people. I suppose you could call it a calling, but I believe for the priesthood you have to be inner-motivated. They chose themselves for this work. My favorite quote from Our Lord is,

"'Even though ye have done it unto the least of these, my brethren, ye have done it unto me.' If Jesus himself were to come back today dressed in his simple garments, presenting his simple philosophies to live by, he wouldn't recognize his church.

"Let me, then, finish up. I never found out where my father went; and whether he left for love or money or simply to escape his responsibilities. But my sister and I did not yield to the fear. We did not become more cynical about life and our parents; if anything our belief in each other, and the mercy and love of Our Lord and Savior, became even stronger. So I'll leave you with that as my contribution this morning to think about, and I pray for all of you in our journey to understand and help each other."

Leonard looked around the room and saw that the participants needed a break; his eyes finally came around to Linda Bell. Linda Bell was shifting in her seat nervously like she'd developed a wedgy. Margaret had affected her.

Debbie Storm, however, was checking her cell phone.

Leonard summarized. "Thank you, Margaret. There were some… impacting perspectives and, if you'll excuse me, Margaret, non-traditional as well, because heresy is illegal in our group sessions. I'll say this, though: you shoot right from the shoulder!

"Now if I may, dear hearts, before our break I would like us in some sense to understand what we have just experienced. Let me try this? From Ms. Bell, Ms. Storm, and Margaret Worthington we had presented three alternatives to the fear factor. They didn't give in. They adapted—in different ways to be sure. In their most difficult existential hour we might find that their reserves of femininity allowed them to survive: Linda Bell with the power of grace, Debbie Storm with the power of assertiveness, and Margaret with the power of belief, a personal faith.

"I've read that eighty percent of our brain reserves are not being tapped on a daily basis—is that a reasonable estimate, Dr. Kiley? These include I presume our abilities to withstand and attenuate how we are challenged emotionally. Translation: you are stronger than you think you are. For example, despite the burdensome sense of being alone, we should cultivate our common awareness that human emotions are not singular, that we are in this together. Therefore may

I suggest, like the metaphysical poet John Donne, that we 'make this one little room an everywhere.'"

With that, Leonard waved his left arm like an orchestra conductor. "Isn't that how the song goes, Carolyn? Metaphysical, metaphysical, I want to get metaphysical?"

"Something like that, Dr. Leonard," Carolyn said, laughing.

Leonard stood up now and placed his book upright on the table almost like a gavel, preparing to call a recess.

"Thank you… Twenty-minute break; be back here or you'll miss the bus to *Truth or Consequences*. Mr. Brader, you're up to bat next."

CHAPTER 16

Norman Rockwell and "Ziggy"

Leonard left the conference room right after his break call for coffee; the others left in couples or small groups: Dr. Balis with Dr. Kiley, Margaret Worthington with Willy Hanson, Carolyn Mayfield with Linda Bell and Debbie Storm. Billy Brader stayed in the conference room writing furiously with his pronated left hand skimming across a yellow pad.

Brader talked to Ozzie as he was writing.

"Hey, this guy is good. I don't always understand what he's saying but the words just flow out of him like, like—"

"The gentle rain from heaven," Ozzie interrupted.

"Yeah, kinda like rain." Brader agreed, and then continued, "But you know what, maybe I've got some male reserves of my own. I've never really had a chance to talk about this stuff except with my kids. Does 'Stoney' have an 'e' in it?"

"I think it can go either way, Billy. You look like you took in a little sun yesterday," Ozzie said amicably.

"Golf. There's a great course up the road here. Do you play, Dr. Ozelts?"

Ozzie went into a minor rant. "I never understood why grown men would want to hack away with long metal rods at a little white ball the size of a small apricot, sitting there on the ground, eventually just to poke it into a hole; and then go through that process seventeen more times. Why not just pick it up and throw it or even roll it? It would be a lot less expensive and less frustrating."

Brader dropped his ballpoint and looked up at Ozzie.

"Frustration is the whole idea. You ought to try it sometime; it's not as easy as it looks. A lot of former pro athletes play it. It gives them an outlet for their competitive urges, and it's popular with beer-bellied weekend warriors because you don't have to stay in shape; they even have little carts to drive you to wherever the little 'apricot' landed. Also it gives them the illusion that they can compete in a sport. Your average score for eighteen holes is normalized to par with a 'handicap' number, which is the difference between a player's average and the par for the course, the number of strokes expected from a good player. No other popular sport compensates for lousy playing like that."

"It's like communism. 'From each according to his abilities and to each according to his needs,'" Ozzie interjected.

"I hadn't quite thought of it that way, Dr. Ozelts, golf as communism," Billy replied, not knowing if Ozzie was trying to be serious, satirical, or funny.

The participants were coming back to the room now; first, Margaret Worthington, then Balis and Kiley, and finally, the Mss. Bell, Mayfield, and Storm. Leonard was outside the door across the hall, talking with Dr. Benedict. He came in when all were more or less seated, and spoke as he placed himself into his chair.

"Billy Brader, you're looking good, sir. Have you something we can learn from today?"

Billy read from a yellow paper pad.

"Thanks, Dr, Leonard. I'll be honest with you people. My whole childhood was around baseball, and even when I was in grade school my social and sporting life was around the Stoney Brae ball field.

"Stoney Brae playground originated out of a sectioned-off part of the first fairway of Rolling Brook Golf Course—probably because there's a large, partially interred boulder in one corner of Stoney Brae. That was such an obstacle, left there by some gentle glacier, that the golfers fenced it off.

"The first fairway of the golf course is formed like the downward slope of a roller coaster. A decent drive from the clubhouse on the top of the hill (out of view from down in Stoney Brae) will send the golf ball rolling down more than halfway to the green; too much club on the next shot to the green, and the ball will disappear into the giant leafy oak and the chain link fence guarding the playground. The second fairway looped above and around the ball field.

"Stoney Brae is shaped like a rectangle with a baseball diamond at one end. No one knows how the rough rocky outline of a diamond got there, but it was probably carved out by the previous generation. On sunny, hot summer afternoons when adults were doing whatever it is that adults do who don't play baseball, we would lose ourselves in the game. Teams were decided by a ceremony in which a bat was thrown into the air by one captain and the other captain caught it at the business end. The captains would alternate grips up to the handle; the last 'gripper' being the first to chose a teammate. There were never enough players for two teams—so much the better, because the boulder in right field made fielding there problematic. Occasionally, little brothers of players were positioned in front of the boulder as a concession, but generally right field was foul territory.

"The frequency of hitting the ball out, over the chain link fence, into the second fairway of the golf course, depended on your age and experience. When I was eight years old it was only a dream, and the bigger, stronger kids who 'had hit one over' had my full respect and admiration. At age nine or ten when I finally 'hit one over,' I reached a new level of status among my friends, as word got around that 'Billy's hit one over.'

"Retrieving foul balls and home runs from the golf course was teamwork too. We'd all stare intently at the baseball flying over into the golf course like a lonely duck into the distant sky, and then huddled together to plan a strategy for recovery—out from under the watchful, paranoid eyes of the golfers and the course caretaker, the infamous 'jeep man.' The person chosen for the extraction had to be fast on his feet. He often turned out to be Brian Kent, eventually the best pole vaulter at our high school. He'd make a run for the ball, make a quick pick-up, pivot, throw, and then run like hell back. He'd leap into the chain link for footing and jump joyfully back into Stoney Brae territory; the cantankerous golfers were peeved, and the jeep man was foiled again. All in a day's work for us though. We were way ahead of them.

"The baseballs of Stoney Brae seemed to have stages of deterioration that we delayed as long as possible, and good baseballs that did not go lopsided had a renewal procedure. The first stage was two or three stitches of the seams coming apart. In the second stage, a flap of the covering started to peel. In the third stage the strings of the interior started to unravel. We usually intervened before stage three with black electrician's tape. This tape worked best because it would stick and it could take a beating. Baseballs got heavier and heavier as they were re-taped, making them heavy to hit and field; you couldn't hit those out. Although these baseballs had a finite lifespan, your favorite bat was 'forever.' Even if it cracked, it was repaired with finishing nails and tape.

"The whole idea of pitching in the 'Stoney Brae League' was to get the ball over the plate (a problem in any league, by the way); for us the plate was a flattened cardboard box with a rock on it. If 'Dizzy Dean' out there was testing the patience of his fielders, you'd hear 'Come on, Dizzy, get it over… let him hit it.' Some fielders were even known to adopt a yoga position and chew on stalks of grass during extended periods of the pitcher's wildness. Pitches to the smaller and younger brothers of players were delivered underhanded.

"What I learned from the Stoney Brae League was acceptance. Political correctness was irrelevant, because we accepted each other without forethought, prejudice, or reservation. If somebody during a game had a problem with his little brother, his dog, or even an uninvited irate parent, we just waited it out. Nothing grew into a confrontation about politics or religion, or why my little Johnny isn't on the starting team. The closest we ever got to performance enhancement was the ice cream man's fudgsicle.

"One day, a family had moved into the neighborhood from Germany. A boy from that family, named Siegfried, or 'Ziggy' as we called him, who wore shorts with suspenders, wanted to play. So we put him in front of the boulder in right field, but we didn't have a glove for him. Then, sure thing, somebody hit a pop fly that rose high into the air toward him in short right field; it hit its apex and was dropping straight to Siegfried. This was Ziggy's first-ever fielding play, but he was a gamer, and spread his arms wide like Kevin Costner on that horse in *Dances with Wolves*. The ball landed somewhere around his forehead and bounced oddly, straight up again. While most of us cringed, one player, Bobby DeBoer, had the presence of mind to catch the ball before it hit the ground, for the out.

"We never saw Ziggy at Stoney Brae again; but I remember seeing him playing soccer, shorts with suspenders, sometime after that. Thinking back, I realized Ziggy may have been attempting a 'header,' a type of soccer pass, to Bobby. Jose Canseco, a steroid-enhanced outfielder for the Oakland A's, was also hit on the head while trying to field a fly ball, but the ball then bounced into the stands for a home run. Ziggy's header was a better play.

"Toward the end of a summer day, at the point of diminished visibility of taped baseballs, you heard reluctant resignations from the silhouetted outfielders and infielders of Stoney Brae: 'I've got to go,' 'Me too,' 'Anybody seen my bat?'

"Each of us would now have to head home for the usual tongue lashing from our saintly mothers about our sweaty, dusty, and bloodied clothes. Our tattered gloves, hung from bats held lazily on our shoulders, threw long shadows against the light of tall lampposts. We were like soldiers returning from the front.

"I present this story because, in my formative years, Stoney Brae was my 'playing field of Eton.' Much of what is a part of my character, in terms of the meaning of competition and sport, came from Stoney Brae.

"All that is gone now. It's not a game anymore. But that's another story.

"Thanks, Dr. Leonard, and I'd like to thank Margaret Worthington for helping me organize some of this story," Brader announced.

"This was your story, Billy," Margaret said, looking at Leonard.

Leonard did his staring routine again, but this time out of simple respect. He spread his hands expressively and said, "What is it about you, Mr. Brader, that brings out my sense of being American? You are this awareness group's answer to the *Saturday Evening Post!*"

Billy laughed. "Thank you, Dr. Leonard, but I'd rather be in *Sports Illustrated.*"

CHAPTER 17

A Dysfunctional Family Implodes

"Dr. Ozelts, I hope your story is digestible because you're taking us to lunch."

Ozzie was ready.

"Dr. Leonard, participants and friends, as I told you my career has had a spiraling pattern to it. But I'm not here to complain, because I don't consider that my life has had that same pattern. Just the fact that I'm alive, just the fact that I'm not juiced up or locked up somewhere, just the fact that I love life and the arts, just the fact that I turned out to be an excellent father, just the fact that I am here with you means that I will win. And I'll try to explain that later on into this.

"My biological father left my mother when I was an infant. I don't remember much about him—just flashes of experiences and dreams—but I did have this sense of the presence of kindness and gentleness, even understanding. And there was a voice, a deep voice coming from a male direction that was comforting. But maybe all that's imaginary or just wishful.

"The new guy she picked to impregnate her into submission was different from the original guy. I was never consulted. I suspect it was 'a shotgun wedding' but I can't prove it. And he was a strict, hubristic, hard-edged ideologue. To him, I was a stupid, misguided little nuisance, and it was his job to set me straight about man, God, and law. It was well put by Ms. Bell or Ms. Storm: children at that age are easily intimidated, and behavior by parents that is inappropriate, or even uncontrolled, is uncorrectable because there is no one to correct it, no Constitution guidelines, rules, no enforcer. There is no matriculation into parenthood.

"Even pathological behavior by parents has to be absorbed by the child's psyche. Pre-schoolers as a rule don't go running to the police regardless of the abuse. I'll give you a simple analogy. How many parents, during the heyday of tobacco, thought it was their prerogative to smoke in the presence of their children, forcing them to inhale toxic substances? So it was, that I started with this monster, thinking all this was supposed to happen, that I should listen to this guy and try to understand the world through him, and his abusive behavior. The problem was that even when I tried doing that, I got my ass kicked for something or another anyway. Further, my mother was getting kicked around as well. I remember police coming into the house to break up fights. And I remember jumping on his back to try to stop him from smashing her with a washbasin.

"I sought refuge in my teachers at school, whom I revered. And it was through schooling that I began to question adults who didn't listen but reveled in their own instant wisdom. I began to see my household as not the rule but the exception. And I began to see my stepfather not as what the kids today call 'a role model', but as 'a psychopathology' to escape. She was married to him… but I wasn't. The first lie he lived, and my first *in personam* awareness experience, was his presumptive authority to abuse women and children in my family. I would run away from home often, even though a whipping was in store for me when it got too cold outside and I had to return.

84

I began to reach out and gather friends; I would take long walks with no particular destination in mind, just for the joy of searching. I still do that.

"I graduated from primary school with the highest score in the building on an academic advancement test, but I was on the edge. The bicycle was my first escape vehicle. The angelic daughter of the landlady taught me how to ride a bicycle, and I rode that Schwinn everywhere. Once in a mindless rapture I rode the bike down the highest hill in our neighborhood, at full speed. At the bottom of the hill there's a stop sign because the street crossing Highland Avenue, Beale Street, is a major thoroughfare. I sped right through that intersection with all the acceleration gained by the descent. Two cars, one from the right and one from the left, alternately missed the blur of red bike, each honking as if, 'what the hell was that?' 'That', was a physical manifestation of my thirst to break away.

"But there was a definitive expulsion and power shift in the family when I was sixteen. And with that long introduction that's a story I want to finish quickly with today. It's about the coming of identity and the power of a kiss.

"It happened in the dark night in my 'old '55' blue Ford on the side of a country road in a lazy seaside town south of Boston called Marshfield. She wore a white dress because I had asked her to. After the kiss I didn't know what to do next. I was suspended in disbelief, that I had finally done it; I had touched Kathy intimately. It was a meta-emotional experience. This event would be famous in my own mind forever.

"After I drove her home, I was still so dazed I drove around the winding roads of the South Shore for half of the night, hopelessly lost— nameless trees, street lamps, marshes, sand dunes. I almost drove the car into the ocean. I don't remember how I found my way home. I do remember being nearly out of fuel when I finally pulled into our driveway. I went quietly around to the back door, slipped off my shoes, and somehow engineered the back door open without its signature squealing noise. I snuck into my room, closed my door, and thought for a minute. Maybe I shouldn't brush my teeth just yet because I had kissed Kathy, and I shouldn't disturb her presence.

"I would wake up intermittently during the night, the two street lamps beaming through my window. Whereas the street lamps were always a beacon from 'reality,' tonight they could hang none of that on me. I'm spending the rest of this night in heaven.

"The next day my family was to go north to a summer camp in New Hampshire to register my little sister. My stepfather would drive. My mother and little sister were in the backseat, and I was in the front passenger seat.

"It didn't take long for my stepfather to notice the gas gauge needle almost to the left of the big 'E.' He became livid. It is in the nature of despotic men that they don't need much to rekindle their hate for those they have injured, who are witnesses to their worst aspects. My mother adopted a simple verbal defense that went something like this:

"'My son took his girlfriend out on a date; they are both great kids. This is a normal and wonderful thing. He lost track of the fuel; give him a break.' This almost perfect maternal argument fueled anger management problems further. The yelling between the front seat and back started to escalate. I then told these lower-middle-class, war-torn absolutists that they could scream at each other as often as they liked, but to refrain from any physical abuse of the kind I had witnessed previously: I was assuming power; I was taking charge.

"Then my stepfather tried something unusually stupid, probably to test my assertiveness. He tried a backhand thrust to the back seat, in an effort to slap my mother. Such a maneuver is unlikely to be successful, because you're working with indirect vision, and the anatomic structure of the elbow limits backward flexing. He was also compromising the control of the vehicle and threatening the well-being of my family. I easily stopped him with a grip onto his right arm with my left hand. Then I let him have it with a right cross to his left cheekbone. The car strayed into the breakdown lane on the downward slope of a hill. The right corner of the front bumper pounded against the side posts, which prevented the car from rolling down an embankment. My little sister screamed, 'The brake, Ozzie, the brake.' I remember my mother screaming, 'Oh, my God, Oh, my God.'

"I held off my grasping, sweating, hysterical stepfather with my left arm. I pulled the emergency brake, and the car jerked, mercifully, to a full stop at the precipice of a ravine into which we all could have plunged. I forced the steering wheel in the direction of the road, and my mother and I got of the car, nervous and tired. My little half-sister would be all right with my stepfather, I thought; he doted over her.

"We walked to the other side of the road. As the blue '55 sped off, my stepfather, blood trickling down his face, yelled epithets back at us that would have made Lee Marvin blush. We would have to hitchhike back home. (Ever go hitch hiking with your mother? It works. There's an irresistible empathy factor.) We had a ride almost immediately. A blue-collar New Englander, probably a carpenter, in a red pickup truck, afforded us a ride:

"'You people look like you've been through hell.'

"'Our version of it,' I said.

"That night the beams from two street lamps poured through my room window with such increased intensity that I woke up suddenly from a post-adrenalin-rush sleep and switched on my bedside lamp. This time I had to face a new reality. My decision to question my stepfather's authority in such a definitive and physical way had separated me from my mother, and my family, forever. It was no longer possible for all of us to live under the same roof.

"The intellectual consequence of such a childhood was an inquisitive mind. Since then I have an aversion to ideologues and zealots, of people absolutely convinced of something. And that's what attracted me to science and physics: the basic perspective that you have to back up a conclusion with evidence. If an opinion or conclusion is not backed by evidence or exceptions to them are found, then you have to revise that opinion or conclusion. In that regard, scientists, or I should say good scientists, are continually amenable to correction; that's how the truth evolves. During a seminar presentation or in a criticism of a submitted paper, it is my prerogative, even my duty, to present contradictory evidence or corrections if I'm aware of them. In contrast, I can't go into a church during a sermon with any degree of credibility, and raise my hand and say, 'After studying the DNA of a variety of biological species I have concluded that Genesis is a fairy tale.' There's no point in arguing based on a system of experimental verification with a system where, as Galileo said, 'You can explain the Universe by merely turning a few pages of a sacred text.'

"Absolutists, by definition, don't like to be corrected. They'd rather go down, clasping desperately to the *Titanic* of denial, than face a new truth or a change in dogma. I think that kind of behavior arises out of the fear of emptiness, the void, non-existence, that Linda Bell, and in a way, Margaret Worthington alluded to earlier.

"Pascal said, 'The silence of infinite spaces terrifies me.'

"It terrifies everyone. So is there an intellectual common ground, some place where we all can take a deep breath?

"Rather than blow my mind trying to conceive of the infinite, for the time being I'll try to appreciate, with John Keats, what is truth... and what is beautiful, with my five senses... six, if you include common sense. I think a benevolent creator would put up with that."

Ozzie sat back; he was out of breath, finished. Leonard made the communicative move again—folded arms, eye contact with Ozzie. "Asking the right questions is the beginning of the learning experience. In that sense Dr. Ozelts, you rose above your childhood terrors, a champion 'Rider of the Storm.'"

Leonard paused, looked around the room, checking his audience for their attention. He scratched his temple, opened his hands, and started his summation.

"One common thread throughout the presentations up to this point has been 'learning' and another, 'adaptation.' As children you were challenged and even threatened, and I get the sense that you were able to adapt and survive through a process. In Dr. Ozelts' case that process kicked in when he had to decide that the behavior of one of his parents was unacceptable. Change doesn't stop, dear hearts. Our faculties don't get together one day and say, 'OK, that's it; I'm done, I quit.'"

Leonard opened his arms in the delivery of that line and paused. Carolyn, Ozzie, Kiley, Brader, and Willy laughed; Linda Bell and Margaret Worthington smiled. They were in good hands.

"Change is probably less dramatic as adults because our buttons are all in place, but there are still increments of embryonic innocence, *stem cells of awareness*, available for empathy and learning; you're using them as we speak."

Leonard paused and thought about his next point.

"Linda Bell, lost in the tall corn, is not alone; Debbie Storm, holding off the grungy guy with her dog, wasn't alone; and Wellington Ozelts, defending his mother from abuse, wasn't alone: 'the life-force that drives the green age' of all children, the force of emotional growth, and the power of ontogeny was with them. And, I might add, the love and respect of all decent human beings.

"We'll reconvene this afternoon; session to begin at 3 o'clock. Thank you, dear hearts…"

Billy leaned over and whispered to Ozzie, "What's 'ontogeny'?"

"The coming to being, Billy."

"The coming to being of what?"

'Your self."

CHAPTER 18

Sharp Edges

B rader and Ozzie grabbed their papers and high-tailed it out of the conference room. As they walked along the corridor Ozzie was exhausted. "Phew, that was tough but I think I got it all out. I wanted to make a definitive statement. I mean… when would I have another audience like this? But I guess I was a little complicated and emotional."

"You're a humanoid, Doc, you're supposed to be complicated and emotional." Brader changed topics. "Hey, why don't we step out and take off in my car for lunch? Maybe we can find a little beachfront cafe. You need a beer? Maybe you're one of these green tea guys."

"If we can get back in a couple of hours, Willy Hanson is next. I told Willy Hanson to tell the story he told me. It's a great story… about his friends. How often do you hear about the blue-collar workers? They're always in the background, like the architecture. Lawyers, doctors, cops, and gangsters get all the glory."

Brader wasn't listening and walking too fast for Ozzie. "OK, let's get out of here. My car's down this way."

They walked out of the building and to the right at the end of the parking area where a beige-colored MGB convertible was parked on the grass. It was tilting up and left on the slope of a mound produced by the roots of a huge oak tree. The license plate read 'SIX.' Brader saw that Ozzie had noticed the license plate.

"My number when I played first base for Rock Hill," Brader explained.

"I haven't seen one of these in a while... Wow," Ozzie said, casting his eyes over the car.

"Jump in."

Ozzie accepted Brader's invitation and slid his long legs in and sat down. He looked around for a seatbelt, but there wasn't one.

Brader said, "I'm working on it."

The sun was out now, and the clouds were dispersing, but there was a breeze. He unbuttoned his shirt, which had a welcome cooling effect because his undershirt was sweaty. They both donned sunglasses as Brader backed the car away from the tree, and then stopped and shifted into first gear. He sped down to the front gate, looked right and left, and then took off with a right turn, north on the coastal road.

It was just past 3 o'clock when Brader and Ozzie rushed through the front door of the institute as Brader checked his watch. Like kids late for practice they didn't want to face the wrath of "The Coach." They ran up the stairs through the doors of the program's suite and down the corridor to the conference room. The door was closed but they slowly pushed it ajar. Leonard, without turning to glance, said, "Welcome back, gentlemen. Please continue, Mr. Hanson."

"Like I was saying, Dr. Ozelts was telling me I should tell a story about the fellas at the yard, but that's not the kinda stories I was listening to this morning. I talked to him about my close friend Brownie dying of lung cancer and how it was tough for all of us to lose him. But most of the stories this morning were about when we were kids, even real small kids. I was going to quit this... program...

I guess you call it, but after this morning I started to get a feeling for what's going on here. Like I said before I don't have the words or schooling most of this group has, but what I want to talk about… it's something I never forgot, that happened to me with my dad, when I was a little kid. So here goes."

Willy smiled at Margaret, and Margaret smiled back supportingly.

"When I was little, my family would go on camping trips together. This particular year, I think I was about ten years old, I asked my parents if we could bring my friend, Terry. Terry was about my age, and we were in the same class in school together. My parents said, 'OK.' Our trips were in August and always around this one mountain near Franconia, New Hampshire. The women would hang around the cabin mostly, while we men would explore and hike and chop wood. In August up in New Hampshire the days can be hot, but the night gets pretty cold. Cool enough that you're going to need firewood. So my dad, who was a salesman by trade, and Terry and I, went out to chop some wood. We found this small, rusty axe in a tool closet in the cabin and went in back of the cabin to look for wood. My dad was what you call kinda blockheaded. You couldn't tell him much… even when he didn't know what he was doing. Besides, we didn't much know what we were doing either. But men are supposed to chop wood to keep the cabin warm. We felt good about this job. But there's a right way and a wrong way to do things I guess, and we started out wrong. First, you got to have the right tool for the job—the axe was too small for the large blocks. Second, I was wondering whether my dad realized where we were while he was trying like crazy to chop these huge blocks with this little axe. You got to watch kids all the time. Terry and I did like he told us: go out and find blocks of wood to chop. We kept piling up wood for him, but he was getting nowhere fast. Then Terry asked him if he could help chop. It was an innocent remark; kids say things that they don't know what they mean sometimes, or they don't know the time isn't right to say something. My father then smashed his axe so hard against the chopping block that the head of the axe flew off and up behind him, where Terry was. Somehow—it happened so fast I can't remember exactly—the blade flew past Terry's head. Terry kind of froze for a minute and then felt the top of his head and blood was pouring out; he just plopped down in a daze. I guess when the blade flew past Terry's head it cut a huge gash in his scalp. Thinking back the kid could have been killed instantly by an axe blade in the neck or in the head. My dad, who was a God-fearing man, cried out, 'Oh God, help us.' We carried Terry back into the cabin, and my mother who was kind of... what am I trying to think of..."

"Squeamish?" Dr. Kiley suggested.

"Yeah, squeamish. Well, she couldn't do much but put on this first aid cream she found. She just spread it all over his head, which didn't stop the bleeding and just made a big white and red mess. We wrapped towels around his head and my dad said, 'I'll have to carry him down the hill, and then to the hospital.'

"'What hospital?' my mom said.

"'I don't know, I'll find one.'

"'Leave him here, he'll be all right, it's just a cut,' My mom said.

"My dad said, 'Are you crazy?' because he couldn't understand my mother, who was just worried about getting in trouble with the police I guess. I've got to say I've never seen my dad like this since. It's the only time I've seen him take over like this. Usually I had the feeling my mom was in charge. He was crazy about her. But this time he didn't even listen to her. He knew what he had to do and faced up to it.

"We wrapped a towel around his head and a bath towel around the kid, and my dad put him on his shoulder and walked him all the way down the mountain, which had to be at least a mile, and it was getting dark. It must have been a long, tough hike in the darkness. My mother wouldn't allow me to go with them. I didn't get much sleep that night, I can tell you that.

"The next day we walked down the mountain and saw a park ranger. We asked her where the nearest hospital was. She asked us what had happened, and she was terrific about it. No interrogation or anything, just helpful. She called the hospital on her radio, and she said that my father and Terry were OK. She arranged a ride for us, and we ran into the emergency ward and then to the room where they had taken Terry. My father was there looking tired, dirty, and bloody. His cheeks were streaked with dirt and tears too, I guess. He had stayed up all night with the kid.

"Terry was going to be all right, though. They had shaved his head and put in a lot of stitches. They said they get a lot of camping accidents there and the axe just missed critical arteries and we were lucky. My father saw us and started to break down.

"'I almost killed a child, for God sakes,' he said.

"'It wasn't your fault, Arthur, it was an accident, you did everything you could afterwards,' my mother said.

"Anyway, Terry's parents came up to New Hampshire and they were just so happy that Terry was OK, that they said just about the same thing my mother said, that it was an accident and my dad shouldn't beat himself up about it. But my dad never forgot that incident, and he never touched an axe again. I think he even wanted to go into a monastery for a while so he could find a way to forgive himself—not only for what happened but for what could have happened that would have been much worse.

"Now, here's the thing. I see this all the time. Bridges falling apart, tunnels leaking, tankers spilling, even buildings falling like dominoes… but people won't admit to ignorance… not knowing or understanding the warning signs before something big happens. I guess it's pride or arrogance, whatever you want to call it. You notice that the biggest infrastructure disasters never get blamed on anybody. It's nobody's fault."

Then Willy paused and looked around the table as he said, "Well, I can tell you right now it *was* somebody's fault.

"But I'll tell you something else while I'm at it. In my line of work at the mill and the shop, I deal with sharp edges all the time; one wrong move and you're done. I've never had so much as a bleeding cut. That's why I figure that experience about my dad was so important to me. I have a respect for sharp edges of the blade. I hone them myself. They have characteristics that can kill you. You work around that. You got to get a feeling for it: call it anticipation or whatever. You work with the danger, but you don't challenge it or get mad at it or lose concentration. I'm always watching and anticipating how the blade is going to cut and the wood is going to split.

"Well that's my story; I don't know where my friend Terry is now but I heard he went to college and became some kind of professor or teacher or businessman... good for him, something like the line of work you guys are in, I guess."

Leonard's face was pale like it was when he was concentrating; he was following Willy's narrative closely.

"I, for one, am glad that Terry made it down the hill. And I am thinking on several contributing levels about your experience, Willy. First, the role of your empathy for your father in this learning experience, second, the power of your father's untimely arrogance to cloud and distort, and finally, 'the vivid, sharp edges metaphor'—we get the big picture, Mr. Hanson, thank you."

"Sounds good to me, Dr. Leonard, I just wish I knew what the hell you just said. If it means that I learned something from this, you're probably right."

Willy gave Leonard a broad, appreciative smile and Leonard answered with a nod of approval. The purpose of Leonard's including Willy into this group now appeared clearer to Ozzie.

Maybe Willy's story was kind of a wake-up call: if you're going to screw up, try to confine the consequences to yourself.

CHAPTER 19

Compassion

"Ms. Mayfield, what do you have for us?"

"There have been some hard stories here, some tough times. We had tough times in Baltimore, too. But today I want to talk about a kind of a love story, and the children of Mozart Street, OK?"

"Please."

"When I was a little girl living on Mozart Street on the South Side of Baltimore—by the way, we pronounced it 'Moze-arr'—we also were a 'dominion of our own,' but we were an extended family that included the whole block. Baltimore was built block by block, with row houses that had marble steps. The steps were more than just a way into the house. They were places to sit and congregate. They were places to define your social group, and they were places to cool your bottom on hot days when the shadows were right. On hot summer days, the doors were flung open and Moze-arr Street was almost a rectangular theater, a Greek theater, and the marble steps all led to our grand stage. All of the kids would gather there for happenings of the extended family. Touch football games, dances, jump roping, hop-scotch, hide and seek… it was like an everyday carnival.

"Then one hot summer day a green convertible Volkswagen turned onto our block. All the kids stopped playing, and jump ropes sagged and footballs meandered into the street gutter; big kids, small kids, and even toddlers turned around and looked, and then stared.

"First of all, the driver was a white guy, and we didn't see a lot of those voluntarily dropping by Mozart Street. And he was different; he was tall and slender and handsome, long brown hair and shorts, and he was a student from the Johns Hopkins University just up the road. We slowly started to gather around the car, and he got out like he wanted to make an announcement. He said he was Dr. Vincent and he wanted to create a baseball team from the neighborhood kids. You should have seen the excitement. We introduced him to the 'Reverend,' the local preacher, and they took names of the kids who were interested. But he did more than that; he talked to everybody, even to me, about our lives, and he joked, brought us ice cream, and even played some of our games with us. He wasn't too good at jump rope though.

"Eventually he did form a baseball team, and got them uniforms and gloves, and with that team he helped the boys develop pride and confidence. He recruited his girlfriend or wife, I don't know which, to work with the church daycare center, and she had kind of an arts and crafts thing going that I got to participate in, usually at night when my mother was working; she was very kind to the little ones. Dr. Vincent also expanded our world outside of Mozart Street. He would take us on trips to Rehoboth Beach on the ocean, he would take us to his laboratory and explain what he was doing at his work, and he would arrange for us to attend banquets where we would be introduced to famous people in the city, including professional athletes. I remember when he came to our house one night to tutor my older brother. He helped him with his homework and then we

97

tried to feed him, but he wasn't too hungry—either that, or he didn't like black-eyed peas, collard greens and chittlins.

"When I was little my father wasn't home much, and then later on when I turned ten he wasn't home at all. Now that I think back, Dr. Vincent and my mother must have had 'a thing going on.' They were always talking, laughing, and one time I couldn't sleep and I looked out from my room door and I saw them dancing together, or… I think it was kind of like dancing.

"Dr. Vincent was important to many lives on Mozart Street. I remember a speech he gave to us from the marble steps. He pointed to the street sign and said that we lived on a street with a special name, close to his heart: Mozart, the composer-and he pronounced the 'z' like a 'c' and also the 't' this time. Mozart also started in a little village, and now he is known for his music throughout the world. He said that each day should be a day of progress toward a larger world, from 'Moze-arr' to Mozart, a world where 'our music' will be heard. He said that just up town, almost walking distance from Mozart Street, was one of the best university medical centers in the world, and we probably didn't even know it; and that wasn't right. Academics had an obligation to the community because they have taken on the responsibility of enlightenment. He said learning was not just an option; it was a necessity, and he said that each of us should get good, or even 'the best,' at a skill or a subject, like Mozart was the best. Finally he pointed to each one of us, like this, and he said loudly, 'Look at me, and trust me when I tell you that I believe in you; you live on a street named after a special person, and each of you is special, and wonderful to me, always.'

"Then one summer he was gone. I asked my mother what happened to Dr. Vincent. She said that his work was finished here and that he had to go.

"I started to cry, and my mother took me into her arms and asked me what was wrong. I said, 'I loved Dr. Vincent, Mamma.'

"Then Mamma said—and I'll never forget this, 'I love him too, precious, that's maybe why he had to leave. But aren't you glad there are people like that in the world, baby? So you stop your crying now and think about this: wherever he is, he's thinking about us, and we're thinking about him. That's what compassionate love is, baby; it doesn't go away when the person you love goes away. It's God's 'gift outright,' yours forever...'"

Leonard, ever keen toward the reactions of the group, noticed that everyone was quiet except for Margaret Worthington, who was blowing her nose, and Debbie Storm, who was checking her cell phone, yet again. If there ever had been traces of tension in the group it was gone now with Carolyn Mayfield's presentation. Leonard skipped his usual summary; that was part of his style. Although he was a word merchant he loved the silence after eloquence; it was a statement unto itself, a statement *beyond* words.

CHAPTER 20

An Inspired Response

"I try to avoid clichés but… tough act to follow, Ms. Mayfield," Kiley said respectfully, looking over to Carolyn.

"Leonard, am I going to do this now or…?"

"Dr. Kiley, you have our undivided attention… right, Ms. Storm!"

Debbie pressed a button on her cell phone and placed the phone under the table. That didn't seem to bother Kiley, who continued.

"In preparing for my presentation today, I was trying to dig back into my memory bank to the first indications that I was going to go into medicine or even the sciences… I think it would have to derive from my fears for my mother's health as a child. She was always sick. Not only that but, strangely enough she wore her vulnerability like a badge of honor, a scepter of maternal bearing. Often I would hear, 'Scotty, what will you do if I no longer exist?'

"This is a frightening question for a kid, I don't know, what, five, six, or seven years old? She was in poor general health. She'd had rheumatic fever as a child in Ireland and suffered from the long-term effects of poor nutrition and neglect as an orphan. That's why Ms. Storm's talk drew my attention.

"Other chronic dysfunctions in her nervous system were probably derived from lead poisoning. And it's interesting how this came about. That's going to be my story.

"We were first-generation immigrants and relatively poor; lower than lower middle class you might say. My father worked in a dry cleaner's, and that's where I got most of my 'new' shirts: customers would sometimes delay picking up their items, but my dad figured two weeks was enough time.

"My mother would try to do odd jobs for people. One such job proved almost deadly. There was a certain Dr. Bussler, a large, rather rotund fellow with metal-rimmed glasses, who looked like a large version of Beria, Stalin's KGB chief. He would make house calls to treat her for attacks of arrhythmia and fatigue stemming from the rheumatic heart. His hobby was sculpturing or carving civil war miniatures out of a lead alloy. He would recreate battle scenes with these figures: cavalrymen, horses, guns, flags, the pageantry, the whole bit. He enlisted my mother, who was a very careful worker, as his finishing assistant for these figures. That way my mother could pay for the house calls and treatments. The problem was that the primary metal in these pieces was lead. She would file down the molded figures and paint them, and she was paid by the number of items she could finish. I remember her hands and fingers being shiny and coated with lead dust. Think of us kids also. You don't get all of that stuff off with soap. My sister was a toddler then. Picture my mother giving a bath to the toddler after an afternoon filing lead miniatures. And the lead dust particles all over the house, on the rug and in the air? Where did they go? Considering that this Bussler guy had a degree in medicine and presumably some training in preventive medicine, and then to have him be the perpetrator of exposure of lead to one of his patients, is unconscionable, inexcusable. I can't prove it, but I think that the lead in her system aggravated her rheumatic heart symptoms, and certainly nervous disorders. She suffered from peripheral neuropathy after that.

Some days she couldn't get out of bed. I had to scrub the kitchen floor and vacuum the house. For years she was in and out of hospitals all the time. I would take buses and subways to see her.

"After the diagnosis I think Bussler lost his license for a while but my mother did not sue. You could settle for millions pursuant to negligence today. Apparently, there was some kind of showdown where he actually broke down when confronted with the evidence, and pleaded for her mercy and good graces. She should have slapped him, maybe just once, and called a lawyer. Lord knows she slapped my butt enough times just for skipping school.

"It makes you think about MDs in those days and what other preventable insults they ignored or even facilitated. The technical term is *iatrogenic*: symptoms produced by the treatment or presence of the physician. Cigarette smoke inhaled from a physician's cigarettes or even transferred from tobacco-stained fingers might have been another source of iatrogenic symptoms. Today one of the major sources of iatrogenic infections is physicians' failure to wash hands between patients. I think my mother's case was useful to med students because of the steady and consistent source of contamination. We're not talking here about chewing on house paint now and then. This is about lead dust every day, everywhere.

"I don't know why my mother didn't sue Dr. Bussler for all he was worth; still amazes me. She had a heart ravaged by rheumatic fever, but yet, supernaturally free of vengeance. Although lead had contaminated her bones, it could not soften her iron will. By her courage and defiance in the presence of the daily pain of chronic disease I was inspired to go into medicine. That would be my response to his professional irresponsibility."

Scattered applause arose from the group. Even Debbie Storm looked up at Dr. Kiley and heaved her breasts.

Leonard paused for the applause and then addressed Kiley in a very business-like tone. "Abusive or negligent behavior can be a powerful motivating force, particularly where the umbilical cord won't let go, Dr. Kiley. You might entertain the possibility of forgiving yourself for something that was not your fault."

Kiley, visibly shaken, leaned back on his chair and took a deep breath as Balis leaned over and gave him a pat on the back.

CHAPTER 21

Balis' First Orgasm

"Dr. Balis... Dr. Balis? Would you finish up for us today, and I'll present my recitation Friday morning?"

Balis' reddish gray hair was now no longer a lie on the fairway but well into the rough. He needed a haircut. He had his charcoal striped, short-sleeved shirt with a cotton, army-green vest, and black baggy jogging pants. Balis was a researcher, and although the scientific method requires rigorous organization, forethought, and logical reasoning, the daily wardrobe and color combinations worn by most scientists make a mockery of minimal sartorial standards. Most male scientists couldn't care less what they wear as long as they don't freeze to death. You get the feeling that they grab whatever polyester falls off the closet hanger and has enough buttons and zippers to support attachment to their neglected frames.

Balis looked up and around slowly and spoke in a kind of exaggerated, pedantic tone. "I have been listening intently to these interesting presentations, and I'm afraid I can't contribute anywhere near that level of psychological impact.

"I will admit, however, to a basic problem when I was a kid, and that had to do with my relationship with the opposite sex."

Now the speaker had the attention of the group.

"From the second grade on, I was subject to a series of crushes on girls that occupied my consciousness to a point that endangered my academic career even before it got started. For extended periods under these spells, I was unable to think about reading, 'riting, or 'rithmetic.

"My first crush was on my first grade teacher, Miss Chisolm. I would stare at her constantly, but I couldn't hear a word she was saying. My 'visual' was shutting out my 'audio.' Thinking back I wonder where I was going with this. The age difference between us precluded anything resembling an affair, and besides, my prepuberal development would have to limit any overt romantic advances to childlike platonic platitudes. I thought she was the prettiest creature in the world. I remember one time when she called on me to stand up and read about 'Zeke raking leaves'; I just kept looking at her. She was very kind, though, and came up to my desk, put her hand on my shoulder, then looked in my book, and said, 'Now, Rolland, we will not be able to read about Zeke properly unless he is standing on his feet.'

"Then she took my book, out of my hands and turned it one hundred eighty degrees, and placed it back into my hands right side up. All the while I was hypnotized by her closeness, and her perfume, her femininity, and became even more helpless than before. Finally, after the giggles of my classmates had subsided, she would coax me into the reading of a sentence or two about Zeke's leaves that could have been on another planet. Obviously the messenger was overwhelming the message.

"I don't know how or why I was eventually promoted to the second grade. I'm sure I was a distant last in my class. Maybe I gave myself away, and Miss Chisolm kicked me upstairs on the theory that, if we broke up, it would re-initiate a normal primary school learning process.

"In Miss Brooke's third grade class, sitting in the first row, to the right near the door, was my next crush. I fell in love with Marjorie Wolfe. As far as I was concerned, she had a smile that could launch a thousand rockets. At least now I was in love in my age bracket, and I had a right to dream about a legitimate relationship.

"Emotionally scarred from my affair with Miss Chisolm, I had to approach this courtship more realistically. I would surround her with my adoration. I would follow her everywhere. I would touch and smell things she had touched. At recess I would deliberately be the last student out of the door so I could retreat and sit at her desk for a moment. I would place my cheek on the magic desk, and try to imagine her presence. It smelled, of course, like erasers, paper, and the old wood of a desk; but it was her erasers, paper and wood. Marjorie must have known that I was crazy about her, but she would not acknowledge my attentions. My theory then was that she was too wonderful to waste her time requiting affections from the unworthy son of peasants. And I didn't blame her, not at all. If anything, the more unapproachable she was, the greater her mystical presence in the classroom. From my amorously tainted perspective, Marjorie filled the room; there were only two people in the third grade that year: myself and Marjorie Wolfe. My studies, however, did improve—not because of any rekindled scholarship, but because I didn't want to be kept back while Marjorie was promoted.

"Something happened in the fifth grade that thrust me into a new level of passion. I was a veteran romantic now and almost accustomed to the burden of yearly crushes. The object of my affections the next two years was Rosemarie Bertolli. In my eyes she was not only the prettiest girl in the class but she was the most intelligent. The fifth grade teacher, Miss Bishop, divided us into groups; the first group was the smartest bunch. Since Rosemarie was in the first group I rose quickly to the top of my class, all on wings of inspiration generated by Rosemarie's eyes. They were dark, mysterious, and made my hands sweat when she caught my glance.

"One day I pulled that trick again where I would be the last to exit for recess. But this time my excuse was that I hadn't finished my morning assignment. Everyone else was out of the room, and I moved to Rosemarie's desk. I was now sitting in the throne of my radiant princess. The left side of my brain tried to calculate long division, while the right side was taking in the atmosphere where Rosemarie breathed… where she placed her *self*. Now for the first time in my life there was a sensual aspect to my adoration. The adrenalin and oxytocin levels of all this kicked in, and I was suddenly overwhelmed with a rush throughout my system. I felt an enormous release, an effluence… I dropped everything and ran to the bathroom.

"No… I was dry. But I was shaking and exhausted as I went back to my seat and somehow finished the math. I must have then dozed off because my next conscious awareness was of students clamoring back into the classroom. I was scolded by Miss Bishop as I passed in my math assignment. But it was worth it.

"To this day I believe I hold the distinction of having the first orgasm in my fifth grade class. After a short review of my career dossier, some may still consider this to be among my greatest personal achievements!"

Leonard was holding back tears of laughter forced by Balis' combination of melodrama, and hyperbole. The story was a refresher from the dramatic presentations of the day's session. Leonard could hardly get the words out as he wiped his eyes. "That's…that's it for today. Please… please be on time Friday. Thank you, all."

Then he threw his note pad up into the air in a gesture of feigned futility. Most other participants around the table did not tune into Balis' drift of humor until he was almost finished because it was so unexpected. Linda Bell "felt sorry for the poor kid," Debbie thought the young Balis "precociously over sexed," but Carolyn Mayfield who was mildly shocked commented, "I didn't know males could get an orgasm that young!"

"Intensity," Ozzie explained.

CHAPTER 22

Eva and the Icons

The King's Pub was starting to increase in population as The Table rearranged chairs to make room for latecomers. A tall, slender blonde, possibly in her late thirties, with long, curly hair and blue eyes, glasses over high cheekbones, with that "efficient intellectual" look, popped into the front door and glanced around. She was in a slight panic as she said, "I locked myself out of my car, can anyone help me?"

Leonard turned left over Suzanne's shoulder to see her and saw this as a recruiting opportunity. "Yes, please join us, I'm sure something can be arranged; as you can see we have a number of endeavoring gentlemen here at the table who would, I'm sure, be pleased to rescue an attractive young lady."

Alex and Bernie got up, but Alex was faster to the trigger.

"Anybody have a coat hanger?" he asked.

"Let's ask Larry, Alex," Leonard responded, and then yelled to Larry, "Hey, Larry, bring two Rollys with a coat hanger on the side down here, will you?"

"I got the first part but was that a 'wall banger'?"

"A coat hanger… somebody locked themselves out of a car."

Leonard tried to make "the distressed damsel" more comfortable.

"Allow me… I'm Myles Leonard, and that's Alexander or Alex, who's been assigned to rescue you; that's Bernie at the end of the table, this is Suzanne… and Ellen… and how shall we address you?"

"Hi, I'm Eva… I was on my way north to the University for a seminar and got off the interstate for some gas and a bite to eat; and then it got complicated."

"You haven't seen anything yet," Bernie muttered.

They found a chair for Eva, and she sat down next to Alex; she looked to the women for a sign of acceptance, and Ellen responded.

"What kind of seminar meeting are you headed for, Eva?"

"It's a seminar on the Civil War. I teach history at State U."

Leonard dropped his arm around Suzanne and turned methodically toward Ellen and Eva. They had his attention. He loved to learn about new people—that was the natural inclination that lead to his life's work—but he also loved to learn from them, about subjects where he had limited knowledge.

Bernie spoke on behalf of the table: "First drinks at the table are on the King, what is your pleasure, Eva?"

"A white wine with some soda water will do, thanks… Excuse me, I didn't get your name, sir?"

"Bernie."

"OK, Bernie …thanks."

Leonard addressed Eva: "Eva, do you believe in historical evolution; are we heading toward something higher, ethically, morally?"

"Wow, Leonard, I just got here. That's a large question, but probably more important than whether I'm going to get into my car tonight."

She turned to Alex as she spoke.

Alex reached out for the coat hanger Larry brought to the table. Larry also brought a pitcher of Rolling Rock. Alex refilled his glass, took a sip of beer, stood his two hundred forty pounds up cowboy style, and said, "I'll take care of this, pilgrim, where's your car?"

"It's the green Volkswagen… Georgia license plates, thanks, Alex."

Alex was enjoying his role as the competent male for the occasion. As a street-wise kid in Athens, Greece, he used to break into cars to steal radios every day. This was a piece of cake.

Eva turned again toward Leonard and launched into an answer to his question.

"I think we all see advances scientifically and economically, especially in Europe and North America, but I don't see that societies and governments of the twentieth century are morally superior to those of the nineteenth century or even the eighteenth. Conversely, I never fully understood why we hold Washington and Lincoln up as gold standards of some kind of moral character and civil generosity."

"Do you have a problem with historical icons in general or just with those guys, Eva?"

"I just think that we ought to see political people in all their colors in whatever century. They were aristocrats, bureaucrats, and manipulators who knew how to inspire, and lead, and even force others to do battle for their political agenda."

"Tread softly on our heroes, Eva," Bernie said emphatically, but Eva was obviously ready for this.

"Well, for starters, Washington was a slave owner. But it doesn't stop there. He was of the aristocratic land-owner class, he inherited probably over one hundred thousand acres in the Virginia Colony and what is now West Virginia. Actually in 1774, Washington made a statement that no one in his right mind should consider independence of the colonies from the crown."

"What changed his mind?" Sue asked.

"He was probably convinced that one hundred thousand acres of Virginia were his, not England's. For example, he was peeved when almost all of his tobacco income went to taxes; that, and pressure from other Virginian aristocrats who felt the same way, changed his mind. By the way, he wouldn't sign the Declaration of Independence, even though there were, I believe, seven or eight signers from his colony of Virginia, including Thomas Jefferson. At least Jefferson tried to put an anti-slavery clause into the Declaration, but was voted down. Washington did sign the original US Constitution because he was the presiding officer of the Convention. This document endorsed the return of escaped slaves to their masters (Article Four section two). I think in The Civil War, he would have been on the side of the South. Robert E. Lee was his alter ego. The powers handed to the States made the Civil War inevitable."

"All's well that ends well, he won and we won," Suzanne said, smiling and starting to feel the glow from the second or third round of Rolling Rock.

"I suppose so; but Washington was no pure democrat, either.

"In his administration after the war, he, along with his sidekick, Alexander Hamilton, favored electoral colleges of aristocrats, the elite land owners, who would decide elections. The uneducated common people were not to be trusted with a vote. Although in this century the franchise has been extended, politicians are still the big land-owners, shareholders, the privileged elite who get the common people to put their lives on the line for their agenda and their wars; I don't think I need to name names."

Bernie was getting fed up.

"You sound like a revolutionary, Eva. What are you trying to do, turn this country upside down? In France, hell, they had at least three revolutions in the nineteenth century, and they're still one of the most class-conscious societies in Europe. The Bolshevik workers revolution in Russia, which was supposed to represent the masses of workers, created a ruling class of ruthless bureaucrats and dictators including Stalin."

"I know what you mean… but that's not what I mean. I remember a line from another historian, G.W. Johnson, in *The New Republic*, written just after JFK's death: '…Washington, the god-like, and Lincoln, the saintly, have been joined by Kennedy, the young chevalier… historians may protest, but they cannot alter the fact that once touched by romance, they are removed from all categories, and comparable only with the legendary.' You can't touch them. If it weren't for the first amendment from the Bill of Rights we'd all be serfs. That was George Mason's initiative, not Washington's. But that's another story."

Leonard tried to head off Bernie who was getting excited. "I think Eva is saying, Bernie, that we have made saints out of the 'founding fathers.' They were courageous and strong-willed, but also, they were a privileged few in the right place at the right time with ambitions and egos. Agents of a work in progress. Am I in your ball park, Eva?"

Eva's wine was kicking in. She was going after a dead white male.

"The monument to Washington, rising up from the city named for him, is a tellingly oversized Freudian tribute from those who in their hagiographic adoration assigned him fatherhood of the country. Listen, the birth of this country had many fathers. The phrase 'United States of America' was coined by the spokesman for the revolution, Thomas Paine, who wrote the philosophical pillar "Common Sense" and contributed the royalties to the continental army. Now there's a guy who put his money where his mouth is... I mean, was."

Just then Alex popped back in, by the front door. He shuffled his way back sideways to his seat next to Leonard, and tossed Eva her car keys.

"You're all set. Here are your keys, and your car is locked."

"Thank you, Alex. These gentlemen have cornered me into revealing my innermost feelings about dead white males."

Leonard cupped his fingers and called out, "Larry, yes please, another pitcher of amber fluid, and a wine cooler to calm the waters."

"I like Eva, Leonard," Suzanne said, turning also to Ellen, who nodded in agreement. "She speaks her mind, and just because we might not agree with her, we have to respect that she doesn't just regurgitate the gospel about these icons. It's refreshing. And now I want to hear what she thinks about Lincoln."

"She'll probably tell us he was a damned liar," Bernie said, forcing a laugh.

"Actually I think Honest Abe lied to himself more than to anyone else,"

Bernie was fiddling with a pack of matches; he didn't want to listen to this, but he had little choice.

"Lincoln's rise to power was totally different from Washington's. He was self-educated and arose from humble beginnings to become president; he was a very literate man, an extraordinary speaker and leader. Having said that, anyone who can carry the burden of presiding over the killing of six hundred thousand young men and teens for a political cause has to think God is on his side. It all depends on how far you want to go to prove your point. He thought that preserving the Union was a sacred duty, and God had placed him in that responsibility: 'God's making me do this.' Ironically, he accomplished it unConstitutionally, scrapping *habeas corpus* and unleashing decidedly unmerciful warriors like Grant and Sherman. Grant wouldn't listen to a delegation of Union prisoners from Andersonville who pleaded for an exchange, and Sherman burned everything in his merciless march through Georgia.

"Often Lincoln's warrior side is justified by those who claim he freed the slaves. But Lincoln wrote in 1862, 'If I could save the union without freeing any slave I would do it.' The Emancipation Proclamation was submitted in September of 1862—which, by the way freed only the slaves in the unoccupied states and territories. My God, if that isn't politics over morality, I don't know what is. Shoot me for not jumping on the fan wagon, but freeing slaves was not his priority; saving the Union of States was his priority. He was a neo-federalist. But he said in 1858, 'I am not in favor of bringing about in any way the social and political equality of the black and white races.'"

"Eva, listen to me." Bernie had had enough, "There's a lot of room for interpretation. I think you've got to remember it's a long way from emancipation to social equality; maybe Lincoln didn't want to scare off the swing vote in the border-states. We all say things under pressure, especially political pressure, and Lincoln was constantly under enormous pressure from all sides. The country was divided; he didn't live long enough for the luxury of moral re-examinations or regrets. He did what he thought was right, and he won. The price was high, but the country stayed united. How much blood would have been shed in future wars with the alliances a free South would have formed? You paper-pushing historians have the pleasure of hindsight to take shots at those who make history."

With that, Leonard broke up the debate quickly by lifting his glass. "Let us raise our glasses to the lessons of history, to the courage of those who make it, and the passion of those who write it."

"Hear, hear, hear..." The table responded with sips of salutation, and Eva released a sigh of relief, glancing at Alex. She hadn't meant to go into such a rant, but everybody thinks they're amateur historians.

"Passion... did you say passion?" Alex asked theatrically.

"Watch out for that guy, Eva, he's a hot-blooded Mediterranean," Bernie warned.

CHAPTER 23

Barking up the Wrong Tree

The table was breaking up into coupled conversations: Alex with Eva, Suzanne with Leonard, and Bernie with Ellen. Leonard's work was returning to his immediate attention as the effects of the beer began to subside. Suzanne suggested that they go to her place, and he was physically too tired to deny her. They left together hand in hand by the back door after Leonard told Larry to defer all his calls, that he would return them. June would probably call The King's Pub eventually, but Larry would handle that.

Alex and Eva left by the front door, leaving Bernie and Ellen at the table. As they turned left and walked toward Eva's car, Alex decided to continue the delicate negotiation for "an extended evening."

"How about something to eat? Hungry?"

"OK. But can you drive? I wouldn't know where to go; I am kind of hungry."

"My car is further down... *You* were great in there, Eva."

"Do you really think so, Alex? I don't know how I got cornered into a heavy-weight history discussion, but I'm not going to sugar-coat my professional opinions."

"Leonard cornered you, I've been at this table for years; as soon as you said you were a history prof, he cranked you up."

"Why?"

"He loves to learn. He's insatiable that way. And the table had a good time too. Most nights are more logorrheic than logical; we don't usually remember much of what we've said the next day. They'll remember this, though."

"Actually, now that I think about it... it felt good to discuss some of this material outside of academia," Eva said, "out among the citizenry where it can get a good hearing without howls of indignation for my treason."

"Yeah, I never understood why some people get angry about suggesting imperfections in 'the founding fathers.' The Constitution has twenty-seven amendments. That's hardly a perfect document."

Alex opened the door to his Corvette for the lady, walked rapidly to the driver's side, opened his door, sat down, smiled at Eva tenderly, turned on the ignition, and set the car heater to medium; the evening was cooling down, and they were both a little nervous now.

Alex was in his element: the woman was in his car. His moves and his words were measured and precise, like a Burt Lancaster scene. He shifted the joystick deftly to "drive" and made a U-turn. He knew a small place that served decent food back south, past the institute.

They talked as Alex negotiated the traffic; an impatient driver was tailgating him.

"Go ahead, buddy, if you want the lane that badly, take it."

Eva laughed; Alex's mockery of road rage made her feel more secure. "A lot of crazies out there", she said.

As they zoomed past the institute sign Eva asked Alex, "Is that where Leonard works?"

"'Doctor Leonard,'" Alex corrected. "His name is Myles Leonard but everyone that he's going to like calls him Leonard. Yes, some of us have thought of seeing him at work but we get the feeling that he wants to keep his private and social life separate from his work. Suzanne once told us that 'he takes his work sacredly.'"

"He has a great respect for individuals. He makes you feel welcome and important in his presence because he has a talent for listening; he has an eclectic ear," Eva added.

"You're saying that because he listened to your history lesson. Does he turn you on?"

"Kind of, but we'd never make it; I'd drive him crazy."

"And you'd have to face the sound and fury of June and Suzanne."

"Who?"

"His wife and his girlfriend."

"The sound may be, not necessarily the fury," Eva said.

Just then Alex saw the sign of the restaurant coming up: "The Sea Bistro" in green neon with a fish wearing a chef's hat.

"I hope you like seafood, Eva."

Alex turned into the lot of the restaurant a little too quickly, and the rear car fender scraped the asphalt driveway. Eva looked at Alex, but he was unfazed, turning the steering wheel athletically to back the car into what he calculated to be the best parking spot available. He popped the car locks, and they both got out of the car, which he then locked with his remote key. They walked up the steps to the dining room of the restaurant, where they were met by a petite, young, blond hostess holding a menu that looked like an oversized diploma.

"Isn't it past your bedtime?" Alex asked her cynically, and then looked at Eva.

"How many?" the hostess asked, ignoring the slight.

"Two."

"This way please."

The hostess walked them all the way past a row of tables to a table opposite the restrooms. Alex was offended.

"I saw a lot of empty tables, and you're going to sit us next to the john? I don't think so, young lady. Let me show you the table we prefer."

Alex walked back to a table closer to a window and a view of the sea cast by the evening light.

"We're sitting here."

"All right, not a problem," she said, defensively. "Your waitress will be with you in a minute, enjoy your meal."

She slapped the menus in front of Alex, and he passed one to Eva.

"You certainly are decisive in your actions, Alex."

"You have to show them who's boss: we're here patronizing their restaurant… You're a very attractive woman, Eva. You're probably married or almost married."

Before Eva could answer that, the waitress, a black-haired beauty, with dark eyes and an East Indian complexion, showed up.

"I'll be your waitress. My name is Raji. Can I get you something to drink?"

"Eva?"

"I'd like a white wine, if you have it."

"A Vouvray, and bring us a bottle."

"We only have Chardonnay," the waitress said.

Alex looked up from his menu. "Oh, Chardonnay… the Coca-Cola of white wines for the muddy-minded middle class. This Chardonnay monopoly reminds me of that *Saturday Night Live* skit about a Chicago Greek Hamburger place. Remember that, Eva? No Coke, Pepsi; chips no fries… cheeseburger, cheeseburger… No Vouvray… Chardonnay, Chardonnay!"

Eva smiled tolerantly and said to the waitress, "Chardonnay will be fine, Raji… So where are you from, Alex? Bernie said you were a hot-blooded Mediterranean, and you seem to know a little bit about wines."

"I'm Greek. My father was an international lawyer. Maybe that's how I have this affinity for Leonard—he and my father are world-class word merchants."

"I'm from the history sector of academia," Eva said. "There's a mountain of verbiage piling up there, as well. How did you end up in the USA?"

"I came over on an international program sponsored by a small college in Ohio that wanted a more diverse student body. I was a party animal there, but I learned how to increase the value of my social stock, how to win friends and influence people."

"You want to elaborate on that, Alex?"

The waitress came with the wine, poured Alex a taste for his approval. He liked that tradition, but tonight he was going to flaunt it. He sloshed a sip in his mouth and said, "It presents itself with a bouquet reminiscent of the glove compartment in a soccer mom's SUV. Its sweetness recalls the confections in a movie theater lobby; and, yes, it sits on the palate like a painted water lily sits on a Monet. Despite all that, it'll do for the time being."

Eva laughed, and the waitress shook her head in "whatever" resignation. "Will you order now, sir?"

Alex ordered the calamari in wine sauce with pasta, and Eva, the flounder *Parisienne*.

They both started buttering the rolls that were wrapped in a napkin in a wicker basket, and Alex continued his autobiography.

"I don't mean this as a put-down of our American friends, but I came here as a college freshman and I damn near flunked out of the place—and now I have houses in Connecticut and Florida and take vacations in Europe and Acapulco. That's an immigrant success story, no matter how you cut it."

"Wow, how did you accomplish that?"

"It took me a while to find out how the game is played. By and large Americans want to be entertained. They want love, money, and a good time. I found out that I was interesting to them. I had a style; I could make a party."

"Lots of people have a style, Alex."

"True, but not everybody can help people enjoy life. I made friends, even in graduate school—or maybe I should say, especially in graduate school. Those geeks and nerds needed someone to light up their lives. When academics finally close their labs and books, and they realize that they haven't had a party or a woman in three weeks, I'm their 'go to guy,' the broker for their suppressed drive to be human, to let it loose."

"I may be profiling here," Eva, prefaced, "but it is true, I suppose, that there's something ebullient in the mentality of Greeks and Italians that maximizes the moment: the music, the dancing, the joy, the laughter, there's no halfway... Oh, here comes your squid."

"Squid?" the waitress inquired.

"That's mine," Alex answered.

The waitress set the plate before Alex and then set Eva's plate. "Looks good," Alex said. "Shall we drink to the King's table and our meeting?"

Alex poured the wine, stylishly turning the bottle so that the last drops wouldn't drip onto the food. They made eye contact and drank a sip of wine.

He renewed the conversation.

"How did you get into American history—I should say, the study of American history, Eva?"

"My father was a professor of English so I had an academic background. I started out an English major but I got more interested in the life and times of authors, than what they were writing. I know that sounds curious and pedestrian but that's how I am, I guess. I also noticed differences in what people write, and what they actually do or how they behave. I got my PhD from Iowa and got a job down here at State University… where I met my partner."

"Your… partner?" Alex asked, almost reluctantly.

"Shauna. She's my best friend in the world."

"What do you mean?" Alex almost gagged on a piece of squid.

"I mean I love her. She's my soul mate."

"So you are…"

"…Assertive, lesbian, and a tae-kwan-do black belt. Are you shocked by male attributes in women, Alex?"

"I'm from Greece. Men over there hold hands. I'm not shocked by anything. Wow, I should have… I don't know. Everybody's different, I suppose."

Alex poured himself another glass of wine, this time ignoring her glass; he ditched his Burt Lancaster role for that of a displaced courtier, and started mumbling.

"Excuse me, did you say something?" Eva asked.

"Well… I was just wondering to myself how I get into these situations."

"What situation? You found me at the King's Table …you liked me… you unlocked my car, for which I'm grateful, and then you took me out to dinner. It's a party, let's enjoy!

"Mmmm… my flounder's delicious."

CHAPTER 24

"He has been shot, Milo...
Stay by my side"

Leonard and Suzanne left by the back door after paying their respects to Larry. Leonard hadn't locked the truck, and he told Suzanne to "jump in." As Leonard started up Betsy and looked in the rearview mirror in order to back up the truck he said to Suzanne, "That was outstanding, Suz, now there's a young lady who looks at our presidential icons with all their warts and wooden teeth in three dimensions. I wonder what she would do with Warren Harding?"

"Wasn't she terrific?" Suzanne said. "It's the same data available out there for everyone about these people; you either include it or exclude it. It's not like she's making this stuff up."

"Patriots are sometimes given to the blind zealotry of religious fanatics. They don't take lightly to their deities being re-examined in the light of objectivity. Like academic science, academic history is not sugar-coated."

Leonard drove to Suzanne's condominium. He was again feeling some discomfort in his chest, but did not want to complicate the evening for Suzanne. He just wanted to rest tonight and prepare for the presentation before his group on Friday. He was able to rest far better at Suzanne's than at home with June. Inevitably with June, even if the evening started quietly, the recrudescence of her recriminations would make it impossible to do homework. Besides, Suzanne was a good critic of his writing, was not unfamiliar with his work, and could contribute a thing or two. They climbed the stairs to the second floor of the split-level that Suzanne was renting. Leonard was accustomed to the ritual at the door, of Suzanne's hard-target search for her keys, deep down into the depths of her bottomless handbag. She would stand on one leg, supporting the handbag on the knee of the other leg while Leonard would patiently cast light upon her portable boutique with his flashlight. He noticed her long, clean hair and how it gleamed in the night. She was very dear to him because he was able to relax in her presence and when he was working, she let him work.

They began to watch a late movie together and laughed when Channel 3 presented its logo: a huge, chiseled-rock "3" that rose, to the music of Strauss's "Thus Spoke Zarathustra," slowly from the bottom of the screen against a background of drifting clouds and blue sky; once the giant "3" had placed itself in the middle of "eternity," it started to revolve slowly like one of those enormous gas station logos on the interstate. Leonard managed a comment between uncontrollable giggles:

"Hail, Oh Great Number 3, lead and we follow, hand in hand to media land."

After laughing themselves into a stupor, Suzanne said she was very tired and prepared for bed. Leonard wanted to work on his presentation to the group Friday. He spent most of the night in the white heat of inspiration and completed a rough draft by 3 a.m. He left his notes and pencil lying there on the kitchen table, relieved himself in the bathroom and brushed his teeth using his fingers, Suzanne's toothpaste, and tap water—an old marine trick. Then he flopped down on the couch and fell asleep and dreamt about his grandfather and the railroad tracks in Sioux City.

Friday morning there was an air of anticipation, and Ozzie, Brader, Willy, and Carolyn were excited at breakfast because Leonard was speaking: "today he would be one of us." The conference room filled quickly, and the man they had grown to respect as their leader and counselor entered, sauntering as usual but this time without the smile. He placed his books and notes down on the table and started speaking slowly without a glance around to see if he had full attention. This was a deliberately difficult mission for him, and he was charging ahead.

"Good morning, dear hearts. I guess it's my turn to relive a lesson in life, so let's get started. Notice that my tone of voice, cadence, and syntax will change as I recall my past. Do not be alarmed; this is a consequence of concentration and focus which I use to identify with my former self. I'm wearing two hats, but I remain yours truly, Myles Leonard.

"This is a story of a near tragedy and redemption.

"When my brother was about eight and I was seven, every Saturday morning we would help my granddad haul the ashes from the basement furnace to the town dump. The dump was on the other side of town. The process entailed shoveling the ashes from the basement furnace into trash barrels, and loading them, along with the old wooden wheelbarrow, onto his ageless battered and rusted red pickup truck, and then hauling everything across town. This was my idea of a good time. I loved my granddad, although he was laconic, a man of few words. He was a worker, a man that knew what he was doing, from the same sub-species, I suppose, as Mr. Hanson." Leonard glanced at Hanson, and Willy smiled.

"He was a burly man with powerful hands and square shoulders, and like Lord Jim 'he reminded you of a charging bull.' There are legends about his barroom brawls, but we knew nothing of that then. With us, dressed in his old St. Louis Cardinals jacket on Saturday morning, hauling ashes, he was our best friend." Leonard looked up at Billy Brader, who gave him a thumb's up.

"My brother and I would compete for how much we could help him load the ashes into barrels; we had our own little toy shovels.

When granddad gave the word in his heavy East European accent, 'Let us move out!' we jumped into the pickup truck, loaded with the ashes and a wheelbarrow, for the ride across town to the railroad tracks and the dump. Granddad always parked at the abandoned terminal, and then we pushed the loaded wheelbarrow across the tracks instead of using the main gate. In order to get to the main gate you had to ride around to the north side of the yard by way of the state highway and a dirt road. Granddad didn't like that, for a number of reasons—the main ones being cars, other trucks and other people. You could approach the dump from the south side by crossing the railroad tracks, behind the abandoned terminal, and there was a place in that part of the dump's perimeter that allowed access.

"For us this was an adventure, and granddad knew it; but he kept a watchful eye. The fringes of Midwestern towns are still 'the wild west.' Dumps and abandoned terminals are not where children should spend quality time. Teens were there out in their motorbikes, poachers were looking for the use of discarded items, and the area was also a favorite place for hunters testing their long-range rifles. They would put soda cans as targets down along the tracks at different distances and test accuracy. So, thinking back, a run to the dump was not unlike what we saw in the news during the Balkan crisis: that race across the Sarajevo town square and back for water, before the sniper hit you. But I exaggerate. Occasionally we would hear a crack and a ricochet and see a tin can in the far distance just fly off into the air. I would even collect some shiny shells in my pocket and make whistles out of them. My granddad wasn't *that* worried about the hunters, because he was a hunter himself and he knew the other hunters in town. And he knew when and where they were practicing and what their shooting range was. It is in the nature of hunters to have an inflated faith in themselves and the security of their weapons. After all, there are only a few hundred accidental human deaths from firearms per year. But there are about fifty homicides per day, and innumerable animal prey killings. The whole significance in carrying a gun resides in the idea of control—to be able to snuff out a living creature not by accident, but by a purpose and will. 'Thou shalt not kill' does not apply to the hunting season, or to vengeance and poor judgment.

"Granddad parked the pickup near the abandoned terminal, and we jumped out of the cab. He unloaded the barrels of ashes and the wheelbarrow off the back of the truck as we tried to help with what strength we had. My brother was stronger than I was and could nudge things further. When the wheelbarrow had been loaded he covered the ashes with a tarp and granddad picked one of us to ride on it, and then the other on the next run. My brother hopped on first this particular Saturday, and I walked alongside, pretending 'to ride shotgun.' Halfway across to the dump my granddad was telling my brother to stop standing on the wheelbarrow, when my brother just keeled over onto the ground; I thought he was toying with us. Granddad dropped the wheelbarrow, knelt, and asked my brother if he was OK, but saw a spot of blood from near his armpit. My granddad had been in the Second World War, albeit on the other side, and he recognized a gunshot wound when he saw one. He picked up my brother with his powerful forearms and said, 'He has been shot, Milo. We have to take him back to the truck and to the doctor as fast as we can; walk quickly but do not run. They will not shoot again. This was an accident, but stay by my side.'

"He told me to walk so that he could shield me from what he figured was the point of origin of the bullet. We got to the truck, and I was able to open the passenger side; my brother was pale and said that his side hurt. My granddad placed my brother onto the middle of the seat and told me to get in and hold my brother's head on my lap, and he would have my brother's legs on his lap as he drove. He closed the door on my side and ran to the driver's side. He gently placed his grandson's legs on his lap, and as he turned the ignition key he said, 'We're going to make it; we're all going to make it, God damn it.'

"Granddad was damning God at a bad time; he should have been damning the kook who was taking target practice on the tracks.

"Granddad drove through red lights, but carefully at turns, to avoid rocking my brother. We headed for Doc Belcher's medical building; the town really didn't have a large hospital—what would you call it, Dr. Kiley, more like a medical group or consortium? As we pulled up at the door, granddad said, 'Just hold him there, Milo, I'll come around and we'll take him in.'

"The blanket that he used for a seat cover was sticky wet with blood, but we wrapped it around my brother anyway and I opened the doors of the office with the help of granddad's elbow as we brought in my brother, who was by now in a daze. The nurse at the desk was on the phone as granddad yelled out, 'Please help us, it is a bullet wound!'

"She cupped her hand on to the phone and said something like, 'I'll be glad to help you, as soon as I'm done with this, please sit down.'

"My granddad said, 'Nurse, this is my grandson, and he has been shot, and if you do not get the doctor here immediately you are going to see a fire from hell. I am meaning NOW.'

"She dropped the phone and ran back to fetch a doctor. He was old Doc Belcher, whom I had seen before for vaccinations. We took the boy back down the corridor and to a room which had a bed, and Doc Belcher started barking orders—and this time the nurse jumped. He was able to stop the bleeding, but thought the bullet had struck a rib and left the body by way of the intestines. We were fortunate that it bypassed his heart. There were probably internal injuries which he couldn't treat there, and the boy would have to be airlifted to the trauma center of the Medical School. Doc Belcher said that we had done well to get him here so quickly. My granddad and I were out of the loop now; it was up to the professionals.

"An ambulance arrived, and all I can recall after that is all these strong young guys dressed in white, coming in with a bed on wheels. They strapped my brother down and started intravenous flow of fluids from bottles hanging on racks, and the last I scene I saw was my grandfather stepping into the ambulance and the door closing behind him.

"The nurse told me to wait there, that my mother would pick me up. The nurse's voice was maternal as she asked me if I wanted a lollipop. I answered by asking her, 'Why the heck would I want a lollipop now? ...you can have one though.'

"I sat down again in the waiting room and stared around, and for the first time I experienced an incongruously combined awareness of fright and relief. I could have been shot like my brother was.

"My brother survived, although he had to have some of his intestines removed, but he still suffers from what I would call a kind of a chronic post traumatic stress disorder. He could never really keep a job and has been in and out of 'rehab' centers nearly all of his adult life. I went on to join the marines for a stint in Vietnam where I was shot at a few times, but not with the accuracy or devastation of that bullet at the railroad tracks. The internal injuries were not only to my brother but to the three us. And the scar tissue remains. My grandfather was severely scolded by my mother, and we never saw much of him after that except on holidays when usually huge arguments about the shooting would come up and he was yelled at again. Finally, I think he went back up to Door County, Wisconsin, where he has his own ethnic crowd. Except for birthday cards, always signed and annotated with the shaking hand of an abiding affection"—Leonard paused here and cleared his throat—"I never saw him again in the house.

"The police investigated the shooting but were unable to come up with a culprit. I venture to assume that the hunters, who included the police, all protected each other. Rumor had it eventually that Waldo Harvey, a teenage wise-guy type, had 'borrowed' his father's rifle and was showing off to his entourage of ne'er-do-wells at the railroad tracks. But that was never proven. Rumor also had it that Waldo's father and my grandfather had an encounter of the most serious kind, and that Waldo's father may also have had some internal organs rearranged. Eventually the Harveys moved out of town.

"My brother and I drifted apart as we grew older. To this day we cannot hold a long discussion without tension building to a breaking point.

"May I conclude however, that although my grandfather bears responsibility for exposing us to the railroad tracks, he also was a hero, in acting quickly to save my brother. Further, although consciously I understand that I need not feel guilty about the shooting, later as a marine, I displayed a possibly correlated disrespect for harm's way. I can also see a connection between my sense of guilt and how I ventured into counseling as a life's work.

"And this brings me to a summary level, to try and integrate my story with all of yours. My purpose in presenting this experience is to demonstrate how a persistent memory can affect our development.

"Childhood memories can retain sharp edges. Remember what Willy Hanson told us." Leonard looked down on his notes. "And I quote: 'I have a respect for sharp edges. They have characteristics that can kill you. You work around that. You got to get a feeling for them. You work with them; but you don't challenge them, or get mad at them or lose concentration.' Unquote.

"Like Mr. Hanson, I'll work around, and with, the sharp edges of the past, exercising my free will to learn."

Leonard made eye contact around the table to regain lost attention, and continued, raising his voice and using his index finger for emphasis.

"But I will not give in to Waldo Harvey... or to any Dr. Busslers"—Leonard nodded toward Dr. Kiley—"of this world, with chronic rage. I will move on."

He took a deep breath and continued, his voice almost cracking.

"My brother was shot in my presence, at an age when the love of life is in first bloom; my best friend, my grandfather, then precipitously left my life at an age when the rapport across our generations was golden. Those memories hurt, and let... them... hurt; you can't fight a feeling. It's like scar tissue; it's there, but I'll work around it.

"I will use the empathy and humanity that he, in fact, passed on to us. I will not give in to intellectual cynicism and fear, and 'to the silence of infinite spaces' as Margaret Worthington and Dr. Wellington Ozelts so eloquently discussed before. When my grandfather left, he was motivated by the same love *that shielded me from another bullet*—to try to take the consequences of the tragedy with him. His love, as Ms. Mayfield's mother explained, 'doesn't go away when (he) goes away.'

"I am a participant in the experience that such love has a life... a force, of its own."

CHAPTER 25

Building toward the Next Level

Leonard's voice now returned to a professional tone as he glanced around at reactions and rearranged his notes,

"I will now entertain questions about my presentation, or any other issue that we have covered this week. Please feel free to comment and to discuss with the group as a whole. This is a forum; please keep it in the spirit of working together. We've been more candid in this group than some families. That's a high level of trust, let's take it from there.

"Yes... Ms. Bell?"

"Dr. Leonard, like you were saying about your grandfather... I felt like that about Michael... remember when my oldest brother appeared in the darkness when I was little, and picked me up in his arms? It was incredible… I mean… why was it Michael who found me in the cornfield?

"All these people looking for me, family and neighbors; it was like… *I* chose him, like… 'OK, I want Michael to find me.' He was my idol. I knew he thought I was something special. You couldn't make up something like that."

"You could, but nobody would believe you, life is stranger than fiction sometimes, that's why a book about all our stories probably wouldn't sell. Ever hear the phrase 'you can't make this stuff up'?" Ozzie commented.

"Maybe Michael had a sixth sense because he cared for you so much," Carolyn Mayfield added.

"Then where was Leonard's grandfather's sixth sense sending those kids into a shooting gallery?" Debbie Storm's confident voice turned heads. Leonard thought the question somewhat provocative, but then he had heard similar questions before many times, in family arguments, his mother screaming at his grandfather. But that was a long time ago, and this was a professional context. Challenges from Debbie Storm were part of the group dynamic, and he allowed the question because it might generate useful discussion.

"Dr. Kiley?"

"Dr. Leonard's grandfather was an immigrant and came to the United States believing in the good will of the American people; something legendary in their own minds and his. There is no reason to expect your grandchild to get shot in peacetime while you do the chores on Saturday morning."

Balis added, "Dr. Leonard's granddad wasn't the problem, Waldo Harvey was the problem… Waldo wasn't supposed to be there, shooting people."

"Waldo Harvey's shot split the family right then and there," Willy Hanson said quietly. The group members turned to Willy, surprised at the depth of his succinct summary. Leonard put his hand up to his earlobe and nodded slowly.

"Carolyn?"

"I'd like to ask Dr. Ozelts whether he ever made up with his stepfather after the big blow-up in the car or was that it… 'Sayonara.' Because I don't think this guy was an evil man. He loved his wife and wanted her for himself; happens all the time. I would think Dr. Ozelts would appreciate that."

"Well, he sent me a letter… no it was a card, maybe a birthday card—and it was a long time later, when I was the father of two children myself—in which he apologized for his sins and asked for my forgiveness and God's forgiveness. I forgot who came first… probably God. Then he enrolled at a night school seminary, got a doctorate in religious studies of some kind and became a creationist Lutheran minister."

"I think it's laudable that a man turns to God for redemption after acknowledging his mistakes," Margaret Worthington said affirmatively.

"You probably have a theory about that, Ozzie," Brader said, giving Ozzie the floor while doing a double take toward Margaret.

"Sure," Ozzie said. "He would then be inaccessible, you know, higher, closer to God, an expert on forgiveness."

"And closer with his wife who was your mother," Carolyn added.

"She couldn't be both a good mother to me and a good, obedient wife to him," Ozzie responded self-consciously.

"Why do you say that? …you sound like you're competing with him; that's an Oedipus complex, buddy," Balis said.

"There's some Oedipus in all of us… give me a break, and don't call me 'buddy'; I'm… Dr. Ozelts," Ozzie answered, slightly irritated now.

"Dr. Ozelts?" (It was Linda Bell.) "I think your mother holds some of the responsibility for keeping him around, even though he was abusing you when you were little; once she discovered that he was like that, she should have dropped him like a rotten apple."

Debbie Storm jumped in. "Unless of course she was enjoying her role as the love object for both guys. If she was an orphan, that would make sense. Orphans are always fighting abandonment, so we learn to manipulate… to survive. The more relationships that are dependent on our affections the better. Can't get enough."

"She *was* an orphan," Ozzie admitted quietly.

Carolyn thought that Debbie was over the top with Ozzie. "Debbie… you're playing 'in-charge' again this morning, aren't you?"

Leonard was pleased that Carolyn had "engaged" Debbie, and hoped that would inspire certain other participants. He saw that Ozzie was now definitely agitated but was at a point where the pain of learning becomes counterproductive. He would have to "put up the stop sign".

"Dr. Ozelts needs a breather here; but I think the comments have been germane; and at least he now might entertain the possibility that both of his parents had complex roles to play in this Greek tragedy. Young Wellington got caught in the middle." He turned to Ozzie. "…I know the feeling, ol' buddy. Nevertheless, the kid prevented the car from going down the ravine, and I, for one, appreciate the avoidance of that catastrophic consequence."

As he said that, Leonard was aware of Ozzie in his peripheral vision holding back tears and almost getting up to leave the room. Billy Brader grabbed his forearm and held him down, leaning over to whisper, "Hang on, Ozzie, it's going to be all right. Leonard loves you, man."

The room was silent for a moment.

"And there's something else that's come up here," Debbie continued relentlessly, "Linda Bell was unable to stay with her husband, and Margaret Worthington never married. In the first case no man could live up to the ideal of her brother Michael; in the second case no man was going live up to the ideal of Jesus, except maybe… that married physics teacher—what was his name?—and he was out of reach. There should be a law against imposing impossible roles on people in relationships. My men and women always know where they stand. I tell them."

"I don't think that's an enforceable law, Debbie," Balis interjected. "I'm an expert on impossible relationships. It's what I do."

Debbie looked around the table. "I think I'm the only person… I mean 'participant'… here that has the balls to ask the tough questions. Most of you are upper-middle-class wimps anyway."

"Watch your mouth, Debbie!" Margaret Worthington spoke up.

Ozzie, Brader, Balis, and Kiley laughed at the exchange; Carolyn shook her head.

Leonard stepped, in raising his open hand in a "Peace" gesture. "OK, good work. We're approaching a level where our learning process is kicking in. Now let's start to think about the next phase of the program. We've all experienced the wish to have one more chance to talk to someone in our past or present. We will start that phase next week. I congratulate each and everyone of you for your outstanding communication, honesty, and grace this week. I was gratified by your belief in each other and the progress in your group dynamics and relationships. Have a good weekend, dear friends."

He used the end of his book as a gavel again.

"The meeting of the Dear Hearts is adjourned!"

Debbie was smiling inquisitively at Leonard, but probably not about the compliment. She was accustomed to dominating conversations and relationships, but in this group she had been contained by "these wimpy losers," and she wondered how. She felt a personal role reversal, as if she were being used. A strange feeling.

Dr. Myles Leonard left the conference room holding his notes and a book under his right arm.

"It's a tricky and fragile business, but you got to love it," he said to himself, smiling and waving at passersby, on the way to his "Betsy."

CHAPTER 26

The Savage Breast

Balis and Dr. Kiley left together but were followed by Linda Bell and Debbie Storm. As they strolled down the corridor, Debbie mentioned lunch to Kiley and Balis, and Linda added, "Good idea, and why don't we go 'Dutch'; that way Doctors Kiley and Balis won't have to pay for the whole thing."

"It's OK by me, as long as I catch my plane tonight. Seven o'clock, to Atlanta. I have relatives there."

"Anytime two attractive women can fit me into their schedule, I'm interested," Balis said, grinning.

"I just wonder if Ms. Storm will be able to put up with the company of 'wimpy losers' for lunch," Kiley quipped.

"Hey, I kicked some butt; that's what they're paying me for, in a manner of speaking. It's not like I came out of nowhere. Dr. Leonard knew I was coming. I get a little tired of the whining, sometimes.

Who said, 'The greatest danger to a group is not the strongest but the weakest'?"

"Nietzsche… is he your guru, Debbie?" Balis asked, but she ignored him.

"Hey, everybody, I suggest the Sea Bistro just down the road. They have a good Chardonnay, the food is digestible… Who's got a car?" Debbie looked around.

"We can take mine, I think everyone will fit," Balis said, "Except for Debbie's boobs; they may have to hang out of the window."

"Shhh!"

Outside on the lot Balis pointed toward his rented car.

Linda Bell then saw Leonard across the lot.

"Look, isn't that Dr. Leonard, over there, in that pickup truck? Hi, Dr. Leonard… Hi!" She waved, but Leonard was too far away and preoccupied to wave back. His truck sped down the exit way and took off quickly with a right turn, and then up the main road. Linda was a little disappointed; she had grown attached to Dr. Leonard this week and wanted his recognition, however slight. She was curious about him personally, like all people she admired.

"He didn't see you Linda, yell louder next time," Balis said. "…Well, here's the car. I went 'big time' this time: an SUV."

"I don't know much about cars; just so they get me there and bring me back; you might as well show off your water heater," Dr. Kiley said.

They all jumped in and talked as the doors slammed and they adjusted their seats and seat belts.

"Then you wouldn't be impressed with my stepfather's Jaguar, I guess," Debbie said from the passenger side, looking back at Dr. Kiley.

"I'm impressed with endangered species of all kinds," Kiley retorted.

Balis stopped the car at the gate and asked Debbie, "Which way?"

"Take a left. It's just a few miles down the road, watch for the big, green, neon fish."

Balis then continued about Jaguars. "I got a ride in a Jaguar once. I almost herniated a disc trying to squirm into the back seat. They should have a warning on the brochure: 'Recommended for dogs and small Englishmen.' They build these fancy engines… and then maybe one and a half midgets can fit into the car. What's the point?"

"The point is that it's got a reputation, it's famous, and most ordinary nine-to-five people will try to get next to or squeeze into anybody or anything that's famous. They figure that's as close as they'll ever get," Debbie concluded.

"Did you ever get close to the famous, Debbie?" Balis asked pointedly.

"It's more like they get famous after I got close to them, Dr. Balis."

Balis softened his voice deliberately now. "…Call me Rolland."

Linda Bell heard that, and smiled at Kiley, but Kiley threw his eyes up, as in "here we go again."

They passed a traffic light, and Balis saw a green neon fish with a chef's hat that reminded him of 'Charley the Tuna.'

"Is that it, Debbie?"

"That's it, Dr. Balis… I mean… Rolland."

Balis was a good driver. He applied the same principle to his cars that he applied to his nuclear magnetic resonance instrument, testing its limits only when necessary. He was reckless with women but prudent with instruments to a fault; this may have contributed more to his lack of creativity than did the timing and exploitation of opportunities he so tenaciously regretted. He signaled for a left turn and drove into the lot for the restaurant. He parked so far from the cars that were stationed there already that Debbie Storm had to remark, "Apparently Dr. Balis thinks we need a short power walk before dinner."

"Hey, why squeeze into a spot when I've got the whole parking lot? Besides I returned to my car after a good dinner once, only to find a deductible-sized dent put there by some guy who had a little too much white wine with his brain food."

Balis backed into his spot, shifted the joystick into park, pulled the brake, and everybody piled out. The group was in a good spirits as they rambled across the parking area. Debbie led the charge up the steps and through the double doors and into the restaurant. Debbie greeted the young hostess with a wisecrack: "I'm glad to see the ponytail coming back; for a while there it looked like we'd all just stepped out of the shower and stuck our fingers into a socket before going to work."

"Excuse me?"

"I think we have four in our party." Dr. Kiley stepped in.

"Hi, guys. Please follow me to your table."

They followed the hostess, who showed them a table not far from the entrance. Everyone took their seats: Linda Bell across from Dr. Kiley, next to the window, and Balis across from Debbie Storm. There was a large, round table with a party of six or seven business types sitting further down from them and toward the middle. The hostess distributed the menus as she spoke.

"The special today is *moules marinieres*; that's mussels in white wine sauce, with shallots and butter sauce."

"Did you hear the way she said that? She must be French. I guess *'moules'* is French for mussels," Linda Bell remarked.

"I used to mess around with a French filly who thought I had big muscles," Balis said.

"What did she think of your 'shallots'?" Debbie shot back, and there some giggles cut off by Dr. Kiley.

"I was going to order the special, but now somehow the small onions have lost their appeal."

Debbie had enough,

"OK, OK, boys, break it up, here comes the waitress."

Their waitress, with librarian's glasses and a dark brown wig, came to the table and asked for drink requests, and everybody ordered the Chardonnay except Dr. Kiley, who ordered a scotch and soda.

The drinks were then distributed by a young man, college age, with curly black hair and huge forearms like a wrestler. Debbie was staring at them.

Linda Bell was curious about Kiley's family ties and asked Kiley, "So, Dr. Kiley, do you have children?"

"Yes, I have two daughters, both out in the working world: one is an English professor at a small college in Maine who can't seem to get tenure and is married to a tree-hugger; and the other is a nurse in New York City married to her job. They're very different, and they are undergoing very different experiences."

"What do you mean?" Balis asked.

"Well, from what I understand from my youngest daughter, people named Morrison, Atwood, and Marx have replaced Shakespeare, Milton and Faulkner in English curricula. English teaching of 'great books' or poetry is considered the pedantry of patriarchal oppression by dead white males. Students should seek to be liberated from 'the classics.' According to the new dogma, the whole appreciation of past western culture is oppressive and needs to be revised and purged to eliminate gender, racial, and cultural qualitative differences."

Balis interjected, "Maybe it all started with free verse. Once that was accepted as poetry, all hell broke loose."

To which Linda reacted by saying, "What... you mean we're going to throw out all the great writers under the banner of male white chauvinist pigs?"

"That's been changed to 'white male essentialists,'" Kiley corrected. "And another thing, which I imagine would disturb Margaret Worthington greatly, is the revisionism in language itself, and how meaning is expressed.

"Every expression based on past literature is in question. Language itself is considered a tool of oppression, and Shakespeare was its master. *The Merchant of Venice*, for example, is a cleverly disguised story about the abuses of incipient capitalism. The beautiful language of Shakespeare is secondary to its political devices."

"That's like saying the New Testament is an advertisement for red wine. If you disintegrate the foundations of Western literature, and even the language with a political agenda, and gender-driven ulterior motives, then it seems to me you might as well call them Political Correctness Departments. All culture is contextual for the human experiences, passions, and perspectives of the time. Even these radical revisionists are subject to their space, time, and social context," Balis said, grinning like he did when he was sure he'd made a good argument.

"Thanks, Rolland, I'll be sure to pass that on to my daughter next time she goes for tenure. Meanwhile, I don't mean to dominate the conversation about my pride and my joy."

Kiley then addressed Ms. Storm: "Debbie, you don't appear to be involved here."

"It's all bullshit to me," Debbie said unabashedly, "I haven't read a book in years. But, I do know that a guy at that table is staring at my endowments. That's what *I* call patriarchal oppression. Besides which, that's probably his wife sitting next to him. Shameless bastard."

Everyone glanced under their eyebrows over to the table in question.

"Take it as a compliment, Debbie. Let's turn to the task at hand—here comes the waitress," Dr. Kiley said, trying again to appease Debbie.

"Are you guys ready to order?" the waitress asked.

"Well, I am. I don't know about the rest of the guys and gals," Balis responded. "I'll have the special. Make sure the mussels are cooked."

"This *gal* will have the seafood pasta," Debbie ordered.

The waitress got the message from Debbie, because she looked at Dr. Kiley and changed her form of address. "And you, sir?"

"I'd like the grilled rainbow trout."

"How about the seafood salad for me," Linda Bell said, proudly displaying her calorie conservatism.

The waitress grabbed the menus and left quickly.

"I think the waitress thinks we're a tough table," Linda observed.

"That's right. We come from the Leonard School of Change through awareness and group dynamics." Balis said, raising his glass. "A toast to the king of awareness and his impossible task."

"Hear! Hear!" And all joined in the toast.

"We're like a Family Karamazov, if you've read Dostoevsky," Dr. Kiley noted. "I get the feeling from Leonard's techniques, sometimes, that we're walking metaphors for Leonard: object lessons for a basic conflict in this society and perhaps in any representative democracy."

"We're listening, Doc." Balis encouraged Kiley, and checked to see if Debbie was listening.

"And that is the following: how to give disadvantaged citizens access to opportunity, while recognizing and rewarding the courageous, the assertive, and the educated. It's a balancing act. Prejudice on either end is a sociological tragedy and must be democratically addressed."

"Are you saying that there is also a prejudice against the educated elite of this society?" Balis asked.

Debbie was still eyeing the "gentleman" staring a laser into her cleavage from the next table.

"Yes. And like all prejudices, it's fueled by ignorance. If you're ignorant about something, by definition you don't know you're ignorant. It's like being deaf all your life. You don't miss the music you've never heard. Conversely, to appreciate great creativity and to accomplish it are two different things. That's why the stunted minds of aging intellectuals are so bi-polar."

"You can't ask *everyone* to understand the molecular mechanisms of cancer or nuclear fission or the genius of a Mozart symphony. Look at Willy Hanson," Balis enjoined.

"No, but you can open their minds to the long-term contribution, discoveries, and concepts. Willy Hanson is special. He intuitively appreciates education. He listens," Kiley answered.

"Then we need an eclectic negotiator between the masses and the educated elite, someone who sees the common ground," Balis suggested, and pointing his index finger with his drink in his hand continued, "Leonard would be perfect!"

The waitress appeared with a cart and the entrees ordered by the group. "Who's got today's special?"

"Here."

"Seafood salad?"

"That's for me."

"And… let's see… guys… the grilled rainbow trout?"

"Over here."

"…And finally the seafood pasta." The waitress placed the dish in front of Debbie, who was still distracted by the obsessed man who kept sneaking peeks; he was relentless. Debbie on the other hand wasn't intimidated into covering her cleavage. She arranged herself to give him better "depth reception."

"Debbie, aren't you going to dig in?" Balis asked pleasantly.

Then… what happened was quick and so unexpected that Balis lurched back from his plate. Debbie Storm jumped up from her seat, which screeched as it was forced backwards. She grabbed her light sweater with both hands and pulled it down from the v-neck and exposed her large, natural left breast toward the man at the table who had been staring at her—or them. Meanwhile Linda Bell and Dr. Kiley were still eating and exchanging pleasantries. (For Dr. Balis this was an instant rare sighting indeed. He thought the breast beautifully symmetrical and voluptuous, like a flower.)

"Here," she said defiantly, "…is that what your looking for, Mister? Come and get it, tough guy?"

With that, the disconcerted man gagged on his food as the others around him pounded his back and fell all over themselves trying to decide what to do, and who should do what. Dr. Kiley, realizing now what was going on, stood up and slid out of his chair, walked quickly over and asked for room to work, turned "the patient" around and performed the Heimlich maneuver. The man spewed something out of his mouth, the wheezing stopped, and he recovered his breathing. Waiters and waitresses came running to the tables wondering what was wrong, and if it was something in the food,

"We told you the food was hot and to be careful, sir."

"It wasn't the food that was too hot to handle," he said haltingly. "Just… just, leave me alone for a minute, OK?"

Everyone backed off and returned to their seats. Debbie had stuffed her breast back into her sweater and was now calmly twisting pasta onto her fork.

Dr. Kiley returned to his seat facing Linda Bell, who was an involuntary spectator of the imbroglio. Ms. Storm had stepped aside of the table in her demonstration, and Linda had initially assumed that she was preparing to go to the restroom. Only when Linda heard the man wheezing and coughing, and her eyes followed Dr. Kiley jumping up to help, did she realize the gravity of the situation.

Balis was aroused by the spectacle, admiring Ms. Storm's panache, but too much in disbelief to react.

Dr. Kiley was upset: "Ms. Storm, couldn't you find a more socially acceptable way to confront the voyeur? The guy almost choked on his food. We're looking at involuntary manslaughter."

"I never thought of my breasts as lethal weapons; but maybe you're right. He never had a chance… the poor jerk," Debbie said insouciantly, as she placed a morsel of twisted pasta into her mouth.

They glanced over, and the male adversary in the battle of the sexes had left the restaurant—probably more out of post-traumatic stress than embarrassment—not even remembering to thank Dr. Kiley.

"Dr. Kiley saved his life," Linda Bell said, throwing her eyes in the direction of the abandoned table. "And saved you from a police inquiry; you ought to thank Dr. Kiley, Debbie," Linda Bell concluded.

"Dr. Kiley practiced his profession, and I practiced mine," Debbie said, winking her left eye at Balis, her best audience.

"You don't mean that you've done this before," Balis asked, feeling another arousal twinge.

"It was a long time ago when I was a lot thinner and I was hard up for a cash flow. I was newly divorced, had two kids to feed and not much to recommend my employment except these," she said nodding down to her breasts. "A lot of strippers do it because they have to, for a car and a savings account, and not necessarily because they're sexual deviates or something."

Linda Bell joined in. "I'm proud of my body, but only in private. Why do men like naked women so much …and it never stops?"

"It's purely physical and hormonal," Balis theorized. "Men never will quit liking women's bodies; it's in the genes. If we weren't attracted to naked women, that would be the end of the human race as we know it. When men first see a beautiful woman take her clothes off there are none of those emotional and symbolic complications, it's just joy… Y-i-p-p-e-e."

"Now wait a minute, Dr. Balis," Dr. Kiley interrupted. "You're not trying to tell us that men, let's say 'normal men,' don't get emotional about women they have sex with?"

"Sure, but for men, sex with a partner for lust, and sex with a partner to express love to her physically, can be two different things. In the second case… no question that men can get very emotional. That's their feminine side. You can start with the physical attraction, or the personality attraction, and then they kind of merge, I guess."

Linda then started "a confession" in response to Balis' conclusion. "At the pharmacy school, I remember a relationship with this guy, Johnny, which started out kind of lustful and then we actually began to enjoy each other's company; I think even 'love' was mentioned a few times, but then it got complicated."

"What do you mean by that?" Debbie was curious.

"Well, he had a lot of friends, and some of those friends liked me too; I mean they'd come on to me when he wasn't around."

"Uh-oh!" Kiley reacted.

"Whatever, you got to understand that I had just left my husband, Rolfe, and I wasn't about to commit to the first guy I got involved with after that Nazi," Linda said in a definitive tone.

"So what happened?" Balis wondered.

"You really want to know? This was a while ago, you know… I was a liberated woman… I'm glad Margaret Worthington isn't here; I'd be ex-communicated from the Catholic Church."

"We'll forgive you, Linda, go on," Debbie said.

"Eventually I went to bed with his best friend."

There were "oohs" and "aaahs" around the table, but Balis said, "Happens in novels and neighborhoods all the time; close friends tend to have many things in common," Balis said.

But Kiley shook his head; Debbie smiled.

"And… Well… maybe there were a couple of other of his acquaintances… that I got a little close to, after that," Linda continued, jabbing at her salad. "Things did get kind of crazy; when Johnny went to bed with my sister after I dropped him, any obligations of sexual protocol went out the window then."

"Sounds like you used sex as a weapon for rebellion, even vengeance," Kiley said analytically.

"Look, I had just left two little children in South Dakota because Rolfe was unbearably dominating. Maybe I got married a little too soon. I loved my children, and there was a lot of guilt associated with that. I was alone and depressed and looking for friends… looking for help… flying off the seat of my pants, so to speak."

Balis and Kiley used their napkins to cover their reactions, and Storm looked up from her plate at Balis.

Linda's eyes and cheeks started to redden, perhaps from the embarrassment of her honesty. She had told them too much.

"What ever happened to Johnny?" Balis asked.

"He wrote me a poem about how the only meaning in his life was my love, and then left the pharmacy department because he couldn't take the pain of being around me—and I wasn't his; you know what I mean? I heard he went to California and became a beach bum. My sister got a postcard with a picture of him and his surf board."

Balis, who had started this topic, was now way over his head.

"I often wondered where beach bums come from," he said resignedly.

CHAPTER 27

The Power of Assertive Femininity

"Linda, you've hardly touched your salad, and we're all just about done. Even Debbie, whose lunch was so dramatically interrupted, has caught up with us. You'll feel better if you eat." Dr. Kiley was pressed for time.

The waitress came back to the table asking everyone if they needed dessert and/or coffee. Dr. Kiley had had a long start to a short weekend. What was supposed to be a pleasant lunch with his colleagues had turned into "the battle of the sexes" and "the confessions of liberated women." He needed some R and R with his favorite aunt, his mother's younger sister-in-law in Atlanta Georgia. He was almost done with his entree and looked at his watch.

"You know what; I think I'll take a taxi back, and then I can use the same one to the airport. Can we give you a lift, Linda? Let me leave a fifty here. That should cover my end. I have some calls to make too. Rolland… Debbie… It's been a scintillating lunch. Waitress?"

Linda acquiesced to the offer for a ride, and they left together with hand waves of "happy weekend" and "see you Monday morning." Balis missed their presence when they went out the door, but Debbie didn't especially. Balis was increasingly physically attracted to Debbie, but he didn't know if he could handle her assertiveness, self-confidence, and panache. He hoped that she wouldn't "pull" anything too outlandish when, after their coffees, he drove her back. Leonard was a professional counselor, and Dr. Kiley was an experienced MD; they had expertise in deviations from the norm. Balis could handle the power and complexities of a nuclear magnetic resonance (NMR) instrument, but right now, Dr. Balis had the feeling that, compared to Debbie, a five-and-a-half-ton NMR machine was a wind-up toy.

"So, did you enjoy your pasta, Debbie?"

"Not bad. Pasta's a caloric way to stretch the seafood. The customer stuffs his face, and the price is right. Everybody's happy, especially if they're Italian. The coffee is good though. Strong."

"Are you ready?" Balis asked nervously. "Let's head back. I'll take care of this," he said, picking up the check and Kiley's fifty-dollar bill.

Debbie picked up her bulging handbag as Balis helped her from the table by pulling her chair back, and she accompanied him to the cash register, where she grabbed some mints and tossed one in her mouth. As Balis negotiated the check payment the cashier gave Debbie "that look," and took an exaggerated breath while giving Balis the receipt. Debbie drew reactions from people.

Balis opened the restaurant door for Debbie and put his arm around her shoulder as she passed him, and for the first time he noticed her perfume, which sent "a yellow alert" to his sensitive hormone sources. They walked side by side to the far side of the parking lot.

"Oh, yeah! …you parked way the hell yonder where no one would fender bend your car. Are you always that cautious, Rolland?" Debbie said.

145

"I try to be," Balis answered, looking down at Debbie (he was taller than she). Ms. Storm was definitely looking attractive now after his two glasses of Chardonnay and strong coffee.

He opened the door on the passenger side for Debbie, but she wouldn't get in; she stood there and looked at Balis. Balis looked down, and then into her eyes. She moved closer to him, and he could smell her breath. It was sweetened with mint, Chardonnay, and his desire. Then Balis' mind went blank and they were kissing deeply. After the kiss was disengaged, she gave him another little peck for good measure and Balis' knees became a little shaky, but he was able to close the car door for her. He walked to the other side, opened the driver side door and flopped down onto the seat, pulled the door closed, and fiddled around his pockets for the keys, which had dropped to the floor. Debbie broke the short silence, and said, "Never mind that, Rolland." Then she reached over, grabbed the back of his neck, and kissed him again—harder and wetter this time. The emergency brake was blocking his right arm, but he was able to take his left arm over to embrace her and then slid it back to feel her right breast. She took his arm and placed it inside her loose sweater, at the same time revealing her breast. He couldn't believe he was there. It had been a fantasy of his to get close to those breasts ever since he had been introduced to them. While kissing him she took the foreplay initiative and started to massage the erogenous zone between his legs. Balis' adrenalin was tapped now, and he began thinking about the condom in his wallet and the difficult logistics of intercourse with her on the two bucket seats and an emergency brake. But she kept relentlessly petting his crotch, and he stopped thinking and kept kissing. She was very sensual and knew exactly where to stimulate him, and Balis was losing even the remotest control of rational thought. Before he could stop himself, his hormones were already signaling for an orgasm, and Balis had to let it go. "Oh God... Debbie...!"

"What's the matter?" Debbie asked quietly.

"I think I spilled my seed." He said as he slowly recoiled back to an upright position in his seat, dropping both arms down.

"Already? ...I just wanted to have some fun before we got back to the institute," Debbie said, busily placing her breast back into her sweater and then flipping down the vanity mirror on her side.

Balis was shaking, and he was trying to catch his breath. "I just lost it... You were too sensual—too early, it's been a while. Couldn't we have picked a better place for this?"

"There is no better place than here, and no better time than now," Debbie responded confidently, checking her lips and eye make-up, "But I guess I did get a little over-enthusiastic. I could feel you wanted me. But I miscalculated how much."

"It's like we're a couple of teenage kids in the car and things got a little out of hand," Balis said.

"What's wrong with that?" Debbie asked mischievously grinning at Balis. She had perfect teeth.

CHAPTER 28

An Invitation to a Party

On his way out of the conference room Leonard gave Ozzie a pat on the back with his right arm as he passed him down the corridor. It was a non-verbal communication, a gesture somewhere between paternal and fraternal, that Ozzie needed after that grueling exchange in group session. Sometimes a well-timed pat on the back is worth a thousand words of counseling. Billy Brader was alongside and wondered why *he* didn't get a pat on the back.

As Leonard continued past them, Brader said, "Margaret and Carolyn say they want to meet us for lunch in the cafeteria and talk to us. I hope Margaret's not bothered by something we said during the week. Margaret's a little conservative for my taste, but she's a trusting soul, kind of like my mother."

"Don't underestimate her; there's a reason Leonard chose her for our group. She's a tough old gal... and bright too. Remember, she represents the generation that brought us through a world war and a few other skirmishes—and spoiled us with all these modern conveniences."

"Yeah, like weapons of mass destruction."

"Cut the crap, Billy, she's an English teacher, not a politician. Anyway, be nice; we've only got one more week to go."

They climbed the stairs up to the next floor, entered the floor through the heavy door with the big "3" on it and then passed through the double doors into the cafeteria. The air was warm and thick with the aroma of soups. They looked around while they were in line and saw Margaret Worthington with a cheerful grin waving to them, at a table back and to the left. She was sitting with Carolyn Mayfield, who was signaling in a sign language of some sort to Ozzie.

"They're over there, Ozzie; that's your pal, Ms. Mayfield, with her too. What do you suppose she's signaling?" Brader answered his own question: "That's woman-speak for 'when you get your food tray, come and sit with us.'"

Ozzie chose the fish chowder over the chicken soup, and he also took some bread and a garden salad, but his suspicion that the women were up to something was dulling his hunger. Brader chose chopped sirloin with mashed potatoes and green beans with chocolate layer cake for dessert. Billy Brader was always partial to red meat and chocolate, and his appetite was not that easily disturbed.

They took their trays over to the table where the ladies were sitting and Margaret said, "Thank you for coming over, both of you, I'm glad to get to talk to you because we've been contacted… with an idea. Sit down, sit down."

"What kind of idea is that, Margaret, a Bible study group?"

"Stop it, Billy, give her a chance," Carolyn said. "Leonard says Dr. Benedict, the head honcho, has invited us to a party at his house tomorrow. Saturday night." Carolyn was enthusiastic.

Ozzie spread a napkin in his lap.

"Great, but are you girls sure we're ready for grind dancing?" Ozzie quipped, and Brader cringed.

Carolyn shook her head. "No, no, no… not that kind of party," she said emphatically. "Dr. Leonard explained something to us. Inspired by his wife, Dr. Benedict holds these musical parties for certain groups that come in here, and it's not your standard cocktail reception. He calls it 'perspectives in music.' She thinks it has therapeutic as well as artistic value. It's a musical encounter party where everyone suggests a piece of music that's special to them, and you listen, appreciate, discuss, or sing and dance if you want. You've heard of a book club. This is the same thing, but for music, everybody's music. Bring a short list. The idea is to get involved into why a piece of music is so important to us. Food and drink provided."

"Whoa, sounds like Music Appreciation 101 to me… where do they propose to have this shindig?" Billy asked.

"You won't believe this: at Dr. Benedict's house, right, Margaret?"

"Yes, and Dr. Leonard told me that Dr. Benedict is an accomplished pianist and his wife is adjunct faculty at the institute, where she's doing research on music as an experimental therapy tool. Apparently they have a huge collection of recorded music of all kinds themselves, but I'm sure they have borrowed from the institute's extensive music library."

"Dr. Leonard said he would try to be there, but couldn't guarantee it. He said his weekends are unpredictable and complicated," Carolyn added.

"Besides us, who'all is coming? Were any of the other people interested?" Ozzie asked.

"Just Dr. Leonard's group; it's strictly voluntary." Carolyn continued, "Dr. Benedict would like to include his own group in these experimental meetings, but he has patients in that group who are under medication. He's a psychiatrist and doesn't want to take his patients out of a clinical context. Our group is supposed to be sub-clinical."

"Is that another word for just plain 'weird'?" Brader jumped in.

Carolyn ignored the wisecrack and continued. "Other than Dr. Ozelts, who I know loves music, I have no idea who else would be interested. You can't force people to like music anymore than you can force people to like themselves. We're still looking for Willy Hanson; he disappeared again," Carolyn said.

"I know Rolland Balis and Debbie Storm went out to lunch with Linda Bell and Dr. Kiley. Some of our group have cars here, so that would help get us to the Benedicts' house. I understand it's not that far from here. Maybe we could use one of the institute's vans."

"This kind of party is a wonderful idea," Margaret Worthington said, "just as a mutual learning experience… But I understand if it's not everybody's cup of tea. I like it as a way to spend an evening; I've lost a step or two in my boogaloo and a turn or two in my twist."

Carolyn laughed and said, "Margaret! That's funny! Save some of those lines for tomorrow."

"OK, Ozzie and I will be there," Brader said checking with a glance toward Ozzie, who nodded. "Did they give a time, Carolyn?"

"Six o'clock. I guess she—I think her first name is Gwendolyn—wants us to eat and chat before we get down."

"You're really into this, Carolyn. Are you sure this whole thing wasn't your idea?" Ozzie asked.

"If it wasn't, it could have been. You can call me an associate producer—my role was inspirational," Carolyn replied gleefully.

CHAPTER 29

Organic Patterns

Saturday, Wellington Ozelts slept until almost noon. He had been out with Brader Friday night, shopping for odds and ends including a couple of music discs, and then they finished the evening with a libation or two at a place north, up the main road, called "The King's Pub."

"Kind of a dive," Brader told Ozzie afterwards, "but it had a neighborhood feel about it, people were happy to be there."

Ozzie was looking forward to the music party at the Benedicts' place as he shaved and hummed a bar or two of "Who Can I Turn To (When Nobody Needs Me)." Usually he didn't like introductory parties, especially cocktail parties, because there was nowhere to hide, to be un-ignored, and everyone talked like they were image-making, competing. This might be different though, maybe even fascinating;

people would reveal their music, it would be like taking a peek into the right side, the aesthetic side, of a person's brain.

He was happy because during this week he had made new friends with whom he had been honest, and open, and they still respected him, liked him, maybe even had some affection for him. He had "a sense of a family," without all that sticky, emotional baggage accumulated from the distant past, like jealousies, rivalries, resentments, and vengeance agendas. It was that wonderful "early spring" part of relationships where everybody was doing their level best to understand, and be understood—Leonard's medium for maximum empathy.

The phone rang, and it was Carolyn.

"Hi, Wellington, I called to let you know we have one of the institute's vans taking us to Dr. Benedict's house. If you want the ride, try to be out there by 5:30."

"Thanks, but I think Billy Brader is going to give me a ride, Carolyn; we might follow you over there. Do you think Leonard will be there tonight? It'll be strange: a group session without him."

"I know," Carolyn agreed, and added, "They ought to call him 'Leonardo' because of how he engineered our group dynamics. What was that Taoist term—something like 'ree'?—for the essential organic patterns in nature: flowing water, the grain of wood, DNA structure, maybe even in your physics equations? He is able to see patterns in a group. We might be able to talk about that tonight. There are certainly patterns in music. Anyway, see you out front, Wellington. Bye."

"OK, Carolyn, thanks." Ozzie hung up quickly but then had a delayed reaction to Carolyn's call, like a rush of affection.

"She has colors everywhere, like a rainbow".

The participants from the group going to the Benedicts', Margaret, Carolyn, Linda, and Balis, were milling around the front steps and the lobby when Ozzie came down at a few minutes before six p.m.. Carolyn was sitting on a couch with a notebook of some kind on her lap--Ozzie guessed, "sheet music." Billy Brader was over by the drinking fountain and waved to him. He dressed in an off-yellow sport shirt and a light brown sports jacket. Ozzie told him he "looked good." Ozzie himself was wearing a long-sleeved white shirt and red striped tie with a dark brown, linen, silk-lined vest. The two of them looked like models for an after-hours picture in *Gentlemen's Quarterly*. They made some small talk with Carolyn and Margaret, and Billy Brader apologized that he only had room for one passenger in his MG.

Ozzie and Brader walked quickly to Brader's car, got in, and slammed the doors shut. They waited near the exit to the lot for the van, which Brader could see in his rearview mirror. The van group was taking its time, and it was now past six o'clock.

"I wonder what the hell they're doing," Brader said. "Get in the vehicle and let's go."

"They're trying to figure out who's going to sit where, and they may be waiting for a straggler… and, here she comes." Debbie came running down the stairs and knocked on the van; they let her in, to a back seat.

Finally, the driver, a security night shift guard, started up the van, which spewed a huge gray cloud of exhaust and then slowly negotiated its way down past Brader's car and to the front gate. Brader followed, and Carolyn waved back at them from a back passenger seat and then pointed for a left turn. They rode about two miles south and then turned right on a country road and passed a pond. After about half a mile the van slowed down in the midst of a wooded area.

But it then turned right, into a dirt drive way you wouldn't know was there… unless, you knew it was there. There was a white fence gate which was closed. The driver stopped the van in front of the gate, stuck his balding gray head out of the car window, pressed a button on a box on a fence post, and identified himself. The gate made a clicking noise and slowly the "gates of Valhalla" opened to reveal a spectacular acreage of rolling grassland like a golf course fairway, and a large Mt. Vernon–style white house set up on a ridge to the left. Straight ahead, the driveway led to a barn-style multi-car garage. In the distance Brader and Ozzie could see tennis courts and beyond the tennis courts a line of hard wood trees. The place looked like it was immaculately manicured.

The vehicles parked on the graveled driveway in front of the closed doors of the garage. Everyone disembarked and climbed slowly up the path to the home on the hill, remarking excitedly on the good fortune of a visit with the aristocracy. For most of the participants, this level of domestic affluence was out of reach and would always be out of reach, so this was a rare adventure for them. Ozzie noticed that Carolyn was dressed royally and leading the way in a white chiffon skirt a bright green blouse with fluffy sleeves and tight cuffs. Debbie was wearing a cream-colored V-neck sweater without a bra, and long, tight, cream-colored jeans housing her generous buttocks.

There was a chained lantern which was lit, hanging from the porch ceiling, and Mrs. Benedict, dressed formally but comfortably in a long, bright-colored cotton dress and a white unbuttoned sweater over her shoulders, opened the door before they even had a chance to approach it. She was a relatively tall, thin woman in her fifties with short, thinning gray hair, and a small, round face that changed structure almost totally when she smiled. Her eyes were hazel, and the crow's feet in their corners suggested an expressive woman.

"Welcome, everyone, it is so good of you to come!"

The participants wandered in to find an enormous living room to the left that they entered by descending two or three steps between two indoor Doric columns. There were couches, chairs, and pillows everywhere with a large but unlit nineteenth-century, colonial-style fireplace. The prevailing color of the room, including the wall-to wall carpeting, was a light beige with off-reds and maroon mahogany furniture. There was a spectacular nineteenth-century landscape painting, probably of the New York State Hudson River School, high above the ledge of the fireplace. There was a white baby grand piano in the corner of the room opposite the fireplace. To the right of the piano were a knotty pinewood cabinets, which Ozzie figured housed a stereo set, books, and music. In the middle of the room was a silver and black metal serving cart with all kinds of hors d'oeuvres and drinks.

Mrs. Benedict introduced herself.

"My name is Gwendolyn Benedict, and of course, my husband Dr. Lincoln Benedict needs no introduction to you. Please make yourselves at home and help yourselves to munchies and drinks."

After about an hour of formalities and small talk—which was just about Ozzie's limit, and beyond Brader's—Gwendolyn called everybody together into the living room.

"Please seat yourselves comfortably, and let's get started while the evening is young," she said.

Dr. Benedict wheeled the cart of hors d'oeuvres into the kitchen, then took a seat at the piano bench and turned toward the group, his elbows on his knees and his hands folded. He was a bit nervous about this kind of "informal therapy," but it was Gwendolyn's idea and if it worked, might be worth developing. While she spoke, Gwendolyn walked back and forth, and at times turned to face the group to emphasize a point.

"By way of introduction for 'Perspectives in Music,' I'd like to start with my perspective… and I'd like to talk about the unity of music, and the artistic and communicative power of music.

"For a long while now music criticism in the press, and by that I mean concert hall music criticism, has abandoned its audience. Critics are so focused on personalities, especially the conductors and the divas, that the music seems exclusive. This turns serious music listening people off. Some music critics should admit they're closer to being gossip columnists.

"On the other hand, critics of the rock scene seldom discuss the music at all; it's all about top forty or top ten; the techniques of emotional expression, chord structures, rhythms and such, the meaning in the music if you will, are seldom if ever discussed. Right now there are deep divides between musical styles: what's called classical or concert music on the one hand, and rock and popular music, pop/rock, on the other. In general, if this gap is going to be narrowed for art's sake, those trained and virtuosic in the classic/jazz repertoire have to open up to the modern and post-modern styles. Some examples of crossovers are Andre Previn, Leonard Bernstein, Keith Jarret, and Wynton Marsalis. I think it's wonderful that Andre Previn can conduct the London Symphony Orchestra in a Haydn symphony and also is then able to sit down with Oscar Peterson to improvise jazz piano, and then again to write a pop/rock hit ("Like Love"). Leonard Bernstein can conduct the Boston Symphony, and also write Broadway hit show tunes. I remember one of his lectures where he discussed the chord changes in the Kinks' rock hit "You Really Got Me." It is the responsibility of the musical elite to come toward popular and jazz music, because they have the capacity, technical facility and the talent to do so. Am I making sense at all or boring you...?"

"Well, compared to the mountainous onslaught of meaningless mush on television and radio these people have been subjected to all their cognizant lives, Gwendolyn, you're a welcome relief," Margaret said.

"Thank you, Margaret, that's encouraging."

Then Gwendolyn addressed Ozzie and Rolland Balis, as much to wake them up as to garner information.

"I understand there are two scientists among you. I'd like to pose a question, and here it is: without a re-education, is it easier for a physicist to do chemistry, or can a chemist do physics experiments anytime?"

Balis answered, "Physics is at the basis of chemistry, and biochemistry is the basis of life. The pyramid of current scientific knowledge arises out of physics, which built a foundation for chemistry, which in turn built a foundation for biology. Ahem."

"So it is with music," Gwendolyn pointed out. "The technical structure, rigor, and discipline which are the foundations of all written and recorded western modern music arose in the sitting rooms, abbeys, churches, recital halls, and concert halls of Mozart, Bach, Vivaldi, Albinoni, Pachelbel, Purcell, Palestrina, and Byrd. These names are as familiar to academic musicians as Washington, Jefferson, and Adams are familiar to politicians; or as Babe Ruth, Johnny Unitas, and Bob Cousy are familiar to sports fans. If you know how to play their works, you know how to play most anything; because they taught us how to write it down, how to transfer the information, and even the expression of emotion through the music. Music is a communication encoded in notes. All you need are the instruments and the players... and the composer communicates as if he were right there talking to you; his personality comes alive again. He summarizes feelings and emotions artistically that we are unable to express otherwise. People that are receptive to music form affections toward particular genres and pieces. There's a sense that the music understands you. That's why I think music might work in group sessions as a communicator tool."

Carolyn raised her hand to ask a question. "Gwendolyn, what about jazz, rock and blues? Sometimes there doesn't seem to be much of discipline and rigor there, even the message sometimes is nothing more than, 'just feel good'; they turned those European guys upside down: Roll over Beethoven, baby."

"Not quite, Carolyn. What would a boogie woogie, or rock, or even rap, be without the rigor of the beat and 'tone'? The beat or rhythm is in the time signature, and the 'tone' is in the key signature. The 'beat' isn't something that started with rock or boogie woogie: Beethoven was a fanatic for the appropriate rhythm in his symphonies and sonatas. Many rock pieces, although they give the appearance and style of being haphazard and improvised, are actually rigorous and specifically structured as to time and tonality. We mustn't confuse style, volume, timbre, and even performance behavior with structure. To give a simple example, my copy of "You Ain't Nothin' but a Hound Dog" is written, I believe, in the key of B flat, with two flats. Signatures with two flats go back at least to the fifteenth century; the piece is also in 4/4 time whether Elvis shakes his booty or not; the 4/4 was the most common time notation in the seventeenth century. I see baby boomers here, so you are all probably familiar with the Rolling Stones and the Beatles and pieces like "Angie" by the Rolling Stones and "Hey, Jude" by the Beatles. These are rigorously structured works, and technically, easily understood by concert musicians. It's like showing a log cabin to an architect; this is not to say that Abe Lincoln's log cabin cannot have a meaning beyond its simple structure. Even variations and improvisations in rock and jazz pieces have a fundamental relationship to the original theme.

"I could give many more examples, but you see what I'm driving at. Take away the apparent informality and tinsel of pop/rock and the hubris of concert music, and the two musical sectors have much more in common than the casual listener would suppose. There are apparent differences in style, presentation, and interpretation, but they arise out of the same quest in man for understanding and meaning… in life, love, and death… in existence and human frailty."

"Or just to dance and have a good time," Debbie Storm interjected, "Do you have a problem with that?"

"Not at all, Ms. Storm," Gwendolyn said, "'Music hath charms to soothe a savage breast,' if I may quote William Congreve."

At that, Brader looked at Ozzie and raised his eyebrows, and Ozzie held back laughter.

CHAPTER 30

Bonding through Music

"I think Dr. Benedict wants to add something."

"I think what you're saying in a way, Gwen, is that American music brought whole new styles to the art form but did not change the fundamental structure. And you can't put interpretation all on paper. For example, blues or boogie woogie cannot be totally read from a score. If you simply play "Pinetop Boogie" from the score it sounds pretty laborious. But the publisher's notation says to play 'brightly.' But one man's brightly is another man's darkly. You have to have a feeling for the left hand base rhythm and the trills in the right hand, or you don't get that driving force typical of that genre. I think that's what's meant by, 'It don't mean a thing if you ain't got that swing.'

"Let me see, I must have a boogie woogie anthology here somewhere."

Benedict got up and turned around to open the pinewood cabinet, which had a plethora of sheet music and discs. He fingered through some sheet music, found what he wanted and placed it on the music stand.

"Now if I play the left hand rhythm simply giving each note its appropriate value, it sounds like this." (He played the left hand of the opening bar of "Pine-Top Boogie" after the introduction, giving each note its mathematical time value.) It sounded plain and uninspired.

"It sounds rather stilted... But if I give it a little bit of emphasis on the first beat of a pair of eighth notes, it lends it more of a drive, almost like a locomotive, let me try that..."

Benedict then played the "Pine Top Boogie" with more of a "beat" and soon he had everybody clapping, and encouragements of "Go, Man!" When he finished, with a run down the scales to a base note, he got a hand from the group. The discussion of the piece and his performance served to get the group relaxed and involved. There were now smiles, commentary, and raised hands.

"That was good!" Carolyn exclaimed.

Benedict stopped the generous ovation by raising his right hand like a politician; he wanted to add something.

"You see, the piece comes out with more joy, determination, and virility. It's the human factor: and that includes interpretation on my part, an active re-creation as to what the composer intended.

"It works in about the same way with Beethoven. I'm not kidding. Let's take the second movement of the Sonata Op. 13."

Dr. Benedict had known he was going to talk about this, because he had the score handy.

"Now for the second movement, it says on top of the page *'Adagio Cantabile.'* Adagio means slow, and cantabile means, and I checked my music dictionary, 'the player should make the music sing.' So literally I'm already told to humanize the piece. I can't play like a robot, like this."

Dr. Benedict played the first bars of the *Adagio* without changing dynamics or expression.

"According to the notation from the composer, I have to try to make the piece sing... Well, I'll try that now."

Dr. Benedict then played a page of the *Adagio* with emotion and expression, changing dynamics to emphasize the melody and the climax of a phrase… including body language. He finished the page to polite applause; the last one of the guests to stop clapping was Margaret Worthington, who turned to Carolyn and gushed, "That was wonderful!"

"You can see then that this is a very emotional piece and Beethoven wants us to express that, when we play it. He 'has the blues' about someone very dear to him. Then—and this might surprise you— listen to the Beatles 'Let It Be' and see if you don't hear some of this Adagio in there."

Dr. Benedict played the first few bars of "Let It Be" on the piano, by McCartney and Lennon of the Beatles.

"And now… the Adagio."

Then he again played the first few bars of the Adagio from the Sonata by Beethoven, for comparison. Benedict stopped playing and turned from the piano. *"Adagio cantabile…* make it sing. Comments… no? Gwendolyn?"

"What is it in the character of the music that has an extraordinary soothing effect—why do some notes soothe and others irritate?" Margaret Worthington asked the Benedicts.

"We're looking into these aspects," Gwendolyn responded. "There's something in the harmonics, something organic in the pattern of notes, that makes cows yield milk and babies stop crying, that resonates within the right side of the receptive brain."

"Resonates as what?" Balis retorted, almost cynically.

But Gwendolyn was ready. "As beauty, as certainty, as symmetry, as a friend, caring about something, or someone, expressing or giving life meaning. When we are happy, contented, and in love, our voice sounds are more often mellower and in a major key. When we are angry and vengeful, our sounds often change to dissonant yelling, arguing and screaming."

A short silence fell over the group, and Gwendolyn knew it was time to stop lecturing. "Well, that's all I have to say, I hope you all have thought about a couple of pieces of music that are meaningful to you, or that you particularly enjoy. Dr. Leonard has told me that you're the brightest group he's ever worked with. He believes in you, and so do I. If we have the recording, or if you have brought some music with you, we'll play some of it, to get a sense of your music, or perhaps Dr. Benedict can provide us with a few bars at the piano. If you want to just sit back and listen, that's all right too. I thought we'd go in alphabetical order.

"Let's see… Dr. Balis?"

"OK… well, I chose an album by Van Morrison called *Astral Weeks*. I love my dictionary's definition of 'astral': 'above the tangible world of refinement, visionary, exalted.' And that's what these songs are. Morrison explores his feelings throughout the course of a love affair. To me the music and metaphorical lyrics seem to fuse. There's the joy of his love, the freshness; it's like being reborn."

"As a matter of fact we do have that album somewhere, don't we, Linc? …He's looking for it already," Gwendolyn said.

Balis continued with his comments: " I heard that originally none of the major record companies wanted to put the album out, but it developed an underground or cult following; and now it's considered a classic, an original. I think it comes out of the Irish tradition of poetic expression. I don't know if you could categorize most of these songs as pop/rock; they're more like poetic ballades with rhythm guitar and drum accompaniment."

"What should we listen to, Dr. Balis?" Dr. Benedict asked.

"Play the title track, 'Astral Weeks,' and then 'Sweet Thing,' and then, a my favorite, 'Ballerina.' That should give you an idea. This man's a genius."

They listened to those three cuts from the CD album. Ozzie thought that the re-mastered acoustics were missing something but didn't comment. Gwendolyn was walking back and forth, concentrating, with her right hand on her chin as she listened, and occasionally nodding to Balis when there was a particularly poignant phrase in the music.

When the three songs finished playing, Dr. Benedict commented on the song "Ballerina": "I liked the way the intensity of the rhythm builds. His consuming obsession is expressed in the lyrics, all the way to helplessness. You get all caught up in his passion. Great stuff. Thank you Rolland."

163

"All right, that was good. Next we have, Ms. Linda Bell. Is there music that you'd like us to hear or talk about, Linda?"

"I don't know too much about music. But I like certain songs; it's weird. I'm from South Dakota, raised on a farm. The kinds of songs that captured my imagination were 'Amazing Grace' sung by Joan Baez, and 'California Dreamin' by the Mammas and the Papas. I've never been to California, although I've been to Oklahoma. Wherever you go, you take yourself with you, so maybe my affection for those songs was more escapism than a real appreciation of the music.

"I have a recurrent dream about one particular piece though; and in it there is a woman singing. There are no words. It's just an 'AHH' sound. There are some kinds of violins playing but most of the time they're plucking with their fingers, like this, you know—" She used her index finger to make a plucking motion. "—instead of using the bow. I don't know where this became part of me. But I wish I knew what it was and where it came from or even if there is such a piece. I know my mother, whose family came from Portugal, used to play music on this old portable record player she inherited from her mother that kept breaking down. When I mention this—what would you call it—sound, in my brain, to people, they think I'm crazy."

Gwendolyn picked up on the clues. She obviously enjoyed "What's my music?"

"Linc, get Bachianas Brasileiras Number 5, Villa-Lobos, out of the collection."

Linda looked back as Dr. Benedict picked out a disc from the collection and placed it into the set. The music started. There was an introduction of cellos plucking softly in unison and then an ethereal soprano voice, singing a vowel sound, "AH," like a musical instrument.

"Oh my God, that's it! That's it!" Linda Bell's hands were shaking a little, and Ozzie saw a flush of her emotion he hadn't seen before.

As the music of the unusual piece continued, almost everyone listened respectfully. Carolyn Mayfield closed her eyes and her lips and hummed to herself in communion with the soprano. There was a pause, and then... like a human Stradivarius, the humming of the last high A.

Gwendolyn commented: "In this work Villa-Lobos weaves Brazilian folk rhythms and tone into kind of a Bachian tapestry. It's an amazing marriage of minds and cultures. In that work there's a recalled sense of his mother's compassionate femininity. Linda, thank you."

"'Who's Bill Brader?'"

"I am, the one and only."

"Mr. Brader, do you like music?"

"Sure… I was going to talk about one of my teeny bopper favorites: 'It's My Party and I'll Cry If I Want to.' Little Leslie Gore sang that. It tells the story of our careers…k-i-d-d-i-n-g, everybody!" Balis booed Brader's remark, and Ozzie shook his head. "But I guess if I were to choose seriously I'd have to go with 'A Whiter Shade of Pale' by a British group called 'Procol Harum.' It's now kind of semi-classic; you hear it all the time. Although I never had any idea what the lyrics mean. Do either of you people remember this piece… Ms. Benedict?"

"Of course… and so does Linc… I know we have the recording of 'Whiter Shade of Pale.' It's an important piece of music; I'll elaborate after we hear it."

Dr. Benedict found the disc easily, placed it in the console, and pushed the start button. The Bachian organ motif began and the singer, Gary Brooker, wailed away. When the organ music stopped Gwendolyn asked Brader, "May I, Billy… unless there's something you wanted to say?"

"No… not really…I just always liked it."

"Well, I'll tell you something about this piece. It was written at a very creative time in pop rock music. But it's not pop rock. It's a fusion of baroque and modern jazz, and it's an Old English style ballade. And Keith Reid's lyrics are more Lewis Carroll than Leslie Gore. I guess I'm not making much sense. Linc, do you have Bach's Cantata Number 147 there somewhere? Can you play the motif there, and compare it to 'Whiter Shade…'?"

Dr. Benedict played the first few bars of the cantata and then the introduction to "A Whiter Shade of Pale." The similarity was apparent.

"This piece re-popularized Bach along with this rock group. Bach is one of these guys that just won't go away. Do you see what happens when you combine two apparently disparate musical styles two and a half centuries apart? These people have embraced a baroque melody and called it their own. As we saw in the Beethoven to Beatles scenario, these 'cross-century communications' are where elite art fuses with popular art. Very effective. That's how often how the edifice of art grows, at the seams of different styles and cultures."

Dr. Benedict wanted in.

"I'd like to say a word or two about the lyrics. When you think about the lyrics today, or even in the big band era, it's almost all about romantic love and love affairs. That's important of course—romantic love can be wonderful, complex, and traumatic; that needs expression. However, these lyrics here are images and metaphors expressing existential aches and pains. The guy's in a room, there's a fandango dance, and 'the room is humming' and then there's 'a miller's tale,' and then there's 'a face just ghostly.' This is almost Salvador Dali and Kierkegaard. What an imagination. This fellow Keith Reid never got Bob Dylan's publicity, but he's every bit as rich in his metaphors, and he's a better poet, more universal, than the more political Dylan. He wrote a magnus opus for chorus and rock band called 'in Held 'Twas I' that I think is the greatest piece of 'existential rock poetry' ever written. Thank you, Keith Reid and Mr. Brader."

"Call me Billy." Billy hadn't realized that he was that deep.

"OK, thanks… Billy."

"They tell me Carolyn Mayfield is a singer. Carolyn might grace us with a song or two."

"I don't know if the group is interested in show tunes. I've brought three of my personal favorites with me here: 'Camelot,' the title song from the musical, by Lerner and Loewe. Then I have, 'Send in the Clowns' by Stephen Sondheim from *A Little Night Music*, and finally, 'One Hand, One Heart,' from *West Side Story* by Leonard Bernstein."

"Well, Dr. Benedict, here's where your accompaniment skills will be tested," Gwendolyn said, pointing to her husband.

"Which of these songs do you want to start with, Carolyn?" Dr. Benedict asked, arranging the sheet music on his piano.

"You mean you want to hear all of them?"

"Sure, what do you think, people?" Gwendolyn asked the audience.

The audience clapped. This was going to be good.

"Let's start with 'Send in the Clowns.'"

"That would seem altogether appropriate for this group," Debbie quipped.

"Hush," Margaret Worthington cautioned.

Carolyn began singing the Sondheim. She wasn't of the stomachache, wailing school of feminine vocalists. Carolyn was a mezzo-soprano of the Sara Vaughn, Roberta Flack school. And she was a stylist, communicating melancholia in her presentation of the song about the farce of acting out roles in relationships. She finished with a pause and an E-flat almost in resignation, making eye contact with the group: "...send in the clowns... don't bother... they're here..."

Everyone applauded enthusiastically, and the evening was getting richer.

Describing "One hand, One Heart" by Leonard Bernstein, Carolyn announced, "This is an affirmation of their belief in each other by young lovers. They are in rival gangs and facing misunderstanding, prejudice, and violence. They have only each other and the timelessness of love on their side; very much Romeo and Juliet."

There was some reaching for napkins among the audience as Carolyn transmitted an almost hymnal sense of empathy for the doomed lovers: "...One hand, one heart, even death won't part us now."

"Interesting, both songs are in the same key and end on the same E-flat note," Gwendolyn said, turning to her husband.

"I'll end my romantic show tune trilogy with the title song from *Camelot*, music by Frederick Loewe and words by Alan Jay Lerner. It is written in a lusty F major key, except when Richard Burton sang it—then it was written in the key of 'conversation.'"

"Particularly lusty with Elizabeth Taylor," Ozzie added.

"OK, OK... Carolyn, please." Gwendolyn interceded.

Carolyn received a standing ovation as she ended the Camelot with its rousing F note affirmation: "...In short, there's simply not, a more congenial spot, for happ'ly-ever-aftering… than here in Cam-el-ot." The song was about a happy place where good men and good women were allowed to be themselves, even kings, queens, and knights in shining armor.

Carolyn bowed, slowly and gracefully bending one knee, like a Lady of the King's Court. *God, what a woman!* thought Wellington Ozelts as he clapped until Brader settled him down.

"Who'd be next, Dr. Wellington Ozelts? Carolyn tells me she found you asleep in the music library. What on earth were you falling asleep to?"

"It wasn't on earth, it was in heaven. The introductory *Kyrie* to Mozart's Great Mass in C minor is the most eloquent plea for mercy in any choral work known to me. Although Mozart was the son of a church musician, this work took him longer to write than most of his pieces. He wrote symphonies in a matter of days or weeks."

"Dr. Benedict, have we got that piece there?

"If it's alright, Gwendolyn, I have the disc with me," Ozzie said, "My favorite version with Kiri Te Kanawa and the London Symphony Orchestra and Chorus, Colin Davis conducting. It is an ambitious and controversial piece. Mozart was thinking to write maybe something on the scale of Bach's Mass in B Minor. He started it in 1782 but never finished it; apparently the Credo and a part of the Sanctus had to be completed by students and scholars. It was published as an unfinished work in 1840, but, get this, one version of the completed mass wasn't published until 1956! Can you believe that? Mozart's Great Mass in C Minor came out when Elvis Presley's 'Hound Dog' came out."

"You're kidding… did it make the top forty?" Balis quipped.

"Since when has the teeny boppers' top forty been a criterion for artistic merit? I wouldn't use the charts for wall paper!" Ozzie answered.

"Wellington, now be nice," Margaret warned.

Ozzie turned to the matter at hand. "Here, Gwendolyn… can you play the first cut, 'The *Kyrie*'? It runs about 8 minutes. Mozart's wife, Constanze, is said to have sung this part for him in a Benedictine Abbey Church in Salzburg. It was dedicated to her, and we know he liked it because he used the score again in another work in 1785."

After a brief introduction by the chorus and orchestra the room was enveloped with a single, mellifluous soprano voice. *"Kyrie eleison..."* And then the chorus answered. When the piece was finished, everyone was silently shifting in their seats for a minute as Ozzie wondered if they liked his choice. Ozzie broke the silence, but confidently. "To me this piece is the musical equivalent of 'The Pieta' by Michelangelo: full harmonic tenderness and compassion."

All eyes then turned to Margaret Worthington, who was the practicing Catholic in the group and appeared slightly stunned by Ozzie's reverence, but recovered her composure to present her choice.

"I am going to choose something we can learn from, and feel good at the same time. It's the song which opens the musical *The Fantasticks*, called 'Try to Remember.' The words are by Tom Jones and music by Harvey Schmidt. I'd like Carolyn to sing it for us if she knows it."

Dr. Benedict opened up his sheet music cabinet and came up with the score. He looked at Carolyn, who walked over to the piano again. They both went over the music, leaning over the piano, humming as he pointed to a bar and a chord here and there. In the left corner of the title page, Dr. Benedict noted that the composer suggested singing the piece "slowly, with tenderness."

They nodded when they were ready and Gwendolyn announced, "Here is a Margaret Worthington production of Carolyn Mayfield singing 'Try to Remember' from *The Fantasticks*, accompanied by Lincoln Benedict at the piano."

The song was about the stages of romantic love, and the stages of life, with the fall and winter as metaphors, September and December, in particular. In the third verse, Carolyn reached out as if asking the heartbroken to take her hand, when she sang, "Deep in December, it's nice to remember, without a hurt the heart is hollow." Even Gwendolyn was taken by the depth of feeling in Carolyn's interpretation. Margaret Worthington, unabashedly moved, was again reaching for her napkins, and Linda Bell was caught by Balis' glance, taking a deep breath as if pining.

No sooner had the clapping and kudos subsided when the doorbell rang.

Gwendolyn excused herself from the group, walked around the furniture and up the two steps through the atrium, and pressed the button for the intercom. "Yes, who is it?"

"It's Myles Leonard. Sorry I'm late. I dropped by to see how my dear hearts are doing."

"Come on in through the gate and park anywhere in front of the barn," Gwendolyn answered.

There were anticipation and cheers from the group as word spread that Leonard was coming up the hill. Meanwhile Dr. Benedict asked if anyone needed coffee or snacks or junk food.

Gwendolyn waited by the door to let Leonard in. Leonard had shaved and was wearing a pinstriped shirt and a woolen, light brown, unbuttoned sweater that was too large.

As he arrived through the front door Gwendolyn greeted him, shaking his hand gently and showing him in. Gwendolyn liked Leonard and respected his competence and intelligence, although she had a natural suspicion of anyone who was "indispensable" to her husband's success. Leonard smiled from ear to ear, and the group hailed their patron as he descended the indoor steps through the columns into the large living room. Leonard spoke as he searched for a seat.

"Hello, hello, hello, I know I'm late, and I apologize."

"Leonard, actually you're just in time for your turn," Dr. Benedict announced from the piano, "The evening is dedicated to music, or more specifically, perspectives and communication through music. Do you have a piece that grabs you?"

"That's easy," Leonard said as he plopped down on an armchair pillow, "'Desperado' by the Eagles' Don Henley and Glen Fry. In some sense we're all desperados on this planet, ol' buddy."

"I have the music," Dr. Benedict said, "but I refuse to submit your group to my singing voice."

"Please don't, Dr. Benedict, the trauma of that experience might reverse all your progress tonight. I like the words to that song. If you have the score there, why don't I recite them, and then we'll listen to the song as a piano solo."

Gwendolyn walked over and got the sheet music from her husband at the piano and went over to hand it to Leonard, who fingered through it and then returned to the front page keeping it open with his left hand. He then started to recite the words to "Desperado," about a loner who has trouble opening up to love. The lyrics were in a kind of cowboy lingo with metaphors of self-inflicted barriers to bonding, such as card games, prisons, and fences. Leonard looked up at his audience and paused, dramatically making eye-contact before delivering the last line of the song: "'It may be rainin', but there's a rainbow above you. You better let somebody love you… before it's too late.'"

Leonard then handed the sheet music back over his shoulder to Gwendolyn who placed it on the piano. Dr. Benedict started playing the ballade straight away in the key of G. Ozzie pictured a cowboy in the twilight of his rugged life, out on the range one night, sitting at a campfire, staring up at the clouds passing before the moon, in a moment of weakness deep in the night wondering if maybe he should have settled down with that gal he left in Abilene, or Dodge, or the one in Wichita.

"We make choices at times in our lives when we are totally unprepared," Carolyn said.

"I think to finish a musical evening properly we should all sing a song together, don't you, Carolyn?" Gwendolyn suggested. Carolyn Mayfield raised her arms alternately in the air like a cheerleader in a gesture of approval.

But Debbie Storm wisecracked, "What? …like, 'Red Sails in the Sunset'?"

"No, no, Debbie; I think I'll suggest a song that has a lot more symbolic importance. But before we do that, can you people believe what we have accomplished here tonight, through the medium and art of music?"

Leonard folded his arms and his eyes opened wider; he wanted to hear this.

"We've discussed the commonality of all western music in the system of key signatures and time signatures; the humanity and styles in music arise from differences in pitch, tonality, dynamics, and prosody in the creative process. Through these tools, and the harmonies and lyrics of music, we can express patterns which recall images of beauty and meaning, and feelings such as power, certainty, compassion, desperation, love, and hope. Although pop rock and elite or concert music appear to be miles apart in style, fundamentally, they really are not. Thus, we found common threads of influence from baroque and classical music to modern styles. J.S. Bach, for instance, has had a powerful influence, across the board, on jazz, rock, and folk music. We listened to modern poetic personal expression in the lyrics and music of Van Morrison, Keith Reid, and the ballades by Sondheim, Bernstein and the Eagles. And we listened to an exquisitely eloquent plea for mercy to a supreme being in 'The Great Mass in C Minor' by Mozart. Any further comment from the group about music or any aspect of this evening?"

There was a pause as Gwendolyn looked right and left. "If not then… yes, Margaret?"

"I think we should give Gwendolyn and Dr. Benedict a round of applause for their hospitality and preparation for this wonderful evening of bonding through music."

Everyone applauded; even Debbie went through the formality although she was tired now and yawning.

"Thank you. And now if you'd just do me, and Lincoln, a favor, there is one more item. Think of it as a benediction of sorts. We like to finish these sessions with a group-sing!"

There were groans from Balis, Brader, and Debbie.

"Can we sing rap music after this?" Debbie asked.

Everyone was now a little over-fed with culture, but Gwendolyn had to finish this.

"Let me introduce and explain the piece. This is by Paul Winter and his consort of musicians and friends. Mr. Winter, who's an outstanding soprano sax musician, admittedly has an agenda, and that agenda is to save the earth. He uses his style of music to express his love of nature and all God's creatures. You might call it 'environmental protection awareness by musical expression.' He's a pioneer in this regard. For example, the piece I want us to participate in tonight, was recorded live as part of the Concert for the Earth at the General Assembly of the United Nations, on World Environment Day, June 5 of 1984. It's called 'Minuit,' which in French means 'midnight.'"

Leonard interrupted,

"In some sense, Gwendolyn, it is midnight for us to act on saving the species on this planet."

"Leonard's right," Gwendolyn continued. "That's exactly what this chant may be about, but in a beautiful communal way. The words are simple and a kind of phonetic blend of Guinean, French and English sounds. We'll sing along with the recording. Dr. Benedict, would you pass out the phonetics sheets to the people?"

Dr. Benedict took some letter-sized sheets from the top of the piano, leaned over and gave them to Margaret who sent them circulating.

"I've tried my best here. For example, I've expressed 'minuit' phonetically, how it sounds: 'minwee,' and so on. Just have fun and sing the sounds along with the chorus and instruments. I'll conduct. We're not doing opera here, just have fun.

"Now, I want the women to sing the opening phrases:

"'minwee sah-ma-say minwee… minwee sah-ma-say-ahh, minwee'

"And then the men to respond:

"'Oh yeah, Oh yeah, Ohhh… Oh yeah, Oh yeah, Oh yeah.'

"Then after, there's a two part harmony as the women repeat, 'minwee sahma-say minwee… minwee sahma-say-ahh, minwee' while the men come in with, 'lala-lala-la (repeat) lala-lala-la (and again) lala-lala-la.'

"Just let it all out… Stop giggling, people, let's be happy campers here. It'll work, you'll see. Ms. Mayfield, you can improvise in the high register if you like."

"This is really a kind of rap song, too, Debbie, trust me… So here's The Paul Winter Consort at the United Nations, backed up by the institute's 'Leonard awareness group,' singing 'Minuit'!"

Lincoln Benedict started the music as Gwendolyn conducted, with a ballpoint pen as her baton. The group was all smiles and laughter, swaying to the acoustic guitars and heartbeat-like base drums, as they joined in the chorus of voices. They really didn't get the timing right until the third go around, when Carolyn soared with vocal scat, singing in a higher soprano register during the two-part harmony (so sensually that Balis and Ozzie got goose bumps).

Leonard enjoyed watching the dissolution of self-consciousness and the communal joy. He was now convinced that there was enough "familial empathy" and bonding in the group for the difficult confrontations of Phase II.

The synergistic power of the ten participants had been constructed and now would be tested.

...

CHAPTER 31

An Introduction to Phase II

The party broke up around midnight, with hugs, appreciation, and good vibes all around. Leonard offered to drive people home, but Dr. Benedict had arranged for the van to take participants back to the institute. The van was waiting down on the gravel driveway as they left the house. The driver, the same security guard who had brought them, was having a smoke leaning against the idling van with his legs crossed when he looked up to see his silhouetted charges making their way down the hill. He flicked his butt to the ground and scurried to prepare for departure.

While driving home, Leonard thought about discussing his recurrent chest pains with someone, maybe Dr. Kiley. But Kiley wasn't there tonight. Dr. Benedict also had an M.D. degree, but Leonard didn't like discussing his health problems with "the pompous bastard."

Leonard reasoned that he would have a physical later; at this critical stage, with this group, he was irreplaceable. He was "kin": these were his people, and he had to finish what he had started for their sake,

"It doesn't matter about me right now."

Leonard and the institute's administration had to find accommodations within an accessible distance from the institute for the phase II encounter candidates. Most were staying at a Hilton Motel up north on the state highway, some were staying in the guest accommodations at the institute—in one case, under close surveillance. One or two others were staying with relatives. Staff was still trying to make contact and complete arrangements with one or two others.

In their grant proposal Benedict and Leonard searched for a precedent for this technique under an academic, experimental, sub-clinical setting, but could not find one, other than the usual empty-chair techniques in individual therapy sessions: "Suppose your father were sitting right there, what would you say to him." Therein lay the originality of the program:

"…Phase 1 will be the construction of support group dynamics by a series of detailed presentations of 'Self,' through which a family level of empathy '*in situ*' is gradually developed, facilitated by a group leader. The purpose of phase II is to use that construct to resolve personal conflicts that were particularly prohibitive to social integration and professional contributions by these underachievers of superior skills and intelligence."

Leonard and Benedict reasoned in their proposal that they could study a process of resolution through a direct confrontation with a critical individual or a source of conflict. These ideas arose out of experiences with most of Leonard's clients and Benedict's patients over the years who, during the course of their therapy, had often said, "If only I had a chance to talk to 'so and so' just one more time."

Phase II was simply one kind of test for addressing the therapeutic value of such fantasies and obsessions.

Benedict and Leonard admitted problems could arise. All cutting edge research had the potential for unforeseen disasters as well as watershed discoveries. But if researchers considered only the negative and detracting possibilities of research projects, then nothing creative would ever get done.

Thus, after careful study of data, transcripts, and notes from the presentations during the phase I sessions, Leonard constructed match-ups of the "encounter pairs" that he preferred for phase II and submitted them to Benedict:

Myles Leonard: Gregori, his older brother and victim of an accidental shooting when they were youngsters.

Dr. Scott Kiley: Dr. Bussler, a negligent family physician.

Dr. Rolland Balis: Rosemarie Bertolli, a "childhood crush."

Wilbur Hanson: Terry Cooper, a childhood friend an accident victim.

Wellington Ozelts: Alberts Ozelts, his stepfather and mother's abuser.

Billy Brader: Siegfried ("Ziggy") Hopmeister, a German immigrant and childhood friend.

Linda Bell: Johnny Linden, a former boyfriend.

Debbie Storm: Rover Carlson, her aunt's companion and a child molester.

Carolyn Mayfield: Dr. Vincent, an academic and a social worker from her childhood neighborhood.

Margaret Worthington: Jesus Christ.

CHAPTER 32

States of Minds

Willy Hanson hadn't heard about the music party until he had gotten back from night of drinking, past midnight sometime. He liked the people in the group, and he appreciated that Ozzie had tried to understand him, but they were too cerebral for him. He missed working with his hands. Anyway, one more week of this and it was a nice piece of cash and back up north to the mill. He reminded himself to pick up a souvenir for his son. He wasn't afraid of any kind of confrontation. He lived in a world of constant confrontation; he lived by an hourly wage. There was nothing that was going to be done here to him that hasn't been done already.

When he wasn't consciously correcting it, Dr. Kiley had a slight lisp. Specific factors that accentuated the minor impediment were environmental and social conditions, and an occasional reversion to childhood inhibitions and shyness. It wasn't a source of constant concern for him because as a rule his lisp was not the type that interfered significantly with his verbal communication. He was almost asleep on his flight from Atlanta to meet his commitment to the program when a flight attendant stuck her face in his and asked him, "Sthir, do you need a dwink?"

Half-dazed, he almost knocked his reading glasses off the bridge of his nose when he reacted and answered her, "Yeth, I'd like a thscotch."

The stewardess, a stocky strawberry blond, stood up and admonished him, "You needn't make fun of my lithsp in my sthothern accent when I take your order."

"Believe me, ma'am, I justht woke up from a nap and I haven't yet the inithiative to mock anyone, esthpecially you… hadn't even entered my mind."

"Sthee, there you go again."

She left in a huff, and Kiley didn't think much of the misunderstanding. His scotches were deferred to another flight attendant, a demure brunette. Toward the end of the flight as the landing procedure was announced the stocky flight attendant approached Kiley again:

"What is your name, sthir? I'm reporting you to the captain, for abusthing me verbally." Kiley was now irritated but controlling his lisp; and the flight attendant was thereby even more convinced that Kiley had mocked her. She had fire in her eyes.

Kiley, recognizing the paranoia, now made an all-out effort to control his speech, and said, "I'm not giving you my name, and I've done nothing wrong. I suggest you pay more attention to the landing procedure than to this counter-productive misunderstanding. I also have a slight lisp when I don't exercise my will. But it's manageable."

The flight attendant stomped off, but the affair was not over. On his way out of the aircraft, a uniformed male who identified himself as the head attendant asked him what had happened between "Becky" and him during the flight. Kiley tried to explain him away, but to no avail; a further meeting was called, at the baggage carousel, a kind of kangaroo court with the captain of the aircraft as judge. The whole crew was present, and Kiley had to explain himself all over again.

He testified that he also had a slight conditional lisp, that he had no intention of mocking the flight attendant, and that he was a physician and would never make light of speech impediments. Finally after twenty grueling minutes of testimony by both plaintiff and defendant, the captain gave his verdict:

"Becky I really don't thwink you have much of a case here, and I would dwop the whole thwing."

A delighted Kiley shook the pilot's hand twice in gratitude. "Thank you, thir, I mean sssir, thank you very much. Phew."

As he left the terminal, Scott Kiley waved "bye" to the crew, wondering if they didn't have more important things to do, like how to conduct a flight without harassing him. He climbed into his cab mumbling to himself, "Maybe another week of introspection with Leonard and the group will help me understand how a simple country doctor gets into these situations."

After arranging her affairs Sunday morning, Margaret Worthington, dressed in white, walked across campus to the institute's chapel. The chapel was in the basement of the business office building. There were rows of pews and a simple altar with a large, looming, oval, blue stained glass window depicting Christ blessing sheep. She took a seat in the first row of pews, because her knees were swollen now and kneeling was impossible. She folded her hands with a rosary and prayed for everyone in the group to learn and improve their lives through this experience. She thanked God for the dedication of workers like Dr. Benedict and Dr. Leonard. She asked forgiveness for her sins and her sinful thoughts, especially her attraction to competent men. And finally she asked for strength and grace from Jesus Christ for the week to come, and a safe passage home for everyone.

CHAPTER 33

The Imperfect Bonding of Brothers

Monday morning there was excitement in the air as the group was gathering in and around the conference room, an atmosphere of an exam day, or a thesis defense. Earlier up in the cafeteria, the talk at the breakfast tables was about "keeping our heads on straight," "don't nobody lose their tempers," and "let's use what we learned last week."

Rolland Balis was heard to have said, "Maybe this is going to be a case of, 'be careful what you wish for, you might get it.'"

Now as the participants took their seats in the conference room they noticed empty seats at the ends of table labeled "For Our Guests." The morning sun shone through the tall windows as Dr. Myles Leonard suddenly appeared at the door; no one noticed him even saunter up the corridor, either because they were so solipsistic in their apprehension or because Leonard was uncharacteristically wearing tennis shoes.

As Leonard placed his notes and book on the table, the buzz in the room subsided. Leonard gave Debbie "that look," and she put down her cell phone. After he checked that all participants from last week were present, he began a formal introduction to the week's Phase II proceedings.

"I am very pleased with what we accomplished last week in terms of communication, interpersonal learning experiences, development of empathy and bonding, and the generation of friendships and affections. For example, Saturday night at the Benedicts' I witnessed togetherness, humanity, and sense of being alive through the medium of music. My Lord, I felt like I had finally arrived at my family reunion."

There were smiles and nods of agreement around the table.

"But before we send you back out there, to the outside world"—he gestured toward the window—"to be challenged again, we want to try something.

"We call it Phase II.

"Please use what you have learned and what skills you have developed from each other; be strong and fair, be positive and negotiate for peace and resolution, and exercise restraint and anger management where necessary. Should the stress of any of these encounters approach diminished returns, in terms of learning and resolution, I will be obliged to intercede, call a recess, or terminate proceedings for the day. If you feel squeamish or faint of heart you may, of course, leave the room, but you may be docked the day's pay per your contract, unless you can convince me of the urgency. Staff are available at a moment's notice.

"But remember, this is an experimental forum to which you have agreed. We are here to find ways to improve lives, not to hurt people. I'll volunteer as the first participant to face the… what should we call it?"

"The Hot Seat!" Ozzie suggested.

"OK, Dr. Ozelts, it's 'the Hot Seat.'

"In good faith I've called in my brother, Gregori. Last week I related to you the traumatic experience, the accidental shooting he survived in my presence with our grandfather when we were very young, about seven or eight. While Gregori is escorted into the conference room by staff, are there any questions, so far?"

Leonard dialed a number on his intercom phone and put it to his ear and spoke: "We're ready in here, Don, bring in Gregori, would you, please?"

There was an increase in the group's intensity and curiosity as Leonard announced his opening gambit. It was clear now why Leonard, even though group leader, had integrated himself also as a participant. He wasn't going to submit anyone in the group to something that he himself wouldn't go through.

Brader whispered to Ozzie, "He's got balls."

Debbie whispered to Balis, "Here's where Leonard breaks."

Margaret Worthington whispered a quick prayer.

Gregori was taller than Leonard and a lot thinner. He had a beard that was darker than his gray hair. The nose was Roman and similar to Leonard's but the main difference in countenance was in the eyes. While Leonard's eyes were warm and inquiring, Gregori's eyes pierced through his beard like darts; they were reddened, possibly from fatigue, or lack of sleep. Leonard's chair scraped the floor as he stood up and shook Greg's hand. He slapped him on the shoulder affectionately and gestured for him to take the empty seat to the left. Gregori, who was wearing a green cotton shirt with a leather vest, jeans and leather boots, sat down slowly, took a deep breath and said, "So what's this all about, Milo? You know I wouldn't be here if you wasn't payin' me."

Gregori also paid less attention to grammar, syntax, and enunciation than Leonard.

"Hi, Greg, thanks for coming, and helping us out. This is the group I've been working with the last couple of weeks. We've been discussing relationships and traumatic experiences in our lives, and trying to learn from them. I thought you could give us your version of what happened that day with us, and granddad; and perhaps your conclusions about it."

"You mean when I got shot, as a kid? …Well, we was takin' the ashes from the house to the town dump, and as we was haulin' 'em from the truck across the railroad tracks with the wheelbarrow some stupid bastard named Waldo Harvey took target practice on me and damn near killed me. Leonard, here, and Granddaddy saved my life."

There was silence in the room, and Leonard kept eye contact with Gregori, because he wanted more. Gregori shuffled his feet and sagged a little in his chair and crossed his hands. Then he continued, "You know, my life got saved but I sometimes wonder if it was worth it. I was more like a pain to the family as a kid after that. Even Granddaddy left. I couldn't eat. I couldn't sleep. I'd get these dizzy spells—well, not really dizzy spells; it was like I didn't know where I was sometimes. I started drinkin' at a real early age. I quite school—that's somethin' I shouldna done. I had a lot of jobs. I was even in jail a couple of times; you know, bar fights and shenanigans. Leonard, here, goes to war and comes back a hero and becomes a professor. I tried to enlist, but on account of the scars and the wounds from that shooting, never passed the physical. Funny how I got shot as a kid, but when I tried to get shot as a man they wouldn't let me. Couldn't even do that right. For a while there I really lost it with the booze and I had to go to a rehab center to straighten out. But I want you to know I'm better than ever now and I'm workin'… nights at a meat packin' plant. It's not far from the place where I got shot up by Waldo. Ain't that funny, Milo?"

Leonard looked at Greg, his chin resting on the palm of his left hand. A tear was rolling down his left cheek. For once he accepted the full force of their differences… and the pain.

Ozzie took the floor. "But I mean your grandfather could have been hit or Leonard or all three of you. You think about the repercussions of stray bullets, and it's stultifying. The Kennedy assassinations, Martin Luther King, Kent State, the recent school shootings, the D.C. interstate shootings, college campus shootings. Stray bullets are everywhere. I'm beginning to think shooting is not a sport anymore than stabbing is. Killing with sharp projectiles is a spin-off, a vestigial corruption, of man as a hunter and warrior. But at some point the warrior part faded. Like the right to bear arms as a revolutionary, or militiaman, faded."

Ozzie paused and then emphasized, "The innocent make convenient targets because they don't shoot back."

"Amen, brother." Dr. Kiley nodded.

Leonard looked up and spoke slowly; he wanted to return to the personal level.

"I guess what I feel most guilty about, Greg, is that I can't say that I wish it had been me. I don't. I wish it had been no one. That's the first thing. Second, my sense of this incident is that this mismanaged miniature projectile changed three lives forever. That's too much power for a small piece of fate. We in the family allowed some of that. We could have discussed these issues more. Family power was not tapped sufficiently for Greg at the time. Blame and guilt won."

"Well, he's got family power here!" Margaret said.

"He sure does," Carolyn Mayfield added.

Then Margaret and Carolyn got up out of their seats, soon followed by Ozzie and even Linda Bell and Billy Brader. They went over to "The Hot Seat" and gave Gregori their hands, hugs, and assurances. Gregori, at first baffled, started to break down from the affection.

"Wow," he said, "I never... I never expected this."

"It's a new, innovative therapy we call 'love and understanding,'" Leonard said, as everybody laughed, relieving intensity of the encounter.

"Are we through? Because I'm not used to this," Gregori asked.

"We're through, except for one thing, Greg," Leonard said.

"What's that, brother?"

Leonard leaned toward Gregori, with typical eye contact when he wanted to dramatize a point. "Is there no place for us, Greg, where all tension fades, where you simply forgive me, where we are simply brothers?"

"I love you too, now... can I go, Milo?"

With that Gregori lifted his lanky frame and, taking rather long steps with his boots, left the room with a wave and a "so long," and then the door slammed.

Ozzie noticed that Leonard was sweating from his brow and upper lip.

"OK, Phew… any comments?" Leonard asked, glancing around the table.

"I thought he was very courageous to come in here," Margaret said.

"Yes, and it showed a certain measure of trust on his part and yours, Dr. Leonard," Carolyn added.

"What if I told you that there's so much we can discuss… and it just stops. I'm a word merchant, except when it comes to Greg," Leonard revealed, smiling wanly.

"That doesn't necessarily have to be because of the bullet. There are a lot of brothers that don't talk. They just have to accept the fact that they're different; they're not twins. I could tell you two were different when he walked in here," Dr. Balis said.

"You did good though, Leonard, you said the right thing; maybe a little late, but the right thing." Willy Hanson gestured with his open right hand in a chopping motion and smiled as he spoke.

Leonard exhaled and said, "Thank you, dear hearts. After a coffee break let's continue with Dr. Kiley and Dr. Bussler."

Kiley sat up and forward on his chair. "What! Where on earth did you find Bussler?"

"We have our means, Dr. Kiley. Are you interested, or should we send him home?"

"No, No, I'll talk to him. I've always wanted to talk to him; I do have a few questions."

Dr. Kiley sat back, looked up at the windows, and let out a barely audible "W-o-w."

CHAPTER 34

A Hypocrite of Hippocrates

All heads around the conference table turned up as Dr. Bussler was escorted in by Don, the male nurse, who was dressed in a white button-down uniform and a ponytail. Bussler was bent over as he managed his way slowly to the "Hot Seat" using a polished briarwood cane. The staff member stepped back against the wall, folded his hands, and looked at Leonard, who gestured with an open hand for him to wait. Dr. Kiley guessed that there was possibly an arthritic spine problem with Bussler aggravated by his obesity. His cheeks were sagging like tiny saddlebags, and he had a double chin. Bussler's eyebrows were so bushy they resembled overused paint brushes. All these components combined to assemble a defiant scowl reminiscent of Charles Laughton's Captain Bligh, but without the dignity and flair. He sat down slowly, holding on to the top of his cane, and glanced around the table. His voice was weak but gruff; it was clear that he

187

would compete for authority here. "I understand that one of my former patients would like to see me. They tracked me down poolside in Palm Beach. I am retired now but I was happy to accommodate the request of this conference for my attendance. Who's running the show?"

"My name is Dr. Myles Leonard. I'm the group leader here. This group is helping us in a research program concerning sub-clinical factors for under-achievement. One of our participants has brought your name up in regard to his mother's lead poisoning."

"I'm sorry, what was the name of the patient?" Bussler inquired.

"Mary Kiley." Dr. Kiley's voice broke in.

Bussler turned to Kiley. "Who are you?"

And for the first time in decades Kiley was face to face with the man who had contaminated his mother's body.

Dr. Kiley was in a dilemma. He wanted to avenge his mother's suffering, but he was a physician, and inflicting pain intentionally was out of the question. Besides, the real purpose of this kind of meeting was a resolution.

"My name is Dr. Scott Kiley. Many years ago you had a patient named Mary Kiley, my mother, who suffered from rheumatic heart disease. During the course of your house visits you interested her in helping you with your hobby, Civil War figure carvings. She would have to file down these little lead-based Civil War figurines, for which service you compensated her by discounts for your physical examinations. As a result of her exposure, she contracted lead poisoning. I remember her hands, glossy with lead dust. There was also the problem of lead shavings and dust all over a house with two primary school–age children. We… I mean, I… was just wondering how a physician could justify such an egregious disregard for a patient's welfare and that of her family; or, how an educated practitioner of medicine could display such a monumental ignorance of human toxicology. You should have had your license to practice revoked and been sued for criminal negligence."

Kiley had worked himself up, and he was red in the face and tapping his fingers on the table. Leonard was carefully monitoring the level of heat now. Bussler's eyes were bulging under his bushy eyebrows. He fiddled and massaged his cane as if ready to leave; his hands were trembling as he spoke, his voice loud.

"You brought me here for this? I have just finished a forty-year career as a physician, and you're going to dress me down like some kind of green recruit? I don't know how many patients I have helped, but there were many them. Do you think I just went around deliberately contaminating people with lead? I took a Hippocratic oath. If there was lead in that metal your mother filed I was unaware of it. I remember your mother. She was a wonderful person and a good patient and I probably prescribed life-saving medications for her a number of times. But I don't recall forcing her to expose herself to toxic levels of lead. Sure, I had a hobby recreating Civil War battles for which the Lions Club awarded me a certificate of merit; they sold hundreds of them to collectors who contributed to Lions' charities. Many people helped me with this hobby—why didn't they report lead poisoning? If she worked for me she needed the money. Those were tough times. If your mother contracted lead poisoning, you'd have a difficult time proving I willfully and knowingly caused the problem."

Kiley was ready with his response:

"It's true that she was a war refugee and they are prone to pick up all manner of toxins and diseases. Notwithstanding, Dr. Bussler, that makes your negligence all the more despicable. You exploited a poor immigrant mother at a vulnerable time in her life to make a few bucks on the side, while contaminating her body and her household with lead particles. There's no telling how many others you contaminated with your damned lead. As far as I'm concerned you're no better than that guy who drove the Exxon Valdez into the Alaskan coast, except he had an excuse. He was ignorant and drunk. You're supposed to be a healer, for God's sakes."

Bussler pressed his lips together a couple of times as if he were chewing on his false teeth. His left hand was still on his cane, and he took a handkerchief out of his pocket with his right hand, wiped his face, and blew his nose. Kiley was still glaring at him. Bussler spoke, this time in a more personable, collegial style.

"I'm an old man, Dr. Kiley. Maybe there were some patients whom I could have managed better. Maybe I underestimated the toxicity of the metal used to make the statuettes. I don't know. I meant your mother no harm. I don't know how I should put this. I'll be honest with you, Dr. Kiley. We were on a first-name basis. I liked your mother very much. She was a special person in my life. I never would have done anything to hurt her, believe me, doctor."

Bussler then took out a handkerchief again and blew his nose so loudly that the conference table vibrated. He then folded it and placed it back into his pocket. The participants stayed out of the encounter, thinking Kiley was doing just fine, but Leonard thought it time to intercede.

"All right, if that's all between the physicians we'll thank Dr. Bussler for responding to our request by coming here to answer to Dr. Kiley. Don, would you escort Dr. Bussler to the business office and to his transportation? Thank you again, Doctor."

When the door closed behind Bussler and the nurse, the group broke out into spontaneous discussions.

"I thought Dr. Kiley was great," Linda Bell said. "He said exactly what Bussler needed to hear and deserved."

"Bussler backed off after Kiley pressed him about the lead contamination. He knew he was a scoundrel and admitted it. How's an MD not going to know about lead?" Balis said.

"He made up that stuff up about loving your mother to get you to lighten up. It's like he hinted at an affair. He's an old bastard," Debbie Storm exclaimed.

Carolyn came out forcefully: "He saw Kiley's mother as an ignorant immigrant and exploited her. He's typical of a self-righteous, white, Anglo-Saxon, male, aristocrat scoundrel."

Leonard raised his left hand to the group.

"OK, OK, everybody relax, let's hear from Dr. Kiley. Doc, have we learned anything? Was this encounter a mistake? What's going on in your head right now?"

"No, this wasn't a mistake at all. I appreciated this opportunity. I almost blew it there for a second, but I decided to keep anger out of it as much as possible. Maybe that's what I learned. In encounters with someone that's hurt you irretrievably, there is no true vengeance, but there is eye contact and the truth; words work better than knives that way."

The group broke into scattered polite applause, and Dr. Kiley finally looked up, with a tight-lipped smile at Leonard.

CHAPTER 35

A Woman for all Seasons

"Dr. Balis, we have a surprise for you. We were able to contact an old friend of yours. According to your last presentation here she played a traumatic role in your development. I'm sure you'll welcome Rosemarie Bertolli."

Balis just about fell over on his chair. And the rest of the participants around the conference table either gasped or shook their heads. Balis was going to re-encounter his powerful fifth grade crush after more than four decades of life. Even Leonard had a mischievous gleam in his eye at the possibility of a fascinating meeting.

"Leonard, where do you find these people? You should work for the FBI," Ozzie gushed.

"They give us a call now and then, ol' buddy," Leonard said, furrowing his brow and folding his arms, feigning arrogance.

But Ms. Bertolli hadn't arrived yet.

"What time is it?" Leonard asked, glancing at his watch. "Let's break for lunch. In the mean time we'll fortify Dr. Balis—he looks a little pale—and locate Ms. Bertolli. I want everyone back here by 14:00 hours on the nose."

Dr. Balis went back to his room at the institute, which was in another building, an upscale dormitory housing VIP outpatients and guest speakers. He had prepared hastily for this morning's session, and now he wanted to spruce up and clear his mind.

"It's not like I have to impress her," he told himself, "but I'll kick it up a notch with my French aftershave... any way, how do I prepare for something like this? How do you tell a woman, that I was so enamored with her that I lost my senses at the age of ten? I'd rather face Burt Lancaster at the OK Corral, than Rosemarie Bertolli; at least I'd know what to say. Why am I suddenly responsible for my obsessions as a child?"

It was a beautiful day, and many patients, outpatients, therapists, and staff were strolling about the grounds. Billy Brader and Ozzie sat on the front steps of the research building, taking in the scene with their sunglasses donned, squinting into the sun and waiting for 2 o'clock and the next encounter session.

"I don't understand the purpose of bringing in Balis' crush. That was so long ago. Do you, Ozzie? Why not just let him move on?"

"Balis is one of these people that doesn't move on. His overwhelming primitive emotions are continually clashing with his superior intelligence. He's not a pathological or evil guy by any means. Actually now, I kind of like him. It's a delicate challenge for Leonard. We'll see the purpose; maybe it's not just about Balis."

Brader looked at his watch: "You're getting pretty good at this yourself, Ozzie, maybe you missed your calling... oops, let's head on upstairs."

The two were the last to make it into the conference room under the gun, before the door was closed. Among his many implicit demands of the participants, Leonard had established a precedent for starting sessions on time. As Brader and Ozzie were pulling back their seats to sit down, Leonard was already on the intercom cell phone informing staff that the group was ready for Ms. Bertolli's appearance. Balis' hands were sweating, and Debbie Storm wished she could light up a cigarette or joint. She wasn't jealous, she was excited. Anytime an empowered woman entered a room Debbie got pumped up.

Then the door opened a crack and stopped, and a voice was heard to say, "That's fine, dear, I can take it from here."

The door opened wider and a woman with a beautiful round face, a perfect complexion, and dark brown eyes, dressed in nun's habit and a modest, but impeccable white coif entered the room, smiling. She bowed slightly to the group and the men—Ozzie, Brader, Balis, and Hanson—tried quickly and clumsily to stand up as she glided her way toward a chair at the head of the table. Margaret Worthington made the sign of the cross as Kiley moved deftly over to help the nun with her chair, but she preferred to address the group standing up, her hands placed on the back of the chair.

"I am Mother Rosemarie of the Convent of St. Jude. Most of the sisters call me Mother Rose. I thank you for your contribution to our orphanage, in return for which I was pleased to come participate in your program. Now, how can I help you?"

"We are honored by your gracious response to our request, Mother Rosemarie. My name is Dr. Myles Leonard. I'm the group leader here. This group is in a research program, concerned with sub-clinical factors for under-achievement. In this phase of the program the participants are having the opportunity to encounter individuals who were influential during their childhood, someone they remember in a special way. One of our participants has brought your name up as an influential individual in his life.

"But allow me then to introduce you to the group. From your left that's Margaret Worthington, a retired teacher, and environmentalist; then that's Dr. Scott Kiley a physician-general practitioner; Linda Bell, a pharmacist,… then there is Dr. Rolland Balis a scientific researcher—you two are apparently old friends. Debbie Storm is to the left of Dr. Balis, and is a woman of many talents; …Carolyn Mayfield, our most gifted artist; Wellington Ozelts, a physicist—and philosopher I might add; …Billy Brader, a former professional athlete and a bread winner in the sales sector now; and last, but certainly not least, Willy Hanson, who is an artist with his hands, carving wood to specifications useful to society."

"Rolland Balis from Miss Bishop's class! Rolland is that you? God bless you, how are you? I don't believe it. That was so long ago," Mother Rosemarie exclaimed.

"Hi, Rosemarie, I mean Mother Rose, I'm glad to see you again. You… you look great," Balis said tentatively in a voice timbre no one had heard before.

"Don't be taken back by this cloak, my dear; I'm still Rosemarie."

There was a pregnant pause in the discourse, and Leonard knew that Balis, though momentarily discombobulated, would recover and see the light—once he had properly processed the irony.

Balis feared that confessing his childhood fantasies or even his affection to Rosemarie Bertolli, the Mother Superior of a convent, might border somehow on incest, or at least blasphemy.

On the other hand, Rosemarie was acquainted with unsolicited adoration. It had almost ruined her life, until she turned to a Supreme Being whom she could adore freely. But she wouldn't impose that kind of discussion on the group unless prompted.

Leonard decided to break this momentary tension with a practical, constructive question: "Mother Rosemarie, what is success; what is it that we so badly want, but we so rarely are able to achieve?"

"You know, my dear friends, I was the Homecoming queen at Archbishop Wilson High School in my senior year, and I thought that was a successful experience. I married an all-American football player, and I thought that was a success, especially when I gave birth to a beautiful daughter. But after his service in the Marine Corps, he changed. He turned out to run the household like a Marine base, with his military and football buddies a constant presence. I began to ask myself the questions you just asked me, Dr. Leonard.

"When I disagreed with his style of household management, he lashed out like a crazed master sergeant, with physical and verbal abuse. This went on until I could stand it no longer and I told him to move out. After a restraining order was issued by a court, he resorted to stalking and even hired a hit man to stalk me and kidnap my child. We were obliged to leave the town I was raised in. Since I was the object of his vengeance, I knew my daughter wasn't safe with me. With strength gathered from prayer, I gave her over to my parents, who then raised her. It was after I knew she was happy with them that I made up my mind to never marry again, and I took the vows and entered into the service of Our Lord and Savior. That was many years ago.

"Today I supervise a convent that provides for the orphaned, needy, the destitute, and desperate. My troubles pale in comparison to these children. Those that I serve in the name of the Lord will be the judge of whether I am a successful person, Dr. Leonard. A famous Catholic president said at his inauguration, 'If a free society cannot help the many who are poor it cannot save the few who are rich.' How we help those many is perhaps the best measure of a successful society, morally as well as economically. So if any among you are looking for a path to success, you might try fulfilling your potential in the service to many who are less fortunate. There is still time."

Leonard saw this was a window of opportunity, and called on Balis.

Balis' words would have to be well-chosen.

"Dr. Balis?"

"I'd just like to say..." Balis cleared his throat "...that what I have witnessed in Rosemarie is the conversion of a beautiful child into a courageous woman, a great person, and through this epiphany I've learned something from the Mother Superior."

Leonard leaned forward, placed his elbows on the table, and glanced right to left.

"Anyone else?" he asked matter-of-factly, as if he had written the script for what had just occurred.

Mother Rosemarie glanced at Dr. Balis, who was now staring at her, this time out of respect.

"Well... thank you all, this has been a wonderful experience, but I also flew down here for the rare opportunity to visit my daughter, who is waiting for me downstairs; my plane leaves this evening."

The men jumped up as Mother Rosemarie started to leave. Her habit ruffled as she started walking around the table to the door, but she stopped in front of Balis; she raised her right hand up to Balis' cheek and touched it gently while looking into his eyes with a smile—the only time in his life she had ever touched him. Balis' pulse was racing as he tried to smile back. Once long ago captured by her immature beauty, he was now conquered by her grace. Leonard got up to open the door for her, but just before leaving she raised her right hand in a gesture of a blessing and said, "Love each other, dear friends, always."

And then she was gone.

"Dr. Balis, are you all right?" Leonard inquired.

"I never felt better in my whole life, Leonard," Balis said softly.

CHAPTER 36

In Great Shape

The door to the conference room swung open, and a tall, handsome, pleasantly plump man with curly blondish-gray hair, a pink complexion, and an ingratiating smile walked in. He was wearing a perfectly tailored, light blue-colored three-piece suit and a silk chartreuse tie neatly tucked into his vest.

"Hi, I'm Terry Cooper. Where's Wilbur, they told me Willy Boy was here?"

Willy Hanson's eyes lit up like headlamps. "Terry... Terry Cooper?"

Willy got up and came around the table, and Terry met him halfway. They gave each other the bear hug. The participants smiled in response to the good feelings resonating from the reunion of two friends.

They looked each other over.

"Well I'll be darned, what have you been doing with your life, Willy? How's your dad?" Terry asked.

"He passed away a while ago, it was his blood pressure—he was too sensitive about everything, I guess. I'm a carpenter, cabinet maker, always trying to wrestle with the lumber, you know. It's amazing how many people get in trouble just trying to do their job, trying to be good."

Leonard stepped in.

"I hate to interrupt such good vibes. Terry, why don't you take a seat at that end of the table; this shouldn't take long. You know this is a federally funded group study on the sub-clinical factors for under-achievement in a competitive society. In this phase of the study we call in individuals who have been influential in our participants' lives to see if they can contribute. Willy Hanson recalled that his childhood adventure with you was a very traumatic learning experience for him."

"You mean the axe incident… well, yeah, sure, I could have been tomahawked right there, but Willy's father got me down off of that mountain, to where I could go on with my life and he could go on with his. But that's all bygones by the boards and spilt milk under the bridge."

Terry wanted to get back to the subject of Willy. "Carpentry, cabinets, huh? I bet you're the best darn wood shaver east of the Mississippi. You know I went to business school at Davidson when my family moved south and then formed my own little company. Now I'm in real estate development, and we buy up big plots of land. Build communities all over Florida. Dry up all the resources. Scatter the alligators and birds. Wilbur, why don't you call my office, and maybe we can arrange for you to help us with the woodworking in our units. You know, the frames, the kitchens, the molding… all that stuff. Should be a piece of cake for you. We have guys that do that now but they're contracted. I need a steady man to run that part of the operation. Somebody I can trust with a saw blade and an axe, somebody with a vision, you know what I mean?"

"Yeah, I know what you mean, Terry." Willy let the inadvertent reference to his father pass.

"...Somebody that doesn't piss in my tent and then nickel and dime me to death. How about it, Wilbur?"

"I never turn down a job offer; especially from an old friend."

"Good... good... Hey let's have dinner after your jaw bonin' here and we'll talk it over... old times and new deals... everything... God love you, Wilbur, good to see you. If that's all... I'll be down in the lobby, Wilbur. Have a nice day, everybody!"

Cooper seemed wary of the group, uncomfortable in this situation and appeared to want to leave the room. Leonard saw no further purpose to the interview and thanked Cooper for his participation as he straightened his tie and left.

Every encounter was not going to be groundbreaking, and it appeared that a resolution had been achieved.

"Well, I'd say that's more or less a happy ending to the axe head incident, wouldn't you say, Leonard?" Ozzie asked the group leader.

Carolyn Mayfield put her elbows on the table and her hands together and said, "You know, Willy was going to quit us early, saying he didn't fit. Willy fits anywhere there's a need for hardworking men of good will; he doesn't have a mean streak in him. I just hope Willy doesn't get in over his head with this big-time operator."

"I hear you, Carolyn, but my control over group dynamics, and worldly affairs, stops outside that door," Leonard added.

Then Leonard upped the volume and addressed the restless group:

"OK, people, perhaps we should call ourselves a 'workshop' like they do at Harvard; it might provide more funding. Let's keep our fingers crossed for the rest of the week. Wednesday 9 a.m. sharp, please. I have Ozelts, Brader, Bell, and Storm on the docket. If preceding presentations by these people are any indication, we will be experiencing more interesting tests of our group dynamics. Stay well."

CHAPTER 37

"It's as Over as It'll Ever Get..."

Wednesday morning shone through Ozzie's window like a second coming. He'd fallen asleep reading and hadn't closed the shades last night. His unadapted eyes hurt as he squinted and looked away while pulling the drapes closed. He navigated his way to the bathroom and gazed at himself in the mirror and smiled. He was beginning to feel the effects of Leonard's group synthesis. Just the humanity expressed in the encounters by Leonard, Kiley, and Balis in this phase of the program had permeated into his awareness; they were processed in his brain maybe even deeper than memories, and now part of his perspective.

He could live with himself and his denial of aging; he could live with the detractors, liars, and manipulators; and, he could even live through a bad day, if there were friends like this, living through all this with him.

He wondered whom he would encounter this morning in the session. *But regardless of who it is,* he thought back to one of Leonard's speeches, *"be strong and fair, be positive and negotiate for peace and resolution; exercise restraint and anger management where necessary."*

Leonard looked tired and a bit haggard as he started the session with hands placed on the table in a resigned body language. He had spent most of yesterday trying to understand his tumultuous marriage to June… then trying to debate Suzanne about her sexuality… finally escaping to the King's Pub. He was wearing a sweatshirt, which was a sign that he was out of clean shirts for the time being, and he had the sleeves pulled up to almost the elbows.

As the level of friendship and camaraderie increased in the group, so did the chatter at the beginning of the sessions.

"Good morning again, dear hearts, let's get settled please, we have a lot of work to do. The resolutions in Monday's encounters were as dramatic as our collective learning experiences. Today might bring some surprises but I hope we remain civil."

Leonard glanced at Ozzie and continued. "May I agree with Dr. Kiley that in encounters or confrontations with someone that's hurt you irretrievably, there is no true vengeance, because there is no reversal of an experience. But there is eye contact and the truth, to regain control of the processing of the experience; in that sense, words work better than the physical…"

Ozzie, sitting next to Carolyn, didn't hear the rest, but looked in her eyes for courage, and Carolyn grabbed his hand and winked assuringly. "It's going to be all right."

A staff member opened the door to the conference room and was heard to announce, "Alberts Ozelts, this is Dr. Leonard."

Ozzie hadn't seen his stepfather for over thirty years. Alberts had gained weight, but he still had that, now gray, wavy hair combed back in the style of a President Milosovic. This had the effect of making his forehead look larger than it was. Now that Ozzie thought of it, an extended forehead might represent wisdom to these people. All those European post-war proponents of God and law combed their hair back. Alberts had a sharp nose, straight and narrow; it was almost like a beak. His face was square except for the jaw, which stuck out and forward slightly. He was dressed in a polyester suit and a dark red and white tie probably representing the fallen of his war-torn country, or the blood of Christ, both absolute symbols to his generation. He bowed politely to the table of participants.

"Thank you for answering our request, Mr. Ozelts. Would you please take that seat at the end of the table?"

Alberts Ozelts pulled his seat back and sat down. His fingers were shaking as he looked around the table. His gaze stopped at Ozzie momentarily as he reached into his coat pocket for a thin, silver ballpoint pen and a small black notebook, and then he turned to Leonard and respectfully waited for instructions. He was a man accustomed to his opinions and beliefs being assaulted in America; that was the price he paid for being "absolutely right." Ozelts was an immigrant from the shores of embattled seas and rivers, steely-eyed and steel hard in his ways.

The East European nationalities which were indigenous to the incessantly and brutally disputed territories from the Carpathians up through the Dnieper, Danube, Neman, and Dvina River valleys to the Baltic Sea have long-maintained traditions. It was a way of rising up out of mere personal survival; it was social, political group survival. But these crossover nationalities suffered recurrent demographic incursions, deportations, and invasions, from the west by Germanic regimes, from the north by the Scandinavians, and from the east by Russians and the Slavs. This cauldron of sociological, political upheaval created classes of inflexible intellectuals with extremes of opinion between the political left and right, between fundamental religion and radicalism, between the traditional and the revolutionary. Adherents of one extreme considered adherents of the other extreme collaborators, conspirators, and infidels.

Thus, Ozelts, on the political far right, viewed himself as a champion of God against all evil and freedom against all communists. And despite the thousands of other religious and cultural lifestyles in this world, he was absolutely convinced that his way was the only way that would eventually assure his soul a place at the right hand of God.

Leonard introduced the members of the group to Ozelts and made the usual statement of purpose for the program, including that Ozzie had named him an influential person in his childhood. He then asked Ozelts whether he had anything to say by way of introduction or contribution. Ozelts spoke "the King's English" with an accent, omitting the article "the" but rolling his *r*'s.

"First of all I would like to thank you for contribution to East European Evangelical Lutheran Church, in return for which I am pleased to accommodate invitation. I see my stepson is here. Hello, Wellington. How are you? Your mother could not make trip. You know we are in our eighties now so that would have been most difficult for her, but she sends you her love."

Carolyn nudged Ozzie to make his move now. Ozzie pulled out a folded sheet of paper, flattened it, and read from a prepared text.

"Alberts, you have had a long and difficult life. Your parents survived World War I, and you survived World War II. You've been a student, a teacher, a soldier, a refugee, a businessman, and now you are the very Reverend Ozelts. Your country has survived brutal invasions from the West by the German military machine and from the East by the Soviet Red Army, and commensurately, the political extremes and exterminations of Nazism and communism. Having said that, you will not receive any medals from me for your adamant adherence to your principles. If your God and your country have survived, it is in spite of people like you. As a family man you were a failure and charlatan. Although you professed absolute belief in the mercy of Jesus Christ, you were merciless in your abuse of your wife and her child. The principles of Christian virtue and democratic open-mindedness which you so proudly hailed as your own were scrapped when it came to your domestic responsibilities. You tortured us with daily tirades about the hate and intolerance you have for people that don't agree with your opinions and absolute truths. I believe you loved my mother, and I can't blame you for that. But the child by her first marriage was a source of your constant retroactive jealousy; I was evidence that she loved someone else. I was a love-child that competed with your male domain.

"On that climactic and fateful day, if I hadn't stopped you, that car would have gone down that embankment, and you would have sacrificed all us for your vengeance. Under current laws of domestic violence you'd have gone to jail a long time ago. There is no defense for destroying the lives of children."

Alberts took a handkerchief out of his coat pocket and wiped his nose a few times. His eyes were reddened as he looked up to speak.

"I am sorry, and I ask for God's forgiveness. I was bad father to you. We were poor refugees, and those times were hard; we lived on church donations until I could get a job at laundry. I came back home many days tired and short-tempered. I loved your mother too much, and I was afraid to lose her. She was all I had in strange land. You were not my natural son, so how could I love you as my own? The part of you I destroyed, I cannot bring back. But, let me say this, Wellington. You are here among these good people. You have highest post-graduate academic degree. You are relatively healthy—at least I hope so. And most important you have raised wonderful children yourself. You know, Wellington—"

"'Dr. Ozelts to you, Alberts," Ozzie interrupted forcefully.

"All right… of course, Dr. Ozelts. You know, you are not only one from post-war generation who has been damaged. Believe me, there are much more tragic cases than yours. If you cannot forgive us, this fire of unfulfilled vengeance will continue to waste your emotional energy which otherwise could be put to more useful purposes. You want to destroy me? Go ahead; I am here. But will that heal you? Only love can heal your heart, not vengeance."

Leonard was listening to the exchange with his right elbow on the table and his palm supporting his chin. He addressed Ozzie when Ozelts finally stopped speaking.

"Well, Doc, it looks to me like you have a choice here. Either shake hands and call it a draw, or go back into your corners, stitch up, and go some more rounds, until somebody throws in the towel across the generations."

"I'll go shake hands with the bastard as long as he doesn't try to hug me," Ozzie said.

Relief in the form of nervous laughter emanated from the participants. Ozzie got up out of his seat and walked over to the old man with his hand outstretched. But Alberts pulled closer, going for the hug: emotional East Europeans hug anything that moves, but

Ozzie pulled back just in time with a precaution: "Ah-Ah-Ah... no hug..."

There was general applause, including Leonard's, as Ozzie made his way back to his seat tight-lipped.

"It wasn't over, but it's as 'over' as it will ever get," Ozzie whispered to Carolyn as he sat down. Then he crushed his prepared speech into a ball and flicked it into the wastebasket.

Leonard called it a draw. "Thank you, Mr... I mean, Reverend Ozelts. You at least had the courage and dignity to face us today. You've been a great help to the program. A staff member will see you to your transportation and accommodations. And don't forget to drop in at the business office for your compensation."

CHAPTER 38

Rocket Science

"Billy Brader!"

"Yes, sir!"

"We have recovered an old friend of yours. Your narrative about your neighborhood ballpark intrigued us so much we went looking for any of your childhood friends who were there with you. And guess whom we found? None other than Siegfried Hopmeister."

"Siegfried Hopmeister? Sorry, Leonard, doesn't ring my bell."

"Ziggy, remember Ziggy?"

"You're kidding… where is he?"

"He should be downstairs by now, let me call." Leonard picked up his cell phone and inquired, "If Dr. Hopmeister has arrived, send him up to my conference room, OK? Thanks, Don."

Brader was worried that Ziggy might remember that a baseball bounced off his head in his debut as an outfielder at Stoney Brae playground, and he might be back for an explanation.

There was a knock on the door, and Leonard asked Dr. Kiley to open the door. A very tall, gaunt, blue-eyed gentleman with balding blond hair combed back, and dressed in a white, long-sleeved shirt entered the room. He had very thin, angular dimples in his smile and walked leisurely to "the Hot Seat" toward which Leonard directed him.

"Dr. Hopmeister is a consultant for NASA. I'm not sure of his field of expertise; I'm not even sure if I can pronounce it. Please, sir, have a seat, and welcome to our session."

Leonard described the goals of the program and that Hopmeister had been a childhood friend of Billy Brader's. Billy waved to Hopmeister but he was not sure, when Hopmeister nodded slightly, that he recognized him as "a Stoney Brae ballplayer." For an instant they were like two self-conscious invitees at a party wondering how this happened. Leonard enjoyed moments when intelligent adults reverted to childhood mannerisms; it corroborated his view about the primitive origins of sub-conscious communication.

Brader opened the conversation.

"Leonard, does Dr. Hopmeister remember playing baseball with us? Remember, sir, when you were just a kid from Germany and had just moved to our neighborhood? We got you into one of our neighborhood baseball games. We admired your gamesmanship, even though you experienced an unfortunate accident."

Dr. Hopmeister had a blinking twitch as he spoke.

"Of course, I remember, Billy, that was a difficult time for me. But you are supposing that a baseball hit me on my head by accident, yes? Because this was the first time that I was playing this game. But this is not precisely the case. At that moment I was calculating that I could send a spheroid with a header to a teammate as in European football—the sport you call "soccer." And I believe I accomplished that. If you will recall your ballistics, ideally, the angle of incidence equals the angle of reflection. However I confess to somewhat miscalculating the hardness of the spheroid, ha, ha."

Then Hopmeister glanced around the table at his audience and quipped, "I had assumed that I was being invited to speak at this institute about our educational programs at NASA, but it turns out that the subject matter was closer to Isaac Newton and his apple, ha, ha."

No one laughed at that except Hopmeister, who was putting Debbie, Linda, and Margaret to sleep. He continued speaking with an air of a seasoned lecturer. Other members of the audience drooped their eyelids in anticipation of a long seminar on the physics of flying spheres. Leonard didn't want to stop him yet because Billy Brader was fascinated.

"The goal of the outfielder is to arrive at a common point with the termination of the parabolic arc of the spheroid. In a paper in the journal *Science* which some of my colleagues published, we used the rendezvous of an outfielder with a spheroid such as a baseball as an approximation for the rendezvous of a capsule with a spacecraft under conditions of a common gravitational influence. Our evidence suggests that the human brain apparently calculates the rendezvous point more efficiently and, inexpensively than the computer systems at NASA. Ha, Ha."

Only Brader smiled appreciatively as Hopmeister continued yet again.

"Returning to my rendezvous with the baseball, I would like to add that in my case not only did I have to calculate the rendezvous point of my head with the baseball, but I had to make a further and immediate calculation of the thrust and angle required for a proper rebound to my teammate."

At this, Brader nodded, as in, "sure thing."

Hopmeister continued, "Too much thrust, and the angle will cause the spheroid to escape from the province of my teammate's grasp; too little thrust and my skull would have to absorb too much of the shock of the collision and my efforts would be counterproductive. So you see, my techniques to play your game of baseball were not as misguided as you have supposed—a bit cerebral, perhaps, but adequate for the purposes of children at play. Are there any questions about this or any other concepts regarding the flight of spheroids under the influence of gravitational fields?"

Brader was expecting a grateful Ziggy to maybe thank him for including an immigrant kid into his circle of friends. Instead, Ziggy, now "Dr. Hopmeister," the astrophysicist, stole the show with a full-blown lecture on the ballistics of a fly ball. While he had him here, Brader was going tap Hopmeister's brain to lower his golf handicap.

"Dr. Hopmeister, how about figuring out how I can rendezvous a golf ball with a four- to five-inch diameter hole in the ground, one hundred yards away, using a five-iron from the rough?"

"Yes, the conditions are different, but the principles are the same. The smaller size and weight of the spheroid…"

Leonard had enough.

"Doctor, why don't you and Billy continue 'the physics of golf balls' after the session. In the meantime we'll thank you for your stimulating and enlightening contribution to our discussion. Our staff will see you out, and don't forget to see the people at the business office. How about a hand for Dr. Siegfried Hopmeister, everybody!"

Everyone clapped politely except for Debbie Storm who was startled awake by the noise. As Hopmeister left the room, Leonard started to jiggle with the giggles as he said, "Oh my Lord, he's a very bright man, but I'm not sure Willie Mays needed to know all that physics before his great catch in the '54 World Series. Do you, Billy?"

"Are you kidding? This guy's a gold mine; he could take three or four strokes off my handicap," Billy Brader gushed.

Leonard, slightly exasperated, said, "What is it with you golfers trying to outthink that little white ball? You set up all these obstacles and then you try to get around them. Why don't you just pick up that quirky little spheroid, walk over, and stick it in the hole, Mr. Brader, and avoid the sense of inescapable frustration?"

"Then it wouldn't be a challenge; it's the imposition of obstacles and limitations that creates the sport, Leonard."

Leonard pushed himself up from the chair with both arms against the table and said, "I catch your drift, Billy. Thank you for your exemplary patience, everyone. Let's launch ourselves out of here for lunch, rendez-vous at 14:00 hours."

CHAPTER 39

"Johnny, I hardly knew you"

Linda Bell, Margaret Worthington, and Debbie Storm ate lunch together as a support unit for Ms. Bell's imminent encounter; she was to be up first when the session reconvened at 2 p.m.

"I'm thinking that Leonard will bring in one of my old boyfriends to pester me about how I broke his heart," she told Margaret.

"It may get more complicated than that, dear. Try to use what you've learned with Leonard in these sessions and you'll be all right. Have presence of mind. Understand what's going on before you jump to a conclusion," Margaret answered.

"Don't take any crap from men, Linda, be in charge," Debbie warned.

At 2 o'clock everyone was seated in the conference room except Willy Hanson, who was apparently off wheeling and dealing with Terry Cooper, his childhood friend and, now, employer. Leonard glanced at Linda and said, "Linda, dear heart, we have located a former boyfriend through a series of contacts that, I confess, were fortuitous. Johnny Linden is here. Will you see him?"

"I tried to explain about Johnny. I wasn't ready to give everything to the first man I met after my separation from Rolfe. I'm sure he's gone on with the rest of his life. But, sure, it might be fun to talk over old times."

It was the first time Leonard had seen Linda confident like this.

"Dr. Kiley, would you open the door and ask the staff person just outside to bring in Mr. Linden?"

"Bring in Mr. Linden for us, please," Kiley said as he poked his head out of the door and to the right.

Johnny Linden was a good looking man, just over six feet tall with a light complexion, square shoulders, and light brown hair graying at the temples. His thinning hair wasn't combed, but it was clean. He was wearing a white and brown plaid shirt and had one hand in his baggy chino pants pocket as he wandered in; he hadn't shaved. He had a guitar strapped to his back and he projected an image of a "neo-hippy."

Leonard said, "Welcome, Mr. Linden."

Leonard introduced the "panel" adding that one member, Willy Hanson, had been unavoidably detained. Unfortunate, Leonard thought, because Willy had a steadying influence on the group and in Leonard's mind every participant had a unique and essential part in the group dynamic he had facilitated in constructing. Willy's absence would test a depleted unit.

"Hi, Johnny, how are you doing?" Linda inquired in a melancholy tone.

Johnny lifted the guitar off his back and placed it carefully to lean against the side of the chair; he turned to Linda, but he was nervous and started rambling.

"Well, let's see, after my hiatus on the west coast I came back east and settled in New Hampshire where I run a marina on a small lake near the White Mountains, and sing at the Mountain Lake Spa there. Want to run a marina with me Linda—you can help pump the gas? ...kidding. I wouldn't want you to soil your hands, or expose you to the some of the gonzos I entertain… God, you bring back great memories. I honestly loved you. I guess too much too soon."

"I loved you too, but your style disappointed me—there was no way we were going to stay together. You had your special circle friends and drinking cronies. There were too many things pulling us apart, and not enough things keeping us together."

Linda spoke facing Johnny. But he was slumped in his chair, his eyes looking down, and his hands folded.

"Just because you said you loved me doesn't mean I have to avoid going to bed with anyone. Since when do you make the rules?"

"OK, OK, but it took me a long time to get over it… I mean over you. That doesn't mean you're that special; it means that I'm that dumb. What I never got over was your screwing around with my closest friends, people I confided in, and then when you got done with them, some of my more distant acquaintances. And then even Bob Anderson. It was like an epidemic."

"How do you know Bob Anderson?" Linda asked quietly.

"I don't. That was a small Midwestern college town. The word among us tequila drinkers was that if our coquettes ended up with a guy named Anderson, then we knew they had finished their first round of the available local male population. We consoled ourselves with the theory that Anderson was somewhere at the beginning of the second go-around. Your next partner had to be someone you'd screwed before, hopefully, one of us. You'd be back with some extra baggage maybe, but the broken-hearted are easy to come back to."

"I ought to come over there and slap you, Johnny. You don't know what depression is like," Linda said.

"Is it anything like not being able to sleep wondering which one of my friends you're with that night? Is it anything like not being able to work thinking about life without you? Is it anything like not caring about the basics of taking care of myself because the meaning is gone without you? Please don't lecture me on depression, Linda."

"That's not my fault. Just because you love me doesn't mean you control my life or limit my choices. Loving me is not a contract to control my life."

"OK, Linda, maybe you're right. I eventually developed a theory trying to explain you, in my head. I was thinking that maybe you were trying to find another Michael, that older brother of yours you were crazy about, the one that saved your life. No man can live up to a saint."

"What?"

"As soon as Leonard's staff contacted me I went to South Dakota, found Michael and talked to him, thinking, if he's such a saint maybe he could help us both."

Linda got agitated, and her hands started moving all around as if she had no place to put them.

"Did you, really? You are crazy, Johnny. Poor guy, you must have scared him half to death," Linda said.

"He's fine. Says he's a little arthritic from years of farming and hard liquor. But he loves you; says you're his favorite little baby sister," Johnny said, more calmly now.

"I don't think this is fair. Leonard, why don't you stop this? It's too much pressure on Linda," Margaret cautioned.

"Be strong, Tiger," Leonard said addressing Linda.

Johnny continued. "Michael and I had a couple of beers, and he told me a story about that night when you were about, what, seven years old, maybe younger. They were harvesting at your farm and you had disappeared into the night. He told me all the tractors to stop, and he set up a search party and he found you. You were huddling with your teddy bear after chasing a jackrabbit into the cornfield."

The room was warming up despite the air conditioning. Most of the participants felt that Johnny just wanted to be understood; he wasn't out to hurt anybody.

"All right, well, I wrote a song about that. I hope you don't mind if I sing it to you. I've been writing poems and songs about you for years. Just let me tune her up a little here."

Johnny reached over and picked up his guitar while still seated.

"Anybody have a glass a water? My throat's kind a dry from talking."

Carolyn Mayfield twisted open a bottle of Evian she had in her bag and passed it down. It wasn't often that a heartbroken "Kris Kristofferson" showed up at an encounter group session.

213

"I was thinking about a title, how about... 'Finding You Again'?" Johnny leaned a little toward Linda, "Because I, also, found you again."

Linda's eyes were already starting to moisten as were Margaret's, and even Balis was getting a little emotional.

And then Johnny sang,

Johnny's Song

There's an empty space
A star has no place
My life's without grace,
'til I find you again.
My thoughts are denyin'
My breathin' turns sighin'
While my heart's dyin'
'til I find you again.
I will march every mile
Bear through all this trial
To see your sweet smile
When I find you again.
Now thinkin' 'bout my woes,
Love's not somethin' that goes.
When she's gone; it still flows.
She may not... but God knows,
Where love is found, again.

There was applause and then a collective deep breath in response to the simple but sincere love song, that ended with a short, ascending riff.

"We've been trying to understand passion since Cleopatra," Leonard said looking at Linda, and continuing. "Romantic love is a deep-seated need, at the level of an addiction. That's why when things go wrong, passing out blame is senseless; are you going to blame blood for circulating? The law and medicine make many more concessions in matters of love and passion than the lovers to each other."

"If it's so powerful then why is there a fifty percent divorce rate and all this heartbreak that people write about in poems and songs?" Debbie Storm asked.

"The relationship has to incubate; too many distractions and other commitments in a global world. And timing... Somebody once said timing is everything. Well, I don't think it's everything. But fifty percent sounds about right," Ozzie figured.

"Why don't we have dinner tonight and kick that around a bit, Linda," Johnny broke in.

All eyes at the table gazed at Linda with almost the same anticipation as Johnny's. Linda thought a minute, more for dramatic effect than indecision.

"Sure, why not... for old times' sake."

"See you in the lobby, about 6 o'clock?"

Leonard was now more pleased with the encounter, which had started out almost vengeful; but then had righted itself with the help of the group. He closed the encounter.

"You two can make specific arrangements later. In the meantime, thank you, Mr. Linden. And especially for your song. I liked it as an adaptation to your experience. Now, if you'll check with the business office, they will reimburse you for your contribution to our program and to the group."

Johnny stood up and shifted his strapped guitar over to his back and left the room walking taller than when he walked in. He had accomplished what he had wanted to do for a long time.

CHAPTER 40

Leonard Engineers a
Predator's Humiliation

After the door closed behind Johnny, Leonard looked around to check if people were ready for the next encounter; he gave a second look at Debbie Storm, who had typically displayed a recurrent attention deficit–type behavior along with her assertiveness, throughout the two weeks. But she was an invaluable contributor to the group dynamics now. She was a protagonist, a source of reality checks without "that romantic squint," and Leonard had learned to contain her manipulation in the context of the sessions.

He started things off.

"As you might imagine, dear hearts, the mental health wing of the institute works with the criminal justice system in some aspects of recovery and rehabilitation. Our next guest was located through that service. There has been precedent for the confrontation of sexual predators by their victims. Examples are the following: the confrontation by parishioners of the Catholic Church who confronted prelates who had abused them, and in legal proceedings confrontations of predators in the courtroom by the abused prior to sentencing.

"Ms. Storm, from your account of his abusive behavior toward you as a child we decided to try to locate your aunt's companion, on the theory that he must be accountable to those whose lives he has damaged. Our crack staff did locate him, but, Debbie, you need to know that Rover Carlson has served his time for his criminal sexually predatory behavior, and even now wears a device which gives his location at all times; he must be registered with local law enforcement authorities. This encounter will be in some aspects a role reversal in that Ms. Storm is now, relatively speaking, in the position of power and even authority, by virtue of the synergistic support of this group and her own devices. Whereas, Mr. Carlson is now in a position of vulnerability, through the processes of aging, incarceration, isolation, and surveillance. Ms. Storm has agreed in principle to this encounter, but I'll ask her again because Mr. Carlson is in the building. Debbie, are you prepared to confront your childhood sexual abuser?"

Debbie's voice was calm and deliberate. "Yeah, bring him in. I have a couple of messages to deliver, as if they're going to do any good with this wacko."

Leonard picked up the cell phone he had placed next to his notes and book. Rover Carlson was to be brought into the conference room. The tension level increased around the table as Dr. Balis leaned over to Dr. Kiley and whispered, "Did you tell Leonard about the incident at the Sea Bistro Restaurant when Debbie went ballistic?"

"No... did you?"

"This could get ugly."

Rover Carlson was about five foot seven and thin but poorly proportioned. He had gray hair that was much more sparse and dispersed on top than on the sides. His eyes were dark brown and receding, and he had bags under them. He had a pug nose and poor teeth except for one gold lower incisor implant. He was wearing horn-rimmed bifocals and a thick weave, black cotton shirt with an open collar, and his blue jeans were hanging below his paunch. His shoes were rubber soled, and he lifted his feet as he walked, like a man accustomed to stealth. If you had "done time" with Rover Carlson, he was probably the guy that suddenly showed up at your cell with library books from a little cart. Leonard directed the male nurse who accompanied Carlson into the room to remain; he backed up against the wall and crossed his hands like a bodyguard. Ozzie recognized the staff worker as the guy who had initially greeted him and shown him around the institute when he had first arrived; it seemed like a long time ago now.

Leonard realized that he would have to monitor this situation carefully. This was an encounter of a male felon, with his female victim. But without her knowledge he had stacked the cards in favor of Ms. Storm. There were two "Hot Seats" at the conference table. Leonard had always directed invitees to the seat at the left end of the table, because the empty seat at the right end of the table was wired with heating coils, a power source, and a rheostat that could be remotely controlled. Leonard had the remote next to his cell phone; with it he could micro-manage the location, intensity, and rate of heating. The testes, for example, are particularly sensitive to heating since they must maintain a temperature about 2° C lower than normal body temperature. This interrogation technique was developed by the secret police in the former Soviet Union and used in experiments by criminal and military psychologists to test the role of environmental stress factors and comfort levels on the reliability of lie detector results. When Carlson entered he had at first turned left when he entered the conference room, but Leonard directed him to the right end of the table.

"No please, Mr. Carlson, that seat has been reserved for you, if you don't mind."

Leonard wanted to increase Carlson's stress level during Debbie's dialogue with him. Published experiments with these wired chairs had shown that responders, even those with minimal empathy or innate sense of morality, were less evasive and dissembling when the temperature of sensitive areas of the lower body was elevated during questioning—in a word, less able to maintain their reserve. The trick was to raise the temperature of the seat at a rate such that the individual would not suspect an external source. They were to suppose that their discomfort was arising from their own physiology, in association with their conning and manipulative answers.

Carlson sat down, crossed his arms and looked around the table, apparently trying to decide who these people were. Debbie was seated four or five seats down from him and made full eye contact as she addressed him; she was impatient, and wanted the upper hand immediately—no fear.

"Do you remember back in Jersey, at a trailer park, my aunt Ruth and a little blond girl and her dog that lived with her?"

"I remember Ruth, but I don't remember no little girl. Who are you?"

"I'm that little girl. You had your hands all over me every chance you could get. If it wasn't for my dog, Puddles, you'd a had me a lot more times."

Leonard now nodded to Don, who reached over and switched the air conditioning off. Carlson started fidgeting in his chair, like he couldn't get comfortable or he had an itch.

"Now look here, lady, I know I been accused of all kinds of things, but I ain't no child molester. If you ask me, it's a way of women gettin' back at me for breakin' their heart."

Debbie recognized that as a lie, and she was ready to let him have it right there. If there weren't restraining factors in the room, Kiley and Balis knew she would be slapping Carlson "silly" by this time. She launched into him:

"Look, you low-life, lying scum, who in the hell do you think you're talking to? I know your kind. Because you recognize that you're such a worthless sleaze-ball compared to the normal citizens of this society, you prey on children whom you can overpower and humiliate. There are verbal abusers, and there are abusers who use violence, and then there's viruses like you who dominate the innocent sexually and destroy them."

Carlson was sweating profusely now and moved the chair closer to the table, trying to adjust his crotch with his hands. Something was wrong with him, and he didn't know what it was. He felt like his insides were boiling. Maybe he was dying. The eyes of all the participants fixed on him seemed to grow larger and burn into his brain. Between heavy breaths he began haltingly to blurt out snippets of uncensored truths.

"You don't know what it's like... Being sick and alone... It's not my fault how I am... I can't help feelin' these things about what I need... I'm not no murderer... You're OK now, look at ya... I paid my price... Everybody's got somethin' they can't control... Now you're actin' so high and mighty... knock yourself out, bitch!"

Carlson's face was swollen and covered with droplets of sweat, and his shirt was now soaked at the underarms.

Leonard raised his voice in anger for the first time in these sessions. "Watch the language you use with my people, sir!"

The room started to smell differently. At first Ozzie, who was seated close to Carlson, couldn't tell exactly what it was. Then it was unmistakable: Carlson was wetting his pants. Ozzie looked at Leonard and pointed to Carlson's seat, spread his hands flat and then pinched his nose. Leonard immediately got the signal and asked Don, the staff worker to turn the air conditioning back on. He then checked his remote control for Carlson's "Hot Seat" and saw a red warning icon flashing "max...max...max" and quickly pushed the "off" icon, mumbling to himself, "Oops, maybe I haven't really got the hang of this gadget yet... I'll have to talk to Benedict's technician."

Carlson was so humiliatingly embedded with his secretions and excretions that Leonard had to close the encounter.

"Well, Debbie, I think you've had your say and Mr. Carlson can relax now... Don, can you take it from here?" Leonard said to the staff worker.

Carlson had not had a voluminous reserve of liquid in his bladder, but his "Hot Seat" was now fuming in any case and the room had to be evacuated.

Leonard gave a wave of his left arm for the participants, who by now had full olfactory awareness of the problem, to follow him out of the room.

"All right, everyone, we've had a minor malfunction. Let's not panic. Follow standard emergency evacuation procedures. Do not run, but exit rapidly. I'm sure by 9 a.m. Friday Don and his crack staff will have this room decontaminated and fresh as a morning in May."

The staff worker stood by the helpless Rover Carlson and called downstairs on the cell phone for backup. It probably wasn't the first time that he'd dealt with such contingencies. Meanwhile the participants were grabbing their notes and other wordly possessions and scrambling out of the room. Debbie was the last to look back at Carlson as she left, Balis tugging at her elbow. Carlson was still stewing in his chair. She pointed in Carlson's direction with her index finger and said, "End of the road, Rover."

Walking down the corridor together, Brader and Drs. Kiley and Balis noticed that Ozzie was shaken by what had transpired in the conference room. It was the first time he had seen such a physical manifestation of Leonard's control over a group.

"Leonard was merciless in there. Anything could have happened. Debbie could have pulled a knife or something... wow," Ozzie said to Balis, Kiley, and Brader walking down the hall.

"It's over now, Ozzie. Don't think about it. Leonard did what he had to do; he was frustrated and angry about all those kinds of guys and how they ruin lives. Mainstream verbal therapy is probably useless," Brader said.

They all agreed to a cold one at The King's Pub, "...but just one."

CHAPTER 41

Dressed Down by the Boss

Leonard walked past Drs. Kiley, Balis, and Ozelts in the corridor in a hurry to get out of the building. Something like that session was not pretty, but preferable to some alternatives Leonard had experimented with before. He knew that there would be controversy surrounding some of his techniques; there always was. But in the case of a victim confronting a felon, he much preferred dialogue to physical violence.

In Leonard's mind, humiliation was a form of emotional violence. That odorous liquid that had flowed from Carlson was a product of a physiological function through which the sexual offender had been humiliated, de-masculinized; castrated in the presence of the victim.

In a young child's mind even abnormal behavior by a parent or an adult must somehow have a reasonable basis; it's the only model consistently available. The demonstrated take-home lesson for Debbie Storm from that encounter was that she had been unjustly and abnormally dominated by a pathological man-child. Her abuse was clearly then not the fault of her 'self' or even of her femininity. Whether that reached her deeply enough to relieve her anaclitic relationships and ameliorate her socio-pathological adaptations remained to be seen. Of all the participants Debbie was the most refractory to group therapy and techniques involving empathy. To the adult Debbie, Carlson was just a "wacko." Debbie would not break down during the face-to-face confrontation because there wasn't enough empathy left in her to fuel that.

Leonard's office was in a row of administration offices, and it was a mess typical of the honest, endeavoring intellectual. In contrast, Lincoln Benedict's lush, walnut-paneled, wall-to-wall carpeted office at the institute on the first floor of the Administration and Research Building was the size of a conference room. Even Connie, Benedict's secretary, had more space than Leonard. In most federally or state-funded research institutions, administrators and their assistants and secretaries had more grandiose offices compared to the researchers by whose very erudition and work their employment was possible. Leonard never understood that, but put up with it.

Although he respected Benedict's professional competence and medical background, Leonard resented Benedict's patrician attitudes and lifestyle. He also resented Benedict because he was the only colleague to call him by his professional first name, "Myles." Musical perspectives defined their differences even further. To Benedict, music was an art form and a passion, a source of complete humanization. To Leonard, music was a structure of sounds, a means of communication, therapy, empathy, a useful tool.

Thursday morning Leonard had been called in by Benedict regarding his use of the wired "Hot Seat" for the predator, Rover Carlson. As Leonard passed the secretary he asked, "Is he in, Connie?"

Connie nodded but threw her eyes to the ceiling—a "warning" look.

The director was not happy about the predator-victim encounter. "Take a seat Myles... Myles, I think we've discussed your use, or

223

should I say abuse, of hardware around here before. If you can't achieve the desired results through your admittedly bountiful verbal and facilitation talents, then come and see me and we'll talk about it. This felon... what's his name?"

"Carlson"

"Yes, Carlson could have attacked Ms. Storm right there, and we would have had physical injury, lawsuits, and the end of the research program as we know it."

Leonard defended his experiment. "I don't know why we're having this meeting. None of that happened. You know, Linc, they once asked Johnny Unitas, the famous NFL quarterback, why he threw a flair pass near the end zone, when it easily could have been intercepted. You know what Unitas said?"

"Myles, do you really think quarterbacks are relevant here?"

"Yes, I do. I'm a quarterback. Anyway, Linc, Unitas said, 'It's not intercepted if you know what you're doing' ...Maybe I cut it a little close to the physical with the use of the wired 'Hot Seat' but I had a goal in mind, and we achieved that."

"What... total de-masculinization, de-humanization in front of the victim? You're playing the role of a criminal justice system. What's going on here, are you judge and jury all of a sudden? Keep it verbal, keep it group-oriented; that's where your talents lie. That's why we hired you. We didn't hire you to induce urinations in our group sessions."

"Linc, you're a cultured man. Have you ever heard of the work called Merda d'Artista by the Italian Pero Manzoni?"

"No, but it doesn't sound like anything Michelangelo might want to be associated with."

"Probably not; Manzoni produced a series of cans which contained his own excrement as a metaphoric humiliation of the packaging and commodification of art."

"What are you trying to say? Rover Carlson's spearheading an art form?"

"No, but it was one of the most successful role reversals I have ever witnessed in a group format. It was as close to a confession of guilt that we'll get in a psychopath. I only wish we had gotten to him earlier," Leonard explained.

Benedict now calmed down and got rhetorical. "And just when I thought he had crossed the line, pushed the envelope too far, the word merchant turns a public urination into a therapy triumph. You never cease to amaze me, Myles."

"I like to think there's an artistry to my craft. May I go back to work now, Mr. Director?"

Benedict looked up, stunned. When he felt aspersed, Leonard liked to leave people searching for words. After realizing that Leonard's imposing but ingratiating self-confidence was every match for his authority, Benedict put a stop to each of these inquiries. "Of course, but try to keep the conference room clean, and free of hardware and secretions this time, will you, Dr. Leonard? At this institute your words are the primary tools of your trade. Even a felon has the right to a trip to the bathroom."

Leonard had long ago resigned himself to the recondite indolence of research bureaucrats. He almost bumped into Connie, Benedict's chubby secretary of many years, on the way out. Connie liked Leonard and thought of him as some kind of gentle genius.

She asked Benedict, "What was that all about?"

"Dr. Leonard and I had a disagreement on the ethics of induced incontinence in predators, Connie."

"Well I certainly hope you two straightened that out!" Connie said cheerfully.

CHAPTER 42

Application of Knowledge Creates Meaning

Friday morning Leonard opened the session with a preface to the last day with his group. It was raining again, and distant rolling thunder and the tall windows in the conference room with raindrops spattering diaphanous patterns added a Gothic dimension for Leonard's short but poignant statement. Leonard had a flair for the dramatic and definitive.

"Dearly beloved, we are gathered here for our last formal group session. It is our final encounter session. I have been privileged to be your group leader and participant. Many of you came from dysfunctional families or suffered abuses as children in one form or another. Thus you were already personally burdened when you engaged the competition in your chosen professions. Through this program, these sessions, and my facilitation, the group has bestowed on you some of the missing pieces in your lives to understand and cope, to redefine your purpose and meaning here on earth. This is the synergy in the power of our ten participants. We were family. Wherever you go henceforth you carry us with you, and what you have learned here. And I remain forever yours, Myles Leonard, a friend and a believer *in* you."

Margaret Worthington was dressed in her Sunday best: a red jacket, white blouse, and blue scarf. She was years younger than when she had started with this group two weeks ago, and had come to form a familial affection for everyone of the participants. Leonard's charisma, competence and talent, his professionalism, the command of his language, had enthralled her. He was the driving force for a new mindset to question ideas and preconceptions she'd assumed for decades. It was as if a new hue were coloring her awareness.

Ozzie was very excited because he could see Leonard was gearing up for a big finish. He too felt empowered with a new emotional intelligence through Leonard's facilitation and the empathy and affections of the group. Now that Ozzie thought about it, Leonard's power to generate feelings in people had an academic style, but a comfortable fluidity, because he did it without judging.

Ozzie glanced around the table, and there was an aura of informal reverence. He turned to Carolyn Mayfield sitting next to him and kissed her cheek for support. He remembered their kiss after the walk on the beach; affection toward her was now natural, and he knew she welcomed it.

Leonard, who hadn't shaved in two days, addressed Carolyn first.

"We have Dr. Vincent on the phone, Carolyn, from Jos, Nigeria, of all places. The phone speakers have been set up so we can all hear your discussion. Please talk clearly; keep your comments cogent. For a true give-and-take conversation, you should wait for him to finish before responding; there's a slight delay in transmission. As soon as I press this button we'll begin. It's been a while since you last saw him, so I'll speak first if you don't mind, dear heart, and introduce ourselves, then I'll hand it over to you."

"Hello, is this Dr. Vincent? Hello…"

"Yes, Vincent speaking."

"Dr. Vincent, my name is Dr. Myles Leonard. We are calling from The Cypress Point Institute of Research as part of research program on subclinical factors for under-achievement in a competitive society. This session is concerned with individuals who have been influential in the lives of our participants. Carolyn Mayfield has named you as an important influence. She'd like to talk with you again."

Leonard pointed to Carolyn.

"It's you from here on in, Carolyn."

"Hello, Dr. Vincent. I wonder if you remember me from Mozarr Street in Baltimore."

"Yes, of course, little Carolyn Mayfield. Cute as a button. Loved to sing and dance. It's so great to hear from you—tell me, how are you? How is your lovely and courageous mother?"

"My mother is well, thank you, and lives with us in Indianapolis. She's a grandmother now, but she remembers you fondly. You were very special to her. I went on to a short career on the stage in an off-Broadway cast of *Hair* in Chicago, but I couldn't make a living out in LA so I came back home to raise a family. I'm working in the church and teaching drama and singing. What are you doing in Nigeria?"

"Carolyn, you know, I was kind of a research rodent after Johns Hopkins and under the wing of prestigious patrons who saw me into various faculty appointments until I landed on my feet. Now I run my own program at the University of New Mexico. Meanwhile, my wife and I were deeply affected by the birth of our son, which was about the time that I was at Hopkins. My son's pristine love made me see things in a different light. The academic research game didn't have enough meaning for me anymore. I had to be doing something that had more of a direct relevance to the well being of the less fortunate on this planet. I started by wandering out of the lab and around the neighborhoods near the University Hospital, and that's how I found Mozart Street, where I organized the baseball team and I met you and your mother. You can tell your people there that story if you haven't already, Carolyn. But let me just tell you how Nigeria came into the picture.

"I thought that the best and most direct way for a trained biochemist to apply his knowledge for the benefit of the poor would be in the area of nutrition and I started sending in grant requests on nutrition projects. The initial diet of the newborn comes from the mother's milk, so I reasoned if you can improve the nutritional value of her milk then commensurately you can improve the health of her newborns. So we are studying that process here in Nigeria."

"Knowing you, Dr. Vincent, it became a labor of love, and you probably got emotionally involved with your experimental subjects," Carolyn added.

"That's exactly right, Carolyn; you still understand me. The Fulani tribes with which I am involved are herdsman and wanderers. The other local tribes that don't get along with the Fulani lifestyle like to settle down and claim a piece of land and farm. There was a bloody skirmish last year when I lost my best friend here, a tribal chief of the Fulani who was killed trying to save his people. I've been shot at too. Reminds me of the Wild West; you know, the homesteaders or 'sod-busters' versus the cattle ranchers. So not only am I chief nutritionist here, but I'm a part-time school master, water-well digger and peace-keeper. But I love it. They named a school after me. I can see results of my work every day. In academic research you're lucky if you'll see a practical application of your work… ever."

Leonard, as was his wont, felt compelled to place the moment into a historical context. "If I may interject here for a moment, Dr. Vincent… this is Dr. Leonard again. I see a fortuitous spin-off of the cultural struggle in both of you; the existential humanism of artists, humanists, and the underprivileged, marginalized or displaced by the materialism, glitz, and entertainment of market forces; the freedom and liberty to self-destruct. You people didn't give in. God love you."

That was over Dr. Vincent' s head, but Vincent understood that Leonard was trying to look at the big picture.

"I'll take your word for it, Dr. Leonard. But let me share with you this much; because on some of these dark Nigerian nights I have time to think, a lot of time. I think in those heady days of Aquarius we represented the forces of change and opportunity, open-mindedness, freedom of expression, shedding of pretense and ideology. That process is frightening to a locked-in political system spawning nine-to-fivers, SUVs, and a lawn to mow."

"I hear you, ol' buddy. Maybe the counterweights and inertia of tradition and dogma were too large to shift." Leonard added.

Dr. Vincent continued, obviously delighted to have a heart-to-heart discussion.

"Yes, but maybe our irresponsible hedonism and drug culture undermined our influence to continue to change things for the better. The assassinations and early deaths of the Kennedy brothers, Martin Luther King, and some of our rock music icons, the Chicago riots, and the My Lai massacre were 'Stop' signs. The 'harmony, understanding, sympathy and trust' of the Age of Aquarius became the solipsism of the X generation, and the trickle-down capitalism of corporate greed. Tolerance of greed is what keeps our tenuous greatness afloat. We gobble up twenty percent of the world's available oil reserves per year. That's more than the next six countries combined. We consume forty-five percent more energy reserves than we generate. And we produce over half of the world's hazardous waste."

"At least some things are getting done. Civil rights legislation, Medicare, the Peace Corps, the women's movement, and a new awareness of global poverty, even the environmental protection and legislation got started with Rachel Carson's wake-up call. There were some structural changes," Leonard reflected.

Dr. Vincent changed subjects and his tone. "Carolyn, are you still there? I guess Dr. Leonard and I cut to the chase and went too far adrift from the magic of our reunion. These phone reunions are too short to cover everything. I just want to say that I'm there with you in spirit, if not in person, and I'm glad you're in good hands."

Carolyn was at a loss for words because she was looking for the perfect thing to say.

"No, no, Dr. Vincent, I was listening, and I learned something. And I'm happy that you found meaning and purpose in the work you are doing for those people. The children and mothers of the Fulani are very fortunate to have you there."

Then, for a moment Carolyn reverted to the little girl in her. "Let's meet again someday on Mozarr Street, Dr. Vincent. And I'm not going to cry when you hang up. I'm grateful that there are people like you in the world, and that wherever you are, you're thinking about us, and we're thinking about you. My mother said when you left, 'that love doesn't go away when the person you love goes away. It's ours forever..."'

There was a noticeable tremolo in the voice on the phone loudspeaker. "I appreciate that very much, Carolyn. And your mother was right, sweetheart, your mother was right about everything."

Carolyn was too choked up to talk anymore and Leonard felt that the conversation had peaked and could end there.

"Well, we thank you, Dr. Vincent, and wish you well in your life's work. You are obviously a special human being."

"Thanks for calling, Dr. Leonard. Take care of Carolyn, and I'll be in touch when I get back from the African Wild West to the American Wild West, unless I get caught up in some range war. Can you just see me standing there between the Fulani herdsmen and the Birom warriors with my arms out like a traffic cop, dictating negotiation: 'Now let's talk this over'? How do you talk people into resolution when it's not in their vocabulary? Anyway, thanks, and Godspeed to all of you."

There was a loud click and a then a dial tone that seemed to darken the room. Carolyn leaned her head on Ozzie's shoulder and tried to dry her tears there. Leonard said, calmly, "Let's take a break here before we move on."

CHAPTER 43

"Jesus, You Got Some 'Splaining To Do"

After a twenty-minute break for coffee and doughnuts, Leonard counted heads and everyone was present, even Carolyn Mayfield, who by all rights should have got a breather after her emotionally exhausting encounter with a modern-day Albert Schweitzer.

"Margaret, I have an idea, and I want to know what you think of it. I want us to have kind of a Jesus Christ Super Star encounter; but not the whole thing, just the part where we get to ask Jesus some questions. This would be for your benefit, Margaret. My educated guess is that Jesus Christ was the most influential character in your life, and it would be altogether fitting and proper that you confront him here in this room. What say you to this, dear heart?"

"I encounter my Lord every Sunday at my church, Dr. Leonard, but if you think it will serve some purpose, and for the benefit of the group, I am pleased to demonstrate my faith."

Balis jumped in. "Leonard, how do you suppose to get Jesus onto the 'Hot Seat,' or should we just assume that his spirit will be with us?"

"No, no, this is virtual reality. We'll need a volunteer to play Jesus... any hands?" Leonard asked.

He got the response he was hoping for: Ozzie raised his hand.

"I love to play famous people. And if I can help Margaret, I'll move to the Hot Seat," Ozzie said confidently.

Brader smiled: "outstanding."

Leonard set down some rules.

"Unlike at churches and religious meetings, we're going to make this an open discussion. Margaret, I want you to inspire the discussion but not necessarily dominate it. Let's try to be democratic; Jesus would have wanted it that way. We may even get a little Socratic here this morning. Jesus and Socrates... now there's a powerful combination of martyrs. When you think about it we've had a rather eclectic list of guests this week: a sexual predator, an astrophysicist, a nun, a doctor, a businessman, a latter-day Dr. Schweitzer, a singer-poet, an east European tyrant and now..." Leonard raised his voice like an announcer. "...a huge influence on many lives as well as Margaret's; a man who, until now, remains a mystery despite an infinite number of interpretations of his statements... Jesus Christ."

Ozzie, curiously dressed in a white, open collar shirt, white cotton pants and sandals, arose to take his place at the left end of the table. He was wearing an Olympic logo necklace, the rings of the five continents, given him long ago. It sparkled, reflecting the window's light as he made himself comfortable. The former supermarket bagger had come a long way in two weeks.

"I hope this seat doesn't get *too hot*. If you catch my drift."

Ozzie didn't wait for questions, but launched right into his role.

"First off, I'd like to make an announcement in the form of a question. The world is a mess, and I came back to sort things out. What do you think my chances are of success?"

"Zero to none. The first thing we'd do is lock you up as delusional," Balis kicked in.

"But what if I *am* the real Christ, not some charlatan lunatic?"

"Then you'd have black curly hair like the rest of the Semites in Nazareth and Judea. And we'd lock you up anyway; we're provincialists, xenophobes, and racists. Besides, too many people today depend on Your absence for authority, influence, and a living. It's your absence that allows their interpretation to dominate and subjugate. Every bishop and pastor is an expert on what you might say or do. Hell, we even have wars about what you meant and whose side you're on. Don't interrupt our agenda of self-annihilation. 'Onward Christian Soldiers,' ready, aim, fire," Balis declared.

Balis was wired up for a rant.

"Listen, Jesus, let me tell you what's been going on today. Greater love hath no God than he should give his only begotten son? Like, wasn't that the theme of your sacrifice? Give me a break! How many sons and daughters have been sacrificed by fathers and mothers in wars due to the decisions of politicians and religious leaders on the basis of demagogic pedantry about morality, right, and wrong? What philosophy courses did they take to make them experts in ethics and morality? As I rant, there are sons and daughters being sacrificed just like you were sacrificed, in wars declared by the rich, condoned by a self-indulgent middle class, and fought largely by the poor. Where is their immortality? How many more need to die for wars and sacrifices flouting 'thou shalt not kill'? How many resources-gouging wealth and assets are enough for the privileged and the corporations, flouting 'thou shalt not covet thy neighbor's house…or any thing that is thy neighbor's'? Why is it politicians and corporations of supposedly Judeo-Christian civilizations and states are exempt from the Ten Commandments? The fact of the matter is that if you obey the laws of God and Christianity, you put yourself at a distinct disadvantage in this society. Shall I go on about this massive hypocrisy…?"

Margaret interjected, waving her index finger.

"Just a minute. I didn't come here to have my Lord and Savior's name defiled. A lot of good is done by the church for the poor, the destitute, the sick and the forlorn."

"Margaret, do you want to continue?" Leonard asked, holding up his left arm to hush up Debbie… and Balis, both of whom wanted to speak.

Margaret inhaled some air to calm herself and continued, with a glance toward Ozzie.

"It's not His fault. Men twisted and dissembled His teachings. Once religions were organized and churches accumulated wealth and influence, that's when all those human frailties corrupted the application of His ideals. Hierarchies and leaders named themselves representatives of Christ or even God. It's now like a huge corporate structure, but that's not how it was supposed to turn out. They run your life from birth, to marriage, to death, on the threat of damnation and the specter of guilt. I wanted to marry and have children like any other woman."

"You mean, Mr. Grayson, the physics teacher?"

"Yes, the Church said that I was a sinner just thinking about it, with at least two major sins on my resume. Tell me, Jesus, am I an evil person for loving a decent man that happened to be married, and happened to be an agnostic physics teacher?"

"No, Margaret, you're not an evil person. You're nothing of the kind. You're a good person, a kind person, and you were a great teacher," Ozzie said.

Margaret was clutching her rosary again, with tears in her eyes. This was a confession. Ozzie left his chair. He didn't want to be Jesus anymore. The job was impossible. But Leonard wouldn't have it.

"Sit down, Jesus. We're not done with you yet."

Linda Bell broke in to give Margaret recovery time.

"I'd like to ask Jesus where heaven is. When I was little I always thought of it as 'up' somewhere."

Ozzie's Jesus thought for a minute and then spoke.

"Obviously it has to incorporate other dimensions than the three we are accustomed to. If you take off, say in a spacecraft with inexhaustible thrust"—Ozzie pointed toward the ceiling with his index finger—"then there's nothing but space, stars, planets, comets, and such. Eternal Happiness, which I gather is synonymous with heaven, would have to arise out of other dimensions, an alternate consciousness, an alternate form and identity. It's like physics, there's matter and then there's anti-matter."

There were whispers and snickers of mockery and cynicism around the table. Billy Brader, however, enjoyed it when Ozzie went off the deep end.

It was part of his charm. Brader said, "Please continue, Jesus."

"Someday physics should dissolve into metaphysics, which will fuse with instinctive religion. The units of matter and energy have been whittled down to mere space; apparently some particles don't have mass. The question I have is, when do we get to nothingness, at what point does something you can define or explain with equations become space? Do you remember Descartes' simple but elegant, 'I think, therefore I am?'

"In physics the analogy might be, 'It has an equation, therefore it exists.' String theory, for example, provides a unifying theory for all natural forces or matter—a common reality. But it invokes space–time with more than three dimensions—ten to twenty-six dimensions, depending whom you talk to. How are you going to prove the existence of ten dimensions? With simultaneous equations? In that sense string theory merges into simultaneous acts of faith."

Leonard was gratified; something had been rekindled in Ozzie: *Doctor* Wellington Ozelts was back.

"Please, Dr. Ozelts, don't bring us down to earth yet..."

"OK, well, then we are left with the converse question, when does nothing become something, which in Christian terms is talking about creation? In physics this might be analogous to asking how did the universe start from an infinitesimally dense black hole? Or, from whatever was there, before the infinitesimally dense black hole.

"Energy?" Dr. Kiley suggested.

"That's what I was thinking. The 'God' of the physicists is formless Energy. But in this universe, Energy is losing to Entropy. The 'devil' of physicists is Entropy, roughly equivalent to disorder, dissipation. The universe is expanding, dissipating. But if I'm Jesus, my job is to give life meaning and purpose."

Ozzie looked around the table; the general attitude was, "Well, OK, so?" He continued. "Life is a highly ordered product of Energy, the quintessential case of order and organization in this universe.

The requirement for the origin and continuation of life is the idyllic coming together of a number of physical variables and then a specific absorption in a narrow wavelength window of the sun's energy. I draw a direct line from the Energy released by the infinitesimally dense black hole at The Big Bang, to…

"the energy in the star called the sun, to…

"the energy infused into the creation of self-reproducing life."

Margaret was excited, and her eyes were wide open and looking straight at Ozzie. She asked, "Christians believe in a benevolent Creator—not some benevolent explosion, and energy absorption. If you're going to be the real Jesus you have to explain yourself and your rather belated intervention, Dr. Ozelts."

"Exactly… Jesus, who, you would agree, represents a benevolent deity in human form, came along more than 13 billion years after the Big Bang, 4.5 billion years after the earth popped out, several billion years after plants, and about 100 thousand years or so after humankind's original African *Homo Sapiens* ancestors. I therefore have reason to believe I was conceived through the energy of empathy. When anthropocentrism reached a critical volume, a critical need. Man's awareness had reached a level that convinced him he was special, at the center of the known universe—hence the term, "in the image of God."

Balis intoned, "Then how come cows are sacred in India?"

Ozzie ignored Balis… he was rolling.

"What appears to differentiate humans from simpler life forms and plants is consciousness and awareness: when a species became so complex in structure and so synergistic and simultaneous in life-sustaining functions that its members began to reflect upon themselves, their existence. I see a direct evolution from The Primeval Energy, to Life, to consciousness, and to awareness. Without consciousness and awareness, empathy would not be possible. And human benevolence and morality arise out of the empathy that we have studied and experienced in the microcosm of this group. That's the human condition that inevitably created the Biblical Jesus. His Golden Rule is, in fact, a definition of empathy."

"What kind of Jesus are *you*, then," asked Linda , pulled in by Ozzie's academic style.

"I'm Jesus, the meta-physicist, Biblical Jesus' twin brother. We have our different perspectives, but we are two peas in a pod, two sides of the same coin. His perspective is, 'They that follow me shall not walk in darkness, but shall have the light of life.'

"My simultaneous interpretation is, 'the force of life depends on the Energy of light.' Time, energy, and matter are all in the same equation, and that includes the energy for the Force of Life. It's OK to be 'Me.' Some miracles aren't based only on faith. I am the Life from the sun's light."

Linda Bell screamed as Margaret Worthington sank to the floor and her chair fell backwards. Dr. Kiley acted quickly. "Give her a little room," he said, backing off the worried participants.

Kiley checked her eyes with his penlight and asked her if she could hear him. Ozzie ran around closer to her and said, "Margaret, you will not leave us, we love you."

Margaret opened her eyes slowly and whispered, "What happened?"

"Dr. Ozelts said he was Jesus' twin brother," Debbie said calmly. "It's the second coming, and you fainted."

CHAPTER 44

"We Have Used Him to the Breaking Point"

After the last session the participants were invited to a farewell get-together at Dr. Benedict's mansion.

Leonard detested social events under the guise of appreciation parties. And "Sir Benedict" would be there. So he appeared at the party only to present his goodbyes to his group, with best wishes, hugs, and kisses. They knew he loved them, and what's more, they appreciated the gift he had given them. They presented him with a laser light pointer for lectures that had inscribed on it "From our heart(s) to yours."

Leonard was reviewing the progress of the group in his mind's notebook as he drove his truck, Betsy, to the usual Friday night rendezvous with his court at the King's Pub. He had tentatively concluded that the appropriate finale to the sessions and true evidence for their success was Wellington Ozelts' unifying confrontation with Margaret; although for a second there he'd thought he'd lost both of them. Wellington came into the program with a beaten, tired, nihilistic self-concept but after two weeks of the group's empathy, familial support, and bonding, a professional drop-out and societal misfit was able to again generate meaning and rekindle repressed learning and thinking processes. The movable "value added" was that he could help others do the same.

The other participants to greater or lesser degrees, also had made important progress, thus justifying the program's format.

Margaret Worthington was not fully "exculpated" but for one brief moment she'd had a meaningful experience with a Jesus outside the Church, a Jesus accepting everyone under the Sun.

Scott Kiley was beginning to see his mother as a human being he didn't have to constantly re-live for. His next model might be Carolyn's Dr. Vincent.

Rolland Balis had learned through Debbie Storm and Mother Rosemarie that his obsessions about femininity were not simply explained by sexuality, but his denial, his refusal to accept manhood. Mother Rosemarie's touch might have helped him there.

Carolyn Mayfield found a place for her musical and artistic intelligence with the group's acceptance, Ozzie's adoration, and Dr. Vincent's reassuring belief in her.

Linda Bell found someone who understood her love for Michael. There were some things you had to live with, and Linda had to live with Michael.

Billy Brader learned the power of precocious social skills, and he was critical as an intermediary for Dr. Ozelts's progress during Leonard's facilitation.

And Willy Hanson turned a near childhood tragedy into a job where he'd be appreciated. His hands were a symbol of workmanship, of the symbiotic relationship man had with trees. "Let's just not kill too many of them; then it's over."

Leonard smiled to himself while passing a glance at a huge cedar tree and thought out loud, "Even their surge toward the sun is bestowed by the benevolent Light Energy Wellington was trying to understand… My Lord, I need a drink, I'm beginning to think like Dr. Ozelts."

Betsy turned into her customary parking place at the back door of the King's Pub. Leonard took a deep breath and felt the usual chest twinges, which now were more frequent after work. But tonight nothing was going to dilute the triumph of having changed the lives of at least eight wonderful people.

He slammed the driver side door of the truck shut, for an instant wondering where he would end up tonight. He dismissed the thought as irrelevant and swung open the screen door of King's. At the far end to the right of the front door he saw that the King's table was booked solid, awaiting his arrival. Suzanne, wearing reading glasses, was there sitting next to Ellen. Bernie and Alex had loosened their ties and were enjoying a repartee; half-filled and near-empty glasses and two empty pitchers were distributed haphazardly around the table. There were two other people sitting with their backs to Leonard as he sauntered toward the group. Leonard had arrived later than usual due to Benedict's benediction party, and the high small-talk noise level in the pub was typical of early evening TGIF clientele. He gave a glance at Larry and spread his hands a measured distance apart vertically, a standard signal to bring him "a cold one."

There were handshakes, waves, and smiles as a chair was prepared for Leonard in his customary place at the end of the table with his back to the front window. The colorful drapes, through which the lighted logo of the pub and the setting sun light filtered through, splashed that corner of the pub with all shades and shapes of red and amber. Suzanne liked to introduce, and sometimes reintroduce, people to Leonard; it was a way of finding out the mood he was in.

"Bernie and Alex arrived early. Ellen and I even had a bite to eat before we got here. Oh… and at the far end of the table we have Eva and Kent. You remember Eva from the other night; and she is sitting next to Kent Paulson, a neuroscientist visiting the institute as a member of a review committee for the NIH. He's from Cal Tech. So even though the conjoint neuropsychiatry project with State University is not in your sector, try to behave yourself."

Leonard, ever interested in new characters, folded his arms and looked across the table perspicaciously. Kent Paulson had a prominent bald forehead but a very long train of white hair flowing back almost to the ground, which Leonard estimated hadn't been cut since Nixon resigned. The locks were tied tightly together at the back of his head by a compounded elastic. He had a small, sloping nose, round, pale pink cheekbones, blue eyes, and an almost childishly fair complexion. He was wearing a spotless yellow cotton shirt with the sleeves rolled up just past the wrists and an unbuttoned high collar with a Western bolo tie. Suzanne thought that he resembled a Jamie Lee Curtis in jeans. Even before the hair, what you noticed were those light blue irises, glinting and reflecting points of light like a cat's eyes. The whites of his eyes were not white but coral, probably from the strain of years of research and reading and maybe contact lenses. His well-manicured fingers were long and thin, and he was licking them intermittently while shucking peanuts and entertaining that end of the table. He had a loud but sincere laugh. Leonard figured him for *another* very intelligent rascal. Suzanne leaned over to Ellen and predicted a clash of charismas tonight between the neuroscientist and the counselor to which Ellen smiled and nodded in agreement.

But first things first; Leonard noticed that Paulson's beer glass was empty and yelled across the table, raising his own recently served beer.

"Can I replenish your glass, ol' buddy… by the way my name is Dr. Myles Leonard and I go by my last name, Leonard."

"My name's Dr. Kent Paulson but my friends call me Kent. I was named after that mild-mannered reporter for the *Daily Planet*."

"If the occasion arises there is a phone booth over by Magoo's Pub," Leonard quipped.

"No, I don't think I'll be leaping over tall buildings tonight—my super cape is at the dry cleaners… you know, it's all that particulate pollution up there; the skies aren't as friendly as they used to be…"

"I always wondered why superman needed that cape." Alex jumped in.

"I think it's a dependency, you know, like Dumbo's feather. A couple of weeks in my sessions and he'd be flying without the damned cape," Leonard said, flicking his wrist back as if shooing a fly.

"Leonard's a counselor and group therapist. They're in the business of mind over matter," Suzanne pointed out to Kent.

Eva was following the topic and decided to politicize… again.

"A heterosexual WASP superman, another iconic power grab by the male establishment."

"Well, there's Wonder Woman too, you know," Bernie interjected.

"Sure but that was an afterthought. When you look up at the sky, exclaiming, 'Is it a bird or a plane?' you don't come up with, 'No, that's a woman.' And speaking of flight, what happened to the first woman to be recognized as a world-class pilot? Took a dive right into the Pacific and disappeared."

"You're not saying that sexist men were behind Amelia Earhart's disappearance!" Bernie exclaimed.

"Well, I can't prove it. But the mechanics were just about all male and still are," Eva continued, with her customary attack on convention. "You see, this all comes out of a biblically masculinized culture. Jesus was male and all of his twelve, hand-picked disciples were male. You can go back even further to the Book of Genesis. Eve came from Adam's rib, which even an uneducated ancient scribe knows damn well is usurping by inappropriate allegorization. It's women that give birth to both males and females, damn it. And if you want to tell it right, Adam should have come from Eve's vagina."

"Whose vagina would God come from then?" Alex asked rhetorically.

"I don't know, good question, and what about the male Son of God who was born by a virgin birth, parthenogenesis?" Eva declared.

"You go, girl!" Suzanne joined in.

"Where would you get the Y chromosome for maleness?" Kent Paulson asked matter-of-factly. "Jesus could have been a female, an XO, Turner's syndrome."

"The chromosome inheritance details have to be worked out, but I agree in principle. We're all humans, and frankly for my first existential experience I'd rather come out of a vagina then a rib," Leonard, concluded addressing Eva.

"Hear, hear, hear."

Bernie raised his glass, as did Alex and Leonard, who threw his head back in laughter at how he was able to attenuate the tension at the table.

In a booth next to the table at Paulson's end listening to this surreal conversation and shaking his head was a huge, broad-shouldered African- American bearded man dressed in a black T-shirt, a black leather jacket, and blue jeans. His size might have been intimidating if not for his large, inquisitive, child-like eyes, which kept glancing at Leonard until Leonard noticed a message.

"Come and join us, sir, we're discussing the gender of deities," Leonard called out.

The man stood up, grabbed a chair, and moved over between Eva and Alex at the table. He spoke as he made himself comfortable and Alex moved his chair laterally to make a place for him.

"Gender isn't the only talking point. The human race probably originated out of Africa, and that's a short hop over to the Middle East. Adam and Eve, Abraham, Jesus, the disciples were all men of color. If man was made in God's original image, he's not going to be no WASP, I'll tell you that. There weren't any WASPs then."

"Wow, how about introducing yourself as you apply anthropology," Leonard suggested

"Sure, my name is Bobby Benton, and I'm from Minnesota. I'm a social worker following up on a case here at the institute that started up north."

"So, Bobby, you believe we're all racists at this table?" Paulson asked.

"In your heart of hearts, of course."

"Believing that the races will never understand each other, or that an individual from one race will never understand an individual from another race is like saying racism is in the genes; it's just another form of prejudice," Patterson intoned.

"I don't think you understand what the black race has been through," Benton responded.

Paulson was ready.

"Maybe I don't, but if guilt is in the genes or transferable across generations, then you're blaming unborn children for selling slaves. That's deterministic, and it's as unthinkable and inhuman as whatever you think has been done to you. People are not perfect social workers. The post-modern world has learned to live with the Germans whose parents and grandparents were responsible for upwards of 30 million deaths during the Second World War, and the Slavs whose Stalinist parents' and grandparents' industrialization and purges cost 20 million lives. As much as those crimes were heinous and abhorrent to me, I'm not going to go up to a German or a Russian six-year-old and tell him that these holocausts were his fault even when he turns twenty-one."

Leonard reacted with his usual philosophically eclectic overview.

"Dr. Paulson might be saying that understanding, love, and empathy are interpersonal. Race is not a person; it's a representation, an image, a gestalt from a series of associations and abstractions."

"You people are crazy," Benton declared. "I leave you to yourselves."

And with that statement Benton dropped his unfinished beer on the table, stood up, zipped his jacket closed, waved at Leonard, glanced scathingly at Paulson, and left the King's Pub through the front door, slamming it shut.

"There goes an angry young man," Leonard surmised.

"When he gets prejudicial about racism, that's where I have to get off," Kent concluded

"Racism doesn't yield itself to science easily. It's an accuser, without due process and reserves the right to be absolutely right *a priori*," Alex added.

"Well, we've covered sexism and racism—why doesn't our fearless Friday panel take a shot at nuclear proliferation?" Leonard suggested facetiously.

"Speaking of atomic bombs, here comes trouble, Leonard," Suzanne warned. She saw June, Leonard's wife, coming in the back door. June probably saw Leonard's truck and charged in.

June was a thin lady, not over one hundred twenty pounds, but very energetic, and she chain-smoked Marlboros, which hadn't help Leonard's cardiac output. She was wearing a red pullover dress that had pale yellow floral designs.

Her dyed light brown hair was in a wavy, fifties, Lauren Bacall style, and this made her head look somewhat oversized for her body. She was not smiling as she marched toward the table. Larry from behind the bar didn't like these confrontations; they disturbed the peace. She glared at Leonard and then said, "Here you are Myles, the once and future King, carousing with your court on Friday night. What am I supposed to do, roost at home sewing socks and baking cookies, a distant third to your job and friends?"

Some people at the table wanted to help, some people wanted to leave, but everyone was silent. Leonard looked up at June and said, "Listen, Tiger, can we discuss this somewhere else or some other time? I am very tired from a great series of sessions, and I need a little down time."

"We'll discuss this here and now. I've had it with you and your head-shrinking bullshit."

"You will excuse me for a minute, dear hearts, as June and I go back to a booth further down and have our Friday night fight.

"If I don't return within a reasonable time, call 911 or my lawyer," Leonard joked.

"Good luck, ol' buddy," Alex said and Bernie echoed, as Leonard shuffled his way past the chairs. They'd seen this scene before over the years. June would say her piece, maybe slap Leonard around a bit, and leave. Suzanne was stunned; she was always intimidated by June, and she grabbed Ellen's hand. She could only wait and hope Leonard would come out of this to save the evening, which had started with some interesting discussion and debate. Now without the facilitator the table was silent. Alex broke the silence with, "Somebody put a quarter in the juke box."

"'Peaceful, Easy Feeling', one of Leonard's favorite songs," Bernie said, digging into his suit pants for a coin. Suzanne could see Leonard and June going at it, at the other end of the pub. Leonard looked frustrated, and he was sweating. Suzanne noticed that Leonard had been sweating more than usual since he had gotten here tonight, but attributed that to the high density of warm bodies at the King's Pub on Friday night. She addressed Ellen with her concerns.

"Leonard doesn't look good. She's all over him. Maybe I should go over there."

"If you go over there you'll just make it worse. They've had these discussions for, what, twenty-five years. If he can handle a complex set of personalities in a group session, then he can handle her."

"That's what's so strange—that he can handle all the complicated characters in group dynamics simultaneously, but he can't seem to figure her out."

Then as Suzanne looked over again June grabbed onto Leonard, but Leonard, trying then to get up, fell to the side out of the booth and onto the floor clutching his chest.

"Oh my God, Oh my God," Suzanne said as she stormed her way past the chairs and to the back of the pub. "Someone call 911! Leonard is down, he's gasping for breath."

Larry immediately picked up the phone to make the call.

"They'll be here in a couple of minutes." Larry started rubbing his forehead anxiously.

Bernie came running from the jukebox. He knew some CPR from the service and tried to get Leonard some more air by loosening clothing, but he needed room.

"All right give us some room here. Back off. Come on. BACK OFF… Keep him flat."

Bernie coordinated with Alex breathing into Leonard's mouth and then allowing Alex to apply pressure with the palm of his hand to the chest.

But Leonard remained passed out.

Alex felt Leonard's jugular. His pulse was weak and arrhythmic. They could hear the ambulance sirens as it pulled up and the pub was invaded with the hovering red "mars light." The medics came running in with a stretcher, which they set up on wheels after Larry had efficiently cleared a path. They checked Leonard's pulse and his eyes and asked if there had been a trauma of some sort that had precipitated the crisis. June nervously explained that she was talking to Leonard and he got up to leave and he just keeled over. She had a handkerchief to her face; her hands and shoulders were shaking, and she was crying.

Suzanne and her friend Ellen were holding each other close and watched as Leonard's stretcher was rolled out of the King's Pub. June went into the back of the ambulance with Leonard. Suzanne wanted to go but they would allow only one individual, and the person had to be a relative. The medic in charge said that, for the time being, they had stabilized Leonard's condition and that there was a weak but steady pulse. They were taking him to the State University Hospital, north up the interstate.

"We're his friends. We loved him. We're supposed to know when to let go. We have used him to the breaking point," Suzanne said to the weary and shocked people left at the King's table, while wiping her tears. "He was… exhausted."

CHAPTER 45

"Vincero"

S unday morning Ozzie was arranging his affairs and preparing his baggage when the phone rang.

"Hello, Dr. Ozelts, this is Lincoln Benedict."

"Hi, Dr. Benedict, How are you?"

"First, just quickly, I would like to thank you for your outstanding contribution to our research program. Dr. Leonard spoke very highly of you, which brings me to the reason for my call. Dr. Leonard collapsed Friday night, and he was taken to University Hospital. I thought it best to let you know before you left the campus. I apologize for the timing but I hope you find my calling appropriate."

"Of course, Leonard is a great man; he did a lot to help us. Would it be OK if I went up there to see him?" Ozzie was flushed with the shock.

"I think that's a great idea, but you'd better call the hospital about an update on his condition and visiting hours… All right, as you might imagine I have other calls to make, Dr. Ozelts. Thanks again for working with us; we'll be in touch."

"Thank you for the call, Dr. Benedict."

There was a knock on Ozzie's door. During their tenure at the institute Billy Brader visited Ozzie often (even when Ozzie hoped it was Carolyn), so it was probably Brader. Ozzie with his maroon tie hanging untied, opened the door.

"Come on in. Leonard's collapsed. He's in the hospital. I'd like to see if he's OK; have you got time to take us there?"

Brader walked in, sat his big frame down slowly on the sofa, and looking up at Ozzie spoke in disbelief. "You're kidding; he seems like such a strong guy."

"He's in a tough line of work," Ozzie said, straightening his tie, "receiving, deflecting, and transforming the expression of powerful feelings and emotions every day. In a group of neurotics I imagine it's like trying to solve simultaneous equations, and if you don't get it right… breakdowns, lawsuits, suicides maybe. It boggles the mind. Not to demean physical courage; but emotional courage is vastly underestimated in this society."

"Let's ride up there, we owe him that much," Brader said decisively.

On the way to the car Ozzie and Brader said little. Ozzie noticed that Brader was walking differently than usual; his gaze was straight ahead and he was using a little more of a charging posture with his shoulders. There was something about the body language of world-class athletes; you could tell when they were aware of a tense or tough situation. They locked out diversions and focused.

"It's funny," Ozzie said as he slammed the car door shut.

"What?"

"Now after the academic and therapeutic role-playing and role reversals of the past two weeks, there appears to be a real-life role reversal. Leonard is hurting, and our counselor needs our support and understanding."

"Yeah, and he's going to get it," Brader said confidently, as he shifted into high gear and pulled onto highway.

It was about 9:30 a.m. when they pulled off the highway at an exit marked by a blue sign with a huge, off-white "H" and another sign in dark blue that read "University Hospital." They had stopped at a Dunkin' Donuts, and the car was strewn with donut wrappers. Brader had his large black coffee between his legs, and Ozzie was clutching his almost-finished large coffee, cream and sugar. Brader looked in his rearview mirror and wiped his face free of crumbs and stains. They were probably approaching the hospital, because there were more traffic cops and people in white and green uniforms jaywalking.

Ozzie's adrenalin level rose whenever he approached hospitals, and he felt his hands start to sweat. He often displaced such anxiety with background music to his awareness, and now it was Samuel Barber's "Adagio for Strings." Once it arose and locked into the replay locus of his brain it was not going away; it was probably going to accompany him throughout this experience. He wondered how accurate these neuronal recordings were, compared to live performances, as he looked over to Brader, who had just pulled into a parking lot driveway and was grabbing a ticket from a distributor.

The main building of the Hospital was red brick with huge cement Doric columns. As they entered through the rotating doors Ozzie noticed that on the high, circular wall of the lobby there were enormous painted portraits of past hospital heads and esteemed physicians. One of them, dressed in a three-piece suit, had a stethoscope hanging from his neck but no watch on his wrist or even a watch chain.

"I wonder how he took a pulse rate? Maybe his nurse had a watch," Ozzie mumbled to himself.

Brader led the charge to the information desk where an elderly lady with a sheen to her gray, curly hair, and "volunteer" pinned to her apron was seated. She smiled dutifully as she asked Brader, "Can I help you?"

"Yes, we're looking for a friend of ours, Dr. Myles Leonard. We heard this morning that he was admitted here. Do you think we could have a visit with him?"

The volunteer began fingering through what looked like lists of patients. "'Leonard'? …how do you spell that?"

"L-e-o-n-a-r-d, first name Myles with a 'Y'."

"Hmmm, he's not listed here. Let me call emergency admissions. Hold on a minute.

"Yes, this is Edna at the Information desk. Was a Myles Leonard admitted recently, because I don't have a room for him? OK, I'll hold."

There was a pause of about a half minute. "Yes… OK… all right then, thank you." The volunteer hung up the phone and looked up at Brader.

"Yes, gentlemen, he was admitted to Emergency and was taken to intensive care for overnight observation and monitoring. He has just been upgraded to 'stable,' and he was moved to a room in the cardiovascular wing of the hospital. You might be able to see him, but not for long. Are you relatives?"

Before Ozzie could explain, Brader jumped in. "Yes."

She pointed back and to her left. "Follow the signs to the elevator for building B and take it up to the fourth floor. Be considerate; remember they're heart patients."

"Yes, of course, thank you, ma'am."

They followed the direction arrows to the elevator doors, and when they found them the indicator lights "up" were already lit, but Brader pushed the button anyway. An elevator door opened, and Brader and Ozzie allowed a coterie of white and green uniforms to almost fill the elevator before squeezing in. Ozzie pushed the "4" button and honored all requests for the other floors. Ozzie thought that these were the most quiet elevator doors he had ever experienced, as if they were gliding up on air.

When the door opened to the fourth floor, Brader and Ozzie exited and looked right and left; across the carrefour of the floor was a large, semi- circular desk behind which there were heart monitors that three nurses, with the backs of their white caps like swans' tails, were busy checking. Uniformed personnel were bustling about on gummed shoes; Ozzie tried to get their attention but to no avail. Finally, a nurse of medium height with short but thick brown-streaked blonde hair under a spotless white cap broke her rapid stride to ask them, "Are you looking for a patient?" She was the prettiest nurse Ozzie had ever seen, like a vision. Between these walls of bone white and pale green there was a comfort in the fortuitous appearance of a biological purpose in life.

While Ozzie was staring, Brader inquired, "Thank you, Miss! We're looking for Myles Leonard, a stocky guy with a large, intelligent head and a Roman nose…"

"You mean the new patient who hasn't stopped talking gibberish since his transfer from IC?"

"Yeah, that's him."

"I'm his nurse. He's in room 405 down there… Easy on the boisterous bonding, please be considerate."

Brader and Ozzie walked down to the room with "405" on the door frame. As they walked in, slowly and curiously, they hardly recognized Leonard in a hospital frock, strapped down with taped tubing. But they did recognize the smile.

"Hi, fellas, thanks for dropping by. Have a seat if you can find one. Join me for lunch?" Leonard said, raising his arm slightly to show his intravenous feeding tube.

Brader and Ozzie found a couple of kitchen chairs and sat next to Leonard's bed. Ozzie had to say something about the nurse. "Jesus, Leonard, they gave you the prettiest nurse in the hospital."

"Oh yes, that's Judy. I've assigned her the responsibility of my sense of being alive."

"Maybe that's what you've given us, at least some of us in your group sessions: a renewed sense of being alive. But look what it cost you."

"At some level, Doc, it's not non-existence itself that's as tough as thinking about it. Once we've been out here, we don't want to return to the silence of infinite spaces. We need that horizon, ol' buddy." Leonard nodded at the window.

At that point, Nurse Judy came into the room with a thermometer.

"Speaking of the wombs of the universe," Leonard quipped, winking at Ozzie.

"Where do you find the energy for all these words, Leonard? Save some for your recovery," Judy said putting her hand gently on Leonard's wrist.

"Dr. Ozelts, I think at this point Heisenberg's uncertainty principle could be applied to Judy's pulse rate determination, don't you?" Leonard quipped.

"Shhh." Judy hushed up Leonard as she looked at her watch for the pulse rate. Leonard opened his mouth to say something, and Judy deftly stuck a digital thermometer in it. She checked the various tubes and the volumes of the reservoirs and adjusted the valves, then went to the end of the bed and wrote down some data.

There was a beep, and she took the thermometer out of Leonard's mouth, which then started talking again: "How are the numbers, Judy?"

"The numbers are fine. Now try to get some rest."

Judy looked up at Ozzie. "Ten more minutes, gentlemen." She then marked something on the chart again, smiled to Leonard, and left the room. There was no question in Ozzie's mind that Leonard was depending on Judy to call on his healing reserves.

"I do believe you'll be her favorite patient, Leonard," Ozzie concluded.

"There's no reason why Judy and I shouldn't benefit from this experience, ol' buddy. We're not giving in to the entropy. Why is it that we spend most of our existential experience trying to understand it, and just when we start to put it all together, it just... flows... away."

Leonard smiled weakly and half closed his eyes as his sedative kicked in from one of the reservoirs Judy had adjusted.

Brader looked at Ozzie and gestured with his head toward the door. Ozzie touched Leonard's bed. "Get well, ol' buddy, we love you. We'll be back to check in on you tomorrow."

He was asleep now, and Ozzie thought maybe Ol' Buddy was dreaming of his grandfather and the perfect friendship... the perfect understanding.

They quietly turned and walked out of the room and toward the elevator doors. Judy was at the semi-circular desk as they entered the elevator, and when Brader and Ozzie turned she looked up and smiled, but then looked down and away as the door closed.

On the way back to the parking lot Ozzie realized that Samuel Barber's "Adagio for Strings" had been replaced by Puccini's "Nessun Dorma" in his brain.

Brader and Ozzie got into the car, and Brader with his hand on the gearshift wound his way laconically through the hospital campus out of town. It wasn't like Billy Brader to be so silent, and reflective, but then he pulled to the side of the road before the entrance onto the highway.

"What's up, Billy?" Ozzie wondered.

"He's dying, isn't he?" Brader said.

Ozzie placed his elbow on the car windowsill, nodded slightly, and looked away.

Brader then jumped out of the car.

"I'm pulling the top down. What do you think this baby can do? ...I just had a tune-up. I haven't really floored the gas pedal for a while. Welcome to Brader Airlines, please fasten your seatbelt."

Ozzie shook his head. Brader was losing it.

"Don't get a speeding ticket," Ozzie warned.

"It might be worth it today," Brader said as he downshifted to third and pulled onto the highway and then after about five miles gradually started accelerating. With the top down in a small convertible the velocity seemed much faster than the speedometer numbers indicated: 60 mph felt like 80, and 75 mph felt like 100. They looked at each other, with the wind gusting through their hair and, this world, for an instant, all in the rearview mirror. As Brader saw his speedometer mount to almost 80 he yelled out a question to his friend.

"So, Ozzie, how are you going to work it out between you and the biblical Jesus? He's already got two billion believers. How many you got?"

Ozzie leaned over and yelled into Billy's right ear, above the noise of the engine and the wind, "I'll teach you a great Italian song about belief in yourself: '*Nessun Dorma*' by Puccini."

"I'm listening... hit it..."

"When I get to the last word in the song, it is repeated three times so you can join in, Billy, let it rip... here we go..."

Brader put the pedal to the metal as Ozzie's tenor voice soared above the din,

Di-legua, o notte!
Tramontate, stelle! Tramontate, stelle!
Al-l'alba vincero

"Hit it, Brader!"

VINCERO!

"Crescendo Molto, Billy!"

V I N C EEE RRR OOOH!

"What does the song say, Ozzie?" Brader asked.

"He says for the night to vanish, he's ready for the dawn, when he will win. He will prevail. Loosely translated it means, 'Nothing can stop me now!'"

"Like 'the Duke of Earl,' Ozzie!" Billy added.

"Not exactly, Billy, more like…

"The Duke of Wellington."

FINE

Printed in the United States
132993LV00003B/421-450/P